The Be  ıgs

ι

www.northcatwriter.com

# Acknowledgements

With special thanks to Lauren Sapala, Tony North, Grace Dolman, Roo Griffiths Coralli, George Costigan, Thalia Suzuma, Kate Burbidge, Sam Turner and everyone else who encouraged me to write and publish this story.

# 1

Kerry Clayton was determined to conquer this illness before it ruined the rest of her life. If she breathed deeply it might help quell her adrenaline spike and slow her stampeding pulse. She inhaled and exhaled for a count of five. Still, her insides squirmed with nerves at the prospect of approaching a stranger.

She loitered on the pavement outside the charity shop, steeling herself to go inside and ask the manager about volunteering. The first step towards repairing her fractured confidence. The shop she'd selected was the South Manchester branch of a mental health charity. Its window display heralded the festive season with an array of Christmas cards and a mannequin draped in a sequinned evening gown.

Her therapist had agreed it would be good for her to get out and meet people instead of being trapped alone in her flat. But now she was here her fears were multiplying. Supposing her brain froze when she got inside and she found herself unable to speak? It had happened the other day at her disastrous job interview. A sickly hot flush came over her at the memory.

Heedless of the winter chill she stripped off her fur-trimmed padded jacket. The rain had stopped and dull puddles rippled in the potholes where dead leaves were disintegrating into copper mush. In the gutter a mottled pigeon pecked at a discarded pizza box. Buses swished along the road, spraying passers-by.

She glanced up and down the road, assessing her escape route. Of course she could just go home. No one was forcing her to do this. Maybe today wasn't the right time. She'd wait until she was feeling less anxious. She turned to leave. A few paces down the road she halted.

On the opposite pavement a woman wearing a hijab was leaving the pound shop with her little boy. An old guy in a raincoat stopped to inspect the buckets and mops lined up outside. A bearded man with a beanie hat sat in front of a boutique, cradling a paper cup of coins. On her way she'd noticed his cardboard sign. 'Homeless and had my benefits sanctioned. Please help me.'

She dug her nails into her palms. There were plenty of people worse off than her. At least she wasn't spending every day out on the streets in the damp and the freezing cold. She was forty-three years old. It was time she got a grip. She returned and hesitated in front of the door.

'Excuse me pet,' said a deep voice behind her. A large woman in a duffel coat was waiting to enter the shop.

'Sorry.' Kerry shrank back to let her pass.

The woman grunted as she heaved the door open and lumbered inside, where she rummaged through the floaty chiffon scarves dangling from pegs. Warm air drifted out of the shop.

Kerry squared her shoulders. She could do this. She'd worked in offices with other people for most of her life. There was nothing whatsoever to be afraid of. She followed the customer inside.

The shop was spacious and spanned two floors. It was one of the better charity shops in the area, which was reflected in its prices. Nevertheless a faint smell arose from the clothes: detergents mingled with traces of sweat soaked into faded cotton and bobbled wool that had been stored in boxes or bags for months.

On the walls behind the rails of clothes were shelves stocked with shoes, sheepskin winter boots and handbags. On top, glass heads modelled wide-brimmed hats. A locked cabinet displayed a tarnished silver spoon set, assorted brooches and a pair of ivory lace gloves.

Behind the counter a white-haired woman wearing a crocheted cardigan and pearl earrings was receiving instructions on how to use the credit card machine from another woman, who had a glass-smooth blonde bob, tanned wrinkly skin and rimless spectacles.

'No Elspeth, if the customer wants to pay contactless, they don't need to key in a number.' The blonde woman pointed at the machine. 'They touch their card on the screen here. Do you see?'

'How does the bank know it's your card and not someone else's you found in the street?' Elspeth asked.

'It doesn't. That's why you can only use it for transactions up to £30.'

Elspeth tutted. 'It was all a lot simpler when I was a check-out girl.'

'Aye well, things change, don't they?'

Kerry stood paralysed. Should she cough to get their attention? At last Elspeth noticed her.

'We've got a *customer*,' she said to her colleague in a whisper.

The blonde woman laid the machine on the counter and looked up, observing that Kerry had brought nothing to be purchased.

'Can I help you?' she asked, unsmiling.

3

Kerry drew in a short breath. 'I'd like to speak to the manager please.'

The woman squinted downwards and then back up at Kerry, with bright and expectant eyes.

'Is it possible to speak to the manager?' Kerry repeated more loudly, confused. Then she saw the badge pinned onto the woman's pink-and-white striped blouse. It read, Sue Heaton: Shop Manager.

Heat rushed to her cheeks. 'Oh I see. You *are* the manager. I'm sorry.'

As Sue continued to stare Kerry's prepared speech vanished from her mind.

'I just wondered if... I heard you were looking for volunteers, and I'm not working right now, so if you liked, I could...'

Her voice tailed off. To Kerry's relief Sue's expression softened.

'That would be smashing, love. We're desperate for help, what with Christmas coming up. Come out the back and I'll get you an application form. Elspeth, will you be all right on your own for a minute?'

'I suppose I'll have to manage,' Elspeth said, her lips setting into a thin line.

Sue led Kerry through a curtain patterned with light and dark bamboo beads and into the back of the shop, where the smell of musty clothes intensified. A black teenager with broad shoulders and a thin moustache was emptying clothes from a bin bag onto the bench that ran along one side of the dingy corridor. A radio beside him played dance music. He turned the volume down as Sue approached.

'This is Joe. He's a little star, aren't you?' Sue said, patting his shoulder as she passed. 'Comes here as part of his college course in retail.'

4

She turned to Kerry. 'I don't think you told me your name?'

'It's Kerry.'

Sue's eyebrows furrowed. 'Why's it scary?'

'No, it *is* Kerry,' she said, flustered.

'Ah, I see. You'll have to speak up, love. My hearing isn't what it used to be. Joe, this is Kerry. She wants to volunteer for us.'

Joe put his bag down and gave her a wide grin. 'How's it going?'

A toilet flushed. From a door on the left emerged a tall, hunched young man. His hair was shaved short and tattoos adorned his pale bony forearms.

'And this is Shaun,' Sue said, her jaw tight. 'Shaun, I want you to meet Kerry.'

'All right,' Shaun said, nodding in her direction. ''Scuse me.'

He shoved past the two women to join Joe at the bench.

'Nice to meet you both,' Kerry said. Joe grinned again. Shaun ignored her.

'Let's go and sit in the staffroom,' Sue said, taking Kerry's elbow and guiding her past the sorting bench. Muffled laughter followed them. Were the boys making fun of her? Kerry told herself to stop being so neurotic. She had no idea what they were amused about.

At the rear of the building stacks of boxes and recycling bags stood waiting to be collected. A double garage door backed onto a concrete yard outside. A chilly draught and the smell of cigarettes crept in through the gap at the bottom of the door.

'Out there's the smoking area,' Sue said. 'Do you smoke at all?'

'No, I don't.'

Sue coughed. 'Sensible girl. Giving up was the best thing I ever did.'

They entered a small room on the left. On the shelves around the sides sat boxes overflowing with toys, tangled costume jewellery and other bric-a-brac. In the corner was a grimy stainless-steel sink. On the table in the centre lay a copy of *The Sun*, open at a double-page spread of girls in bikinis.

'Have a seat,' Sue said, hastily folding the newspaper and tucking it away on a shelf. 'Do you fancy a brew?'

'A coffee would be great thanks, if you've got time.'

Kerry sat at the table while Sue put the kettle on and spooned instant coffee granules into a stained chipped mug. She handed the drink to Kerry then ferreted through a drawer.

'This place is crying out for a tidy-up,' she said. 'But there aren't enough hours in the day. I'm here until gone seven most nights as it is.'

'That's very dedicated of you.'

Having located the paperwork Sue drew up a chair.

'I can't complain. At least I get paid. Only me and the deputy manager do.' Sue handed Kerry the application form. 'We need two references. One from a previous employer if possible.' She took a gulp of her tea. 'So how come you're not working at the moment?'

Kerry ran the tip of her finger along the crease of the form. 'I was made redundant at the end of the summer. The company I worked for had financial troubles and they had to let me go. I'm looking for another job but nothing's come up yet.'

Sue peered over her spectacles. 'What have you got in the way of qualifications?'

'I did an English degree,' Kerry said. 'Only that was a long time ago now.'

'So is it office work you're after?'

'I guess so. That's what I've always done.'

'And are you signing on at the job centre?' Sue asked.

It was beginning to feel like an interview. 'I'm claiming jobseekers' allowance. My savings ran out pretty quickly.'

'So you want to volunteer until you find a job?'

'If that's okay. I could do a few days a week. I don't have much retail experience, I'm afraid.'

'That's all right. We can train you up on the till in no time. We're so short of volunteers; I struggle every week to fill the rota.'

Kerry wondered if she should ask to work in the back of the shop until she got used to being around people again. Or would Sue think she was being daft? Perhaps she'd better not if they were already short-staffed.

'You could help me price up the clothes too,' Sue said. 'Do you know much about fashion?'

Sue looked up and down Kerry, taking in her nose stud and earrings, her leggings and lace-up boots. Kerry was wearing her favourite old tunic in turquoise nylon with a peacock feather design. Although it was fraying at the sleeves she liked the way it flattered her waist and flared over her hips.

She flicked back her fringe, conscious of the wisps of grey showing beneath the burgundy dye she hadn't got round to re-applying for months. Suddenly she saw herself through Sue's eyes. A scruffy middle-aged woman still trying to look like a student. Sue must be wondering why she wasn't better put together at her age.

'I get a lot of my clothes from charity shops.' Her breathing was shallow and her mouth was dry from the strain of maintaining the conversation.

'Great. Then you'll have a sense of the prices we charge.'

Kerry cradled the mug in her hands, drawing comfort from its solidity and warmth. 'So how long have you worked here?'

'Getting on for six years.' Sue paused to rub the side of her nose. 'I wanted to work for a mental health place because my son has schizophrenia.'

Kerry forgot her own discomfort as she placed her cup down on the table and looked at Sue. 'I'm sorry. That must be hard.'

'Aye well. You've got to get on with life, haven't you? He was in and out of hospital for years. But he lives on his own now, with help from his support worker.'

'I think it's amazing you're raising money to help other people with mental health problems,' Kerry said, picking up her drink again.

'Thanks.' Sue gave her a sudden smile. 'What about you? Got kids of your own?'

'No children, I'm afraid.'

'Are you married?'

She tightened her grip on the handle of her mug. 'I separated from my husband earlier this year.'

Sue clicked her tongue against the roof of her mouth. 'I know what *that's* like. On my second marriage myself. At least you're free to have some fun. Plenty of wild nights out with the girls, eh?' She chuckled.

'Not so many these days, to be honest.'

'Are you from round here? Your accent sounds northern, but I wasn't sure.'

'I've moved around a lot, but I grew up down the road in Chorlton. My parents have moved out to the countryside now.'

'Sounds nice.' When Sue had drained the dregs of her tea she scraped back her chair. 'I'd better go and check on Elspeth, bless her. Are you all right to head off?'

'When shall I come back?' Kerry asked as she retrieved her coat.

'You can start as soon as you've got your references. Why don't you give us a ring when you're ready and we'll arrange your first shift?'

Kerry zipped up her jacket and swung her satchel over her shoulder. Sue led her back past Joe and Shaun at the bench and through the bamboo curtain.

'All the clothes, accessories and bric-a-brac are down here,' Sue said as they emerged onto the shop floor. 'We always have a seasonal promotion at the front. And that's the vintage section.' She indicated a rail of embroidered smocks, crushed velvet jackets and polyester shift dresses in geometric patterns.

Kerry gazed around. So many things purchased then discarded once they no longer fulfilled their owners' needs. And now here they hung, waiting for another chance.

'On the first floor is the furniture, electrics, books and music,' Sue said. 'I'll show you up there another time. I'd better get on now. But thanks for coming in. It'll be smashing to have an extra pair of hands around the place.'

Sue went over to Elspeth behind the counter. Kerry made for the door, where she almost collided with a man coming in. He wore black-framed glasses and a volunteer's badge on his chest.

'Sorry, I wasn't looking where I was going,' she said in a rush.

'That's all right. Nor was I.'

They exchanged smiles. Glancing up at him Kerry saw a broad nose, sunken cheeks and gold stubble, which gave him a leonine appearance. He had thick untidy hair the colour of sand mingled with pebble-grey.

'Thanks,' she said, unsure what she was thanking him for. She scurried out of the shop before she could make a fool of herself.

As she breathed in the cold damp air in the street, the tension she carried in her neck and shoulders ebbed away. She'd done it. She'd fought her fears and applied to become a volunteer. Sue had been easy enough to chat to, once she'd abandoned her initial frosty manner. The others would be okay too when she got to know them.

A lightness of spirit she hadn't experienced in months took hold as she put up her hood and hastened through the drizzle. She paused beside the boutique but the homeless man had gone, no doubt moved on by the shop owner so he didn't scare their customers away.

# 2

A ten-minute walk along the main road brought Kerry to Fallowfield where she lived. It was a vibrant urban area on a busy traffic route a few miles from the city centre. Close to both Manchester University and Manchester Met, it was home to thousands of students. Bars, takeaways and late-night convenience stores lined the road.

In her student days she'd been familiar with the interior of every bar on the high street. These days she watched with wistful envy as young people headed out for a night of drinking. Their laughter reminded her that too many years had passed for her to enjoy that carefree spirit any more.

A group of men stood outside the newsagents, smoking and swearing. She flinched, then psyched herself up to pass them. Her spine stiffened as she walked past, feeling their hostile eyes on her.

'Cheer up love,' one said. 'You'd be a lot better-looking if you smiled.'

The others guffawed. Avoiding eye contact she hurried on. She turned left opposite the old red brick building that had once been a railway station but now housed a supermarket. At last she reached the detached house in which she rented an attic flat. She collected her post from the table in the hall. It looked like credit card statements. She shoved them in her bag to deal with another day and climbed the stairs past floors occupied by postgraduate students.

The walls of her apartment were magnolia and the carpets the standard beige favoured by landlords. The space comprised one bedroom, a bathroom and an open plan living area with a tiny kitchen at one end. Kerry loved the sloping ceiling in her bedroom, which looked out onto a garden shaded by trees and overgrown with ivy. She'd brightened the place up with potted plants, a fringed lamp and a silver incense burner she'd bought at a flea market. Framed art prints hung on the walls. On the chest of drawers coloured bead necklaces dangled from twisted wire stands. Her worn leather jacket hung on the door.

Beside her bed stood a small bookcase. It had been a wrench to leave behind her extensive library when she left Stuart but there wouldn't have been space for it. She'd kept only the authors she couldn't bear to part with: the Bronte sisters, Tolstoy and the Romantic poets.

They'd separated six months ago and Stuart was still living in the house they'd once shared. He owned most of the property and he was paying the mortgage but she knew she ought to be pushing him to sell it in order to get her share, however little it was. It was only the guilt over walking out on him that held her back.

At the desk in her living room she switched on her computer. The PR firm at which she'd had the awful interview had sent her an email. It was bound to be a rejection. She'd been in such a state by the time she'd arrived that she was hardly able to speak to the woman on the front desk, who'd asked her if she was all right. Somehow she'd stumbled through the interview, her voice cracking and her hands trembling as she sipped from a glass of water.

She opened the message.

'Thank you for attending an interview for the position of administrator. Unfortunately you were not successful. We are unable to give individual feedback but on this occasion other candidates better demonstrated their suitability for the role.'

Kerry had to admit that her first response was relief. The place had felt so pressured. Phones ringing constantly. Staff hunched over close cramped desks. The worst environment for someone with anxiety. If by some miracle they'd offered it to her she'd have been sick with nerves at the prospect of going in.

But she desperately needed a job. Her debts were mounting alarmingly and she was struggling just to make the minimum repayments. She couldn't stay on benefits forever and she wasn't ill enough to be signed off work: her doctor had made that clear. Therefore she couldn't afford to be fussy about potential workplaces.

She turned her attention to the new adverts that had come in based on her search criteria.

'You'll be a confident communicator, capable and calm under pressure.'

'Must be assertive with good negotiation skills.'

'The job will involve out-of-hours work and extensive travel across the region.'

As she opened the file containing her CV, she sighed. The exhilaration she'd experienced on leaving the shop was waning. But she wasn't going to accept defeat. She'd give the applications her best shot. What else could she do?

She was eating a sandwich and filling in forms when her phone rang, making her jump. Approaching it with caution she saw her sister's name on the screen and answered.

'Hey Fran.'

'Kez. How are you doing? How's the job hunting going? What happened with that interview?'

Kerry perched on the edge of the sofa. 'They offered it to someone else.'

Fran tutted. 'Idiots. I bet you were the most qualified candidate they had. Over-qualified, I expect. Did they say why?'

'No. But something good happened today.' Her voice brightened. 'I went into a charity shop and offered to volunteer.'

'Really? I guess it's good to keep yourself busy while you're looking for work.'

'That's what I thought.'

Much as she loved her sister there was no question of telling Fran the hurdles she'd overcome to go into the shop today. Kerry imagined her sitting at the table in her white-and-chrome kitchen, a pot of fresh coffee beside her, tapping away on her laptop or flicking through the lifestyle pages of *The Guardian*, which probably contained one of Fran's own articles.

'You won't lose your unemployment benefit because of this volunteering, will you?' Fran asked.

'I already checked. The job centre won't mind as long as I'm still available for work.'

'Cool. So was it full of little old ladies?'

'I only met one. In fact, I saw rather an attractive man.'

'Really?' Fran said with a giggle. 'A charity shop isn't the first place I'd consider looking for a date.'

Kerry pictured Fran laughing, tilting her pointed chin upwards and flicking back her shiny black hair, which she wore in a chic layered style. Like Kerry, she still spoke in a recognisably northern accent, although hers was fading the longer she spent in the capital.

'I wasn't looking for a date. I don't know anything about him. I just thought he looked nice.' She paused. 'So how are you?'

'Busy as always,' Fran said. 'Still no luck with you-know-what. My period was late this month and I got all excited, but it started yesterday. I'm beginning to think it'll never happen.'

'Don't give up hope, love,' Kerry said. 'You're not forty yet.'

'I will be this summer. After that your fertility drops off a cliff.' She sighed. 'Anyway, enough about that. We ought to catch up soon. Why don't you come down to London and stay with us?'

Kerry chewed at a loose fragment of thumbnail as she considered the idea. 'I'll have to see if I can get a cheap train ticket. I'm so broke at the moment.'

'I'll pay for your ticket,' Fran said. 'It's a shame you never learned to drive. It must be hard now you haven't got Stuart and his car.'

'Stuart never used to drive me everywhere. I manage fine on the bus.'

'All right Kez. I wasn't having a go at you. Are you all right? You sound stressed.'

She blinked and swallowed hard. 'I'm fine,' she said in her brightest voice. 'I guess I should let you get on with your work.'

When Fran had gone Kerry went into her bedroom and lay on the bed staring at the ceiling. After a while she got up and pulled on her boots and jacket. There was no point moping around feeling sorry for herself. A walk before the afternoon light faded might help clear her head.

Wandering north along the main road led her towards Rusholme, where the warm scent of spices drifted from the Indian, Pakistani and Middle Eastern restaurants and shisha bars that marked the start of the Curry Mile. She entered Platt Fields Park and wandered around the boating lake. In the centre was an island on which herons nested. Grey geese honked as they pecked the grass. Shrill cries drifted from the nearby children's play area. Two little Asian girls danced among the puddles on the tarmac, their red polka-dot dresses bringing vividness to the dull landscape.

Kerry sat gingerly on a damp bench near the lake. A young couple wandered past, arms entwined, and stopped by the water's edge to exchange a kiss. As usual she was reminded of Stuart and everything she'd given up when she left him.

# 3

Kerry had met Stuart at a friend's house party not long after she turned thirty. Following a decade of disappointing dates and flings she was beginning to despair of finding a life partner. She'd gone to the party reluctantly and was lingering alone in the kitchen beside the drinks table, unsure how to join one of the conversational circles that had formed. Stuart came over to the table to help himself to a glass of wine and noticed her.

'Can I pour you one too?'

'Thanks.' She cast a glance at him from behind her fringe. He was neat and athletic in his chinos and polo shirt, with tidy thinning hair and grave grey eyes.

'Are you here on your own?' he asked as he handed her the wine. 'I can introduce you to some of my colleagues from the university if you like. I lecture there in economics.'

He led her over to his group of academics, who asked Kerry what she did. She told them she worked in an office, and since she could think of little else to say, they soon lost interest. But Stuart must have seen something in her because he persisted in asking her about her career aspirations.

'That's the problem with arts degrees,' he said when she told him how she'd struggled to find work after graduating. 'They're not much use unless you want to teach.'

'Why does everything have to be about getting a good job?'

'Because that's what the economy needs. People with skills to contribute.'

Flushed from the wine, she flicked her hair out of her eyes. 'I'm not sure about that. I think education has value for its own sake.'

He gave her a smile. 'I agree with you on that. But anyone can read books in their spare time. They don't need three years to study literature at the taxpayer's expense.'

They debated for some time. Kerry realised it was because she felt secure in his company that she was able to disagree with him. He wasn't crude or brash like many of the men she'd dated; instead his quiet confidence reassured her.

When the party drew to a close and people collected their coats, Stuart got out his phone. 'I've enjoyed talking to you tonight. How about a coffee some time?'

She looked up at him. Why not? He seemed nice enough, and quite attractive. She had nothing to lose by giving it a go. They exchanged numbers, and after a few months' casual dating she felt comfortable enough to sleep with him.

Stuart lived in Didsbury, an affluent suburb boasting tapas restaurants, wine bars, coffee houses and a specialist cheese shop. His flat was meticulously organised and equipped with expensive gadgets. She lay in his bed reflecting that if they were to have a future together, she'd have to move from her run-down neighbourhood and her shabby bedsit full of books into this immaculate place. Her lifestyle would inevitably be tailored to fit around his.

'I've always known what I wanted and worked towards it,' he said one day while discussing her move. 'A successful relationship is the last missing piece.' He turned to her and gave her a kiss. 'You can rely on me not to mess you around or let you down. I'm not that kind of guy.'

Despite her reservations she managed to settle into his apartment. There was plenty of space for her stuff, and Stuart spent long hours at work so she often had time alone to read. He was agreeable to her family and friends when they visited and impressed them with his cooking and domestic skills.

A year later when he proposed, she hesitated before agreeing. She'd never been swept off her feet with passion for him but she'd long ago given up expecting that. She respected and trusted him, and over time she'd developed feelings of attachment and love. And that was what mature adult relationships were all about.

'He suits you down to the ground, love,' her mum said. 'You've always been a worrier with that over-active imagination of yours, and he's so calm and level-headed.'

They agreed not to have children. Stuart made it clear he didn't welcome the disruption to his routine, and when Kerry imagined coping with the stress of small babies her intestines coiled with tension.

'I don't have any maternal instincts,' she explained to her sister.

'It's funny, isn't it?' Fran said. 'You were the one who loved looking after your dolls. Now it's me who's desperate to have a family.'


Two years into their marriage she and Stuart relocated to Oxford for him to take up a new academic post. The move south and away from everything familiar unsettled Kerry for a long time. Five years later she'd made close friends and found a job she enjoyed when they moved again to London. She did her best to embrace the capital, appreciating the galleries, museums and music. Stuart discovered an enthusiasm for rock-climbing and with increasing frequency he disappeared to the countryside on camping weekends with his friends.

Another four years passed and they returned to their home town of Manchester, where Stuart was offered a senior lectureship at his former university. Kerry still had a few friends there but most had moved on or lost touch with her.

The house move was fraught with complications, and a week later she started her new job as an administrator for a graphic design agency. She sensed from the start that she wasn't going to fit in with her colleagues: a clique of hip young designers. Moreover, her manager, who was twig-thin and dressed all in black with animal-print accessories, was assertive to the point of being terrifying.

'I feel queasy at the thought of going in this morning,' she confessed to Stuart in her third week. 'It's horrible being stuck in a room all day with people either ignoring you or harassing you about deadlines.'

They were in the dining room eating breakfast before work. Kerry's throat was too constricted to swallow her cereal. As usual Stuart was glued to his laptop.

'It's because you're new and they don't know you,' he said, wrenching his attention away from the screen. 'I'm sure you'll settle in eventually.' Working in academic communities he'd never had trouble meeting like-minded people.

'Yesterday we went out for someone's birthday lunch. They had to invite me or it would have looked rude but they spent the entire time gossiping about people who used to work there. I tried to join in but I couldn't think of anything to say. I felt so excluded. The longer I sat there without talking the more embarrassed I got.'

'They're only work colleagues. They don't have to be your best friends.' Stuart returned to his computer. 'If you hate it that much, you can always get another job.'

'There aren't many around. It was hard enough finding this one, if you remember.'

Stuart wrinkled his brow as he continued typing. 'Why don't you try asking them questions about themselves, instead of expecting them to think of stuff to say to you?'

She'd given up trying to make him understand that she needed his support more than she wanted him to offer her solutions. She cleared away her untouched bowl and retreated into the bathroom, where she sobbed silently into a tissue. Then she repaired her smudged eyeliner, pulled herself together and went to work.

Her first task that morning was to update the blog on the company's website. It was supposed to be her manager's job, but once her boss had discovered Kerry was the more competent writer she'd dumped the bulk of the communications work on her. Kerry had soon learned that taking on responsibilities outside her administrative role didn't gain her more respect.

'Any trained monkey can send out press releases,' she overheard her manager saying to a colleague. 'I don't see why I should waste my time on it when she's sitting there twiddling her thumbs.'

Next Kerry had to phone a client to inform him of a delay to his project. He wasn't going to be pleased, but she'd dealt with situations like this a hundred times before. Although she never looked forward to those calls, her polite apologetic manner usually managed to smooth things over.

The office was subdued as her colleagues sat at their desks, sipping lattes and scrolling through their social media timelines. As she picked up the phone to dial the number she became aware that everyone, including her manager, would be listening to her call and judging the way she handled it.

Under the desk her knee trembled. She felt stifled, as if she couldn't breathe. Her heart pounded in her head and there was a buzzing in her ears. The temperature in the room soared. A wave of dizzying fear washed over her as she began to hyperventilate. Her stomach clenched like a fist and she realised she was going to be sick.

She hurried out to the toilet, leaned over the bowl and retched. Sweat prickled on her forehead. She remained crouched on the floor until she cooled down and the nausea subsided.

Perhaps it was low blood sugar from skipping breakfast, or the result of weeks of disturbed sleep. She splashed cold water on her face and returned to her desk, where she tried to push the incident out of her mind. But she decided to send the client an email instead of phoning him.

The second time it happened she was in a crowded restaurant with Stuart and his university friends.

'Was there something wrong with your meal?' Stuart asked when she emerged, still shaking, from the toilets into the lobby where he stood waiting for her. She remembered those toilets so well. They had the original ornate green Victorian tiles on the walls. She'd stared at those tiles for ages, wondering if she was going crazy.

'It wasn't the food,' she said, wiping her damp eyes on her sleeve.

He gave her a sharp look. 'You're not pregnant, are you?'

How could he imagine she was? She was forty-two and used contraception and they'd only had sex once since they moved house. She wondered how he'd react if she said yes.

'I wasn't ill. It was just so loud and hot and I felt uncomfortable because everyone was watching me eating.'

'No one was watching you eating. Why would they be?'

'I felt like they were. Then I panicked and had to escape. I'm sorry if I embarrassed you.'

Stuart kissed her forehead and patted her on the back.

'Never mind. It's all right. I just don't understand what you were so scared of.'

'Nor do I.'

He leaned against the wall, his arms folded and his face serious as he considered the problem. 'If it happens again, try to focus on something else. Imagine all the people in the world facing real danger.'

'Okay,' she said, though she didn't see how it would help to imagine other people in danger when her ribs were already so tight with fear she could hardly breathe.

'Shall we go to the bar and get you a drink?' Stuart said.

'I'd rather go home, if that's all right.'

They sat in the car, rain spattering down the windows. As he drove home Stuart told her about his ideas for redesigning their living room.

'It'll look much better once the floors are sanded and varnished. We could put in some more shelves for your books. What do you think?'

'That would be nice.'

'And we could get some bigger speakers for the TV.'

'Okay.'

Stuart swivelled in his seat. 'Are you even listening to me?'

She twisted the strap of her handbag in her fingers. Her adrenaline levels were rising and rising, as if the spike would never end.

'Sorry, I can't really concentrate on the living room right now.'

Silence. The car sped under the flyover and onto the main road towards their house. The windscreen wipers swept back and forth and suddenly they were evil, like giant insect legs in a horror movie. She breathed hard until they returned to normal. What the hell was happening to her?

'Stuart,' she said, 'why don't we talk any more?'

'What do you mean? We talk all the time. I was talking to you just now, only you didn't seem at all interested.'

'I mean about anything important.'

'Such as what?'

'I don't know.' A lump rose in her throat. 'Like the fact I'm so miserable all the time. And what happened just now in the restaurant.'

He kept his eyes fixed on the road as they approached a roundabout.

'I've no idea why you're so unhappy. But if this is about your job, I've told you what I think. You need to get out of there.'

She fiddled with the zip on her bag. 'I feel like you don't care.'

'Of course I care,' he said with impatience. 'But I can't solve this problem for you.'

'I'm not asking you to solve it. That's what you never seem to understand.'

Stuart stared at the traffic ahead. Kerry examined her thumbnail. The skin around it was red and inflamed from where she'd picked at it. For the rest of the journey home she sat in silence.


A fortnight later they were in front of the television when Stuart asked Kerry to call and order a takeaway from their favourite Indian restaurant, as his phone was upstairs charging.

Anxiety tingled in her insides. 'Can't we do it online?'

'They don't have a website.'

She handed him her phone. 'How about you do it? You're better at this than I am.'

Stuart leaned one elbow on the armrest of the sofa and regarded her with a puzzled frown. 'What's the big deal? All you have to do is ask for a curry.'

'I know.' Her pulse sped up. 'I've been getting this thing recently where I find it hard to talk on the phone, especially in front of other people. I know it sounds weird. I think it's to do with feeling uncomfortable at work.'

She looked at him, longing for him to respond sympathetically, but with a scowl he thrust the phone back at her.

'You're not at work now, are you? Go on. Make the call. You need to get over this before it becomes a problem.'

Her breath caught in her throat. She felt on the verge of tears.

'Stuart, I can't.'

'Well, I'm not doing it for you. So I guess we'll have to eat whatever's in the fridge.' He got up. 'I'm going to do some work before dinner.'

'Hang on a minute. I want to ask you something.'

He stopped at the doorway. 'What?'

'I've been thinking,' she said. 'I'm sick of office work. I've been doing it for over twenty years. I need more fulfilment out of life than this.'

Slowly he came back into the room and sat beside her.

'I've been telling you for ages you should apply for a better job.'

'That's not what I mean.' She twisted a loop of hair in her fingers. 'What I'd love is to go back to university. To study for a PhD in literature. It's something I regret not doing before.'

'But what would you do with it afterwards? Academic posts in the arts are extremely competitive.'

So far he was reacting as she'd anticipated. But she was desperate enough to push the idea.

'I don't want to do it for a career move. Just something to give life meaning. I'd carry on working a few days a week.'

'Do you realise it would take you at least six years and cost you thousands of pounds?'

'Yep. I've looked into it.'

'And who's going to pay for that? Me, I suppose?'

'I'm not asking you to pay for it. I'm asking if we could manage on less money for a while.'

'That's effectively the same thing.'

'It was you who insisted we take out a huge mortgage to buy this place, remember?' She gestured around the living room with its gleaming oak floors and stripped pine furniture.

'Yes, since it appears I'm the only one of us who cares about investing in our retirement.' He got to his feet. 'I understand you hate your job, but quitting work to sit at home reading isn't the answer. You're an adult, and that means making adult choices.'

As he disappeared upstairs it came to Kerry in a flash that if she stayed with him for the rest of her life their lack of intimacy would destroy her spirit. She sat still for a while, overwhelmed by the enormity of what she had to do.

# 4

It took her another month of sleepless nights and agonising before she worked up the courage. They sat on the sofa together again, and before her brain could freeze in panic, she forced the words out.

'I'm sorry, but this isn't working for me. It hasn't been for a long time. I think it would be best if I moved out.'

She regarded his stunned face, unable to believe what she'd done.

'Please, Kerry,' he said, his lips trembling and tears filling his eyes, 'I know things haven't been good lately, but can't we keep trying?'

The sight of him weeping for the first time since she'd met him twisted her heart. But this was her only chance. If she went back on it now she'd never be able to put him through this again. And she'd never know what might have become of her life.

'I'm sorry,' she said, closing her eyes, 'but it's over.'

When he saw he couldn't change her mind Stuart channelled his hurt into a cold and bitter manner. Although difficult to endure, this was easier than the tears. Over the next few weeks Kerry began the painful process of searching for a flat and separating her belongings from his in preparation for moving.

'I wasted twelve years of my life on you,' Stuart said one day, standing over her as she sat cross-legged on the floor next to their shelves, going through their film collection. 'I put so much effort into building our future, and it turns out it was all for nothing.'

Her guilt mutated into resentment at his refusal to take any responsibility for the failure of their marriage.

'So everything we did together was a waste of time because it didn't pay off?' she said. 'You realise it was a relationship, not an investment portfolio?'

He treated her to a condescending smile. 'I bet you don't even know what an investment portfolio is.'

'I forgot, I don't know *anything* useful, do I?'

'It's not like you've ever been interested in making any contribution to our finances.'

Kerry stood up and faced him. 'That's a very unfair thing to say. I've worked full-time and paid my share of the bills. What more did you expect?'

'I suppose I should have realised from the start you had no ambition.'

'I *do* have ambitions. You've just never supported them.'

Stuart spread out his hands and then dropped them to his sides. 'I've literally no idea what that's supposed to mean.'

She kneeled on the floor again and pressed her palms to her eyes in frustration. 'You know exactly what I mean. We talked about it not long ago.'

'You mean your idea for us to sell this place and move into some poky terrace so you could study for a useless degree you didn't need? Well, good luck with finding a husband who's prepared to do that.'

He stood with his arms folded and his eyes narrowed, and in that moment she despised him.

'Has it occurred to you that I don't need a man's permission to do it any more?'

Stuart gave a hollow laugh. 'I don't see you doing it on your own. You haven't got the money, let alone the drive or the self-discipline.'

Kerry told herself not to rise to his bait. She held up a film about Virginia Woolf, which she couldn't remember how they'd acquired. 'Do you mind if I have this?'

'I don't give a shit,' he said, walking out. 'Take whatever you want.'

Moving into her new place in Fallowfield brought her a sense of liberation and pride. She'd considered herself too fearful or too day-dreamy to initiate major life changes, yet she'd taken this bold step into the unknown. It was a lesson she'd remember: that she had the power to influence her fate.

Soon however the reality of the separation struck home. Despite everything she missed him and obsessed over how she'd hurt him. The anxiety that had been preying on her now dug in its claws. She worried about everything: electrical fires, burglars, having to telephone the letting agents to request repairs.

Leaving her husband had left her more isolated than she'd anticipated. The couples she'd met through Stuart's work and socialised with now drifted away. One woman she'd considered a friend came to check how she was but after the initial expressions of sympathy, the visit turned awkward.

'Were things really *that* bad?' her friend asked her as they sat drinking tea. 'I mean, no relationship is perfect. We all have to work at it. And there's a lot worse men than Stuart out there.'

It was clear that since Kerry was the one who'd called time on the marriage, she'd be expected to justify her decision to everyone who knew them.

Her few remaining friends from school and university stayed loyal and invited her to parties and dinners to cheer her up. But despite her growing loneliness she couldn't face eating in front of people or making small talk with anyone she didn't know intimately. She often found herself lost for things to say when conversations centred around careers, marriages and child-rearing. So she turned them down, hiding away in her flat and distracting herself from her troubles as she always had by getting lost in a book.

'I feel guilty for breaking up with him,' she confided to Fran on the phone one day, after she'd related what her friend had said.

'Sod them,' Fran told her. 'Do what makes you happy. Who cares what they think?'

That was typical of Fran, who forged ahead without regard for others' opinions. It was this strength of character that made Kerry not only envious of her sister but also reluctant to admit that irrational worries were taking over her mind. How could Fran understand what it was like to feel breathless with nerves at the thought of talking to strangers?

Soon they noticed the changes in her at work, and that was when things got serious. Her intimidating manager called Kerry into her office.

'I was disappointed you didn't get this month's report to me on time. I told you I needed it for the board meeting.'

Kerry shifted in her chair, stung by the criticism. She'd never been in trouble at work before. In her previous jobs she'd enjoyed a reputation for conscientiousness.

'I had trouble getting information from some of the designers. I sent several emails but they didn't get back to me.'

'And what do you think you should have done when they didn't reply to your emails?'

Kerry swept her hair from her hot forehead. 'I should have called them and insisted it was urgent.'

She had in fact tried, but on picking up the phone she'd felt dizzy with nerves again and had to go outside to calm down. But how could she tell her boss that?

Her manager crossed her slender bare legs and leaned forward in her chair. 'If you're going to be effective in your role, you need to work on your assertiveness and time management.'

'I will,' Kerry said in her best efficient voice. 'I'll make sure it doesn't happen again.'

A few weeks later they hauled her in again. This time the chief executive, an older woman in a pillar-box red jacket, was sitting next to Kerry's manager. Kerry had suspected something was going on earlier that day when sombre men with briefcases arrived for an unscheduled meeting.

'We've had the accountants in to discuss the company's finances,' the chief executive told her. 'Unfortunately we've had a run of bad months and we need to make some cutbacks.'

Fear pinched her insides. 'Are you making me redundant?'

'We looked at all the options and decided we can't afford the luxury of a full-time administrator. So yes, I'm afraid we're going to have to let you go.'

Kerry could think of nothing to say. She bit the inside of her cheek. The red of the chief executive's jacket reminded her no longer of a pillar-box but of fresh arterial blood. Her manager was staring out of the window, as if it was nothing to do with her.

The chief executive shuffled her papers. 'As you've only been with us a short time, you're not eligible for redundancy pay. But you'll be paid until the end of the month. I hope you manage to find something else. Do contact me if you need a reference.'

The chief executive stood up, shook Kerry's hand and left. Her manager showed her out of her office.

'You may as well take your stuff and go home,' she said, avoiding eye contact. 'There's no point you staying on for the rest of the week.'

Kerry collected her belongings from her desk and walked slowly home, numb with shock. Back in her flat she couldn't face calling anyone to tell them what had happened.

For the next two days she remained holed up indoors in a state of panic. Every sound in the street outside made her jump. Half the time she couldn't tell what she was so scared of. She only had a sense that something terrible was happening.

She paced constantly around the flat, since whenever she sat down a tidal wave of adrenaline engulfed her. Her thoughts raced. How was she going to find another job? And how would she pay her rent and bills when her savings ran out, which wouldn't be long in coming?

She couldn't ask her retired parents to support her. Not at her age. They were working-class northerners who'd brought her up to stand on her own two feet, just as they had.

How then had her life ended up in such a mess?

At the end of the week she found herself in the doctor's surgery, shaking and in tears.

'I'm scared I'm losing my mind,' she told him as she dabbed her eyes with the tissue he'd handed her. 'It's taken me days just to pick up the phone and make an appointment with you.'

The elderly doctor commiserated with her on her marriage break-up and redundancy. He prescribed her an anti-anxiety drug, as well as diazepam for emergencies, and referred her for cognitive behavioural therapy. Warning her there was an extensive waiting list, he gave her the number of a low-cost counselling service run by a charity, which she could refer herself to in the meantime. Another phone call she'd have to steel herself to make.

'I feel so ashamed of not being able to cope,' she confessed as he signed the prescription. 'Everyone else seems to handle life better.'

'I wouldn't be so sure of that. I see people every day with symptoms like yours. But they usually respond well to medication and therapy. Do you have friends and family you can talk to?'

'My parents will want to help. But I'm not sure how well they'd understand *this*.' She indicated the slip of paper in her hand.

'Did you know there's an anxiety support group in your area? The people there will know what you're going through. I'll give you the details.'

Kerry took the information to be polite but there was no way she could travel somewhere new and introduce herself to a room of strangers when she could barely face leaving the house.

Slowly, however, things improved. The pills helped her feel calmer, and she made an appointment to see the counsellor. She told her parents and her sister about the redundancy but not about her financial problems, not wanting to admit she'd accumulated so few savings during her working life that she had nothing to fall back on. She also couldn't bring herself to tell them she was receiving treatment for a mental illness.

Eventually she recovered enough to sign on at the job centre and commence her search. Her CV won her three interviews straight away but each was a shattering experience ending in rejection. As her confidence dwindled she guessed this must be coming across in her applications somehow, because the offers of interviews dried up. The one at the PR firm had been the first in ages. It seemed her nerves were making her unemployable.

Now, sitting on the park bench, Kerry forced her memories out of her mind and gazed around at the muddy water rippling on the lake and the stark bare branches of the November trees rising from the island. By springtime everything would be lush and green and alive again. Hopefully by then she'd be well and have found a job where she felt settled. Hopefully. Because she wasn't sure how much more of this she could take.

# 5

Having obtained her references Kerry turned up on Monday morning for her first shift at the charity shop. As she entered the building she inhaled deeply, fighting the nausea that seized her once more. She'd been unable to eat breakfast, her stomach tense at the prospect of new people and responsibilities. Since it was unpaid work she didn't have to stay if she hated it, but she'd resolved to make a go of it. Quitting too soon would only reinforce her fears.

'One of my regular volunteers is off sick and I haven't got time to train you on the till today,' Sue told her briskly. 'So you'll be out the back with me pricing up the stock.'

Relief came over Kerry that she wouldn't have to deal with customers yet. 'That's fine with me.'

'I'll give you a quick tour of upstairs too. We didn't get a chance last time.'

'Ruth and Alex manage this floor,' Sue said as they ascended the stairs. 'They're both in today.'

*Alex.* Was he the volunteer she'd bumped into last time on her way out?

'Here we are,' Sue said as they reached the landing. 'This is the furniture area.'

In a large space stood two solid old wardrobes, a couple of cabinets and a round table in burnished mahogany with bevelled edges and clawed feet.

Sue gestured at the table. 'That's Edwardian, that is. We had an antiques dealer come in to value it. We've priced it at two hundred quid. I've had to deal with a few stroppy customers who expect everything to be cheap as chips.'

'What do you say to them?'

'That we're here to raise money for charity, not put on a jumble sale. It'd be wrong of us to let that table go for a tenner.'

They approached the counter where a small woman with lank fair hair stood behind the till. She wore a drab olive-green linen dress with a cardigan that hung loosely on her slight frame. Kerry guessed from the creases in her neck that they were of a similar age.

'Morning Ruth,' Sue said. 'This is Kerry, our new volunteer.'

'Hi there,' the woman said in a subdued voice. She offered her tiny hand to Kerry and they exchanged a limp handshake.

'Ruth helps Alex price up the music and the books,' Sue said. 'Speaking of the devil, where is he?'

'He's in the stockroom,' Ruth said.

'We'll pop our heads round and say hello. Ta Ruth,' Sue said, and she led Kerry to a corner containing a library of books, records and CDs.

The door to the stockroom stood ajar. Sue peeped in.

'Alex, could you bob out of there for a second? I've got someone for you to meet.'

'Hold on a minute,' a man's voice replied. 'Damn,' he added as what sounded like a stack of books collapsed onto the floor. He came out and saw Sue, and then Kerry.

In the days since their brief encounter her memory of him had grown hazy. But now his slender figure seemed as familiar to her as that of someone she'd known for years, though his hair was greyer and his face more lined than she'd pictured. He wore jeans and a black-and-silver striped shirt.

Alex removed his reading glasses to look at her. She noticed his eyes were a warm brown, almost amber colour. He smiled, and she felt the long-forgotten sensation of having stepped unexpectedly off a high kerb.

'Hi. I'm Kerry,' she said. 'I'm a new volunteer.'

'I'm an old volunteer. In every sense of the word, I'm afraid.' The crevices splitting his forehead suggested he was a good few years older than her.

'Never mind, eh? Age is just a number. Or at least that's what I keep telling myself.' Kerry gave a self-deprecating laugh as she winced inside. *Jesus.* How had she managed to come out with such an awful cliché?

'Alex has been here longer than me,' Sue said. 'How many years is it now?'

He ran a hand through his hair and frowned. 'I think it's eight. Possibly nine even.'

Kerry found herself mirroring his actions as she swept her fringe out of her eyes.

'Kerry here's a brainbox like you,' Sue said, making Kerry cringe. 'She studied English at university, didn't you love?'

'Yes. Though that was years ago.'

'But you like to read?' Alex was watching her intently.

'I love second hand books,' she said, turning towards the colourful spines lining the shelves. 'What kind of things do people bring in?'

'A lot of mass-market paperbacks,' he said, 'but some unusual ones too. Just this morning I found a beautiful old illustrated encyclopaedia of herbs. I think it could be valuable, given its age and condition.'

'Wow. That sounds interesting.'

'I could show it to you if you like.'

'That'd be lovely,' Kerry said, charmed by his enthusiasm. He turned to fetch the book.

Sue pursed her lips. 'Maybe another time.'

'Okay,' he said, although he didn't seem pleased. 'Would you like to help me sort through the books sometimes, Kerry?'

Before Kerry could reply Sue interrupted. 'Alex, you don't need an assistant. You and Ruth are hardly rushed off your feet, are you?'

Apart from a man browsing through the CDs, the floor was deserted.

'Oh, I know we're not busy,' he said with a grimace. 'I just thought since Kerry's giving up her time to help us, perhaps we could make use of her skills and interests?'

He raised his eyebrows at Sue and twiddled the arm of his black-framed glasses in his fingers.

'I'm sure Kerry's as bright as a button. But I can't spare her to hide up here with you,' Sue said firmly. 'I need her on the till downstairs and helping me price up that mountain of clothes out the back.'

'Fine. I appreciate you need her more than I do,' he said.

'All right, Alex love,' Sue said. 'We'll leave you in peace now to sort out your books.'

Kerry followed Sue downstairs.

'Poor Alex, bless him.' Sue exhaled through her teeth. 'He's a sweetheart really.'

'He seems nice to me.' Why did Sue speak about him in that pitying tone? And what was behind the uneasy relationship she'd witnessed?

. They stopped at the sorting bench in the corridor, which was piled high with clothes.

'Joe and Shaun aren't in today, but they've done the initial sorting and chucked out the worst of the crap,' Sue informed her. 'They leave the rest for me to go through and price. It's a lot of work, so I could do with someone to help.'

'Can't the boys do the pricing?'

'Nah. Joe's a good lad, but he's not got much of a clue about ladies' fashion. He's learning, mind. As for that Shaun,' she rolled her eyes, 'he makes a pig's ear of everything he touches.'

Kerry recalled the lanky tattooed youth she'd met last week. 'I guess it's nice he's volunteering though.'

Sue gave her a grin. 'Bless you, love. Do you really think Shaun's here out of the goodness of his heart?'

Kerry didn't reply. Sue's comment was intended to make her feel naïve but she hadn't wanted to assume too much about someone she didn't know. Sue glanced towards the beaded curtain and lowered her voice.

'Shaun's here on a community rehabilitation programme. He's not long out of prison for taking part in a robbery. Used to be a crack addict.'

'But he's not now?'

'His probation officer assured me he's clean.'

'Then he's done well to beat an addiction.'

Sue grunted. 'I'll give him credit for that. Still don't trust him as far as I could throw him, though. Sometimes I regret taking him on, but I thought we should do our bit to help young offenders. Some of them have got mental health issues, like my Ian. Mind you, Shaun hasn't. Not unless you count being lazy and sullen. Of course he comes from a useless family. None of them's ever done an honest day's work in their lives.'

Sue was reminding Kerry of her dad when he got started on politics. Quick to judge and very certain of his opinions.

'Then I guess Shaun didn't have the easiest start in life,' she said.

'No, but neither did Joe. He comes from a deprived area too, but he's not into drugs and gangs like half the kids on his street. He's going to college and getting a qualification. You've got to respect that, haven't you? A young lad trying to make something of his life.'

'Yes, you do,' Kerry agreed. She turned to the clothing on the bench. 'So where do I start with these?'

'This is your pricing guide,' Sue said, handing Kerry a laminated sheet with three columns of clothing brands on it. 'Low range is your cheap crap from the supermarkets. Medium range is standard high street. If we come across anything designer, we charge as much as we can get away with.'

'What if it's torn or dirty?' Kerry asked, eyeing a gingham dress with yellowish stains on its white collar.

'Bung it in the blue bag for recycling.' Sue pointed to the bin bags mounted on metal frames. 'Same if it's got broken zips or missing buttons. Unless it's top of the range, in which case we might put it out with a note on the label about the fault.'

Sue fished in the pile and dug out a pair of women's jeans. 'All right Kerry, what price would you put on them?'

Kerry examined the jeans. Sue watched over her rimless spectacles.

'I can't see any faults,' she said, testing the zip and inspecting the hems at the bottom of the legs. 'They're in good condition, but they're not an expensive make. I'd say maybe five pounds?'

Sue tilted her head to one side. 'Not bad, though I'd probably go with six.' She rooted through the clothes again and held up a purple woollen dress. 'And this?'

'Six as well?'

'Nah.' Sue pulled a face. 'Look at it. It's all stretched and baggy round the waist, and there's a hole in the sleeve. That goes straight in the bin, that.'

'I see what you mean,' Kerry said, feeling she'd failed the test.

'You'll get the hang of it, love. Always ask yourself whether *you'd* buy it.'

'Although I suppose people have different standards.'

'Aye, but no one wants clothes full of moth holes.'

Sue gave Kerry a labelling gun, some plastic tags, a pen and a stack of printed price labels. 'Write the date on the back of the label. That way we know how long it's been out when we restock.'

Kerry held up a tasselled bohemian vest top. The sort of thing she'd have worn to a festival in her twenties. She was about to check its label in her guide when Sue stopped her. 'That's summer stock, that. We store it till the season changes, so it needs to go in a box.'

A while later the phone on the wall behind them rang, making Kerry jump. Sue answered. 'All right love. I'll send some up.'

'That was Ruth upstairs,' she said to Kerry. 'Run out of change on her till. Can you take her some bags of coins?'

'Sure.' Nervous anticipation seized her at the thought of seeing Alex again. 'Where do I get the coins from?'

'I'll fetch them. Only Dan and me have access to the safe. Dan's the deputy manager. Takes charge of the shop when I'm off and does all the computer stuff. I'm what you call a technophobe, me.'

Carrying the plastic bags of change Kerry ascended to the first floor where she found Ruth behind the till.

'Hi there.' Ruth took the bags from her. 'I'm sorry; I've forgotten your name.'

Her soft voice sounded polite but possessed no warmth. There was no hostility about her either, or anything in her body language to indicate shyness. In fact it was difficult to discern much about her at all.

'I'm Kerry.'

'That's it. I remember now.' Ruth opened the till drawer and tipped the coins into their correct sections.

Kerry supposed she should try to make small talk with Ruth before departing but her mind had gone blank. Why was she so tongue-tied with people she didn't know?

Instead she glanced towards the book corner and caught her breath. He was there. Standing with his back turned, taking CDs out of a cardboard box and stacking them on the racks.

She lingered near the counter, conscious of Ruth's eyes on her. She couldn't stay there staring at him but there was no way she was brave enough to go over and interrupt him. Then Alex turned and straightened his back. He put down the box and wandered over.

'Kerry. How are you getting on?'

'Good thanks.' She flicked her fringe off her flushed forehead, willing herself not to freeze up in front of him too. 'Which days are you usually here?'

'Monday, Tuesday and Wednesday. I prefer it during the week when it's quiet. On Saturdays it gets too crowded in here.'

Kerry glanced surreptitiously at his left hand as he raked it through his hair. No wedding ring.

'So how do you spend your time when you're not here?' she asked.

His eyelids flickered. 'Me? Oh, I'm a photographer.'

'That's cool. What sort of photography?'

'Mainly portraits and street scenes. But I do all sorts really. Anything that captures my interest.'

'And you sell the images?'

'Yes, though not as often as I'd like.' He laughed. 'But I get by. I used to do weddings and events, but I got tired of working so many weekends. I prefer the balance I've got now. Coming in here stops me getting lonely. I live on my own, so I wouldn't see many people otherwise.'

So he wasn't married or living with a girlfriend. Though that didn't mean he was single. If he *was* attached, she'd have to forget about him straight away. One thing her instincts assured her was that he wasn't gay.

She shouldn't be thinking of him that way at all. She had too many problems to fix in her life first. He was unlikely to be interested in her anyway. She wasn't making a good first impression, standing there twisting her fingers together, not sure what to say next.

'What about you?' he asked. 'Sue told me you were looking for work.'

'That's right. Just an admin job. I don't know why it's taking me so long to find one.'

'I'm sure it's not your fault. I hope something comes up soon.'

'Thanks. Me too. Though it's not really what I want to do with my life,' she added on impulse.

He leaned in towards her. 'Go on then. Tell me your dream.'

This conversation had gone deep quickly. Kerry turned to the counter behind her to see if Ruth was listening but she was busy with a customer.

'I'd like to do a PhD in English literature,' she said. 'I've thought about it on and off for years, but I never had the courage. Now I feel like I've left it too late.'

'That sounds like a fantastic thing to do. Are you *sure* it's too late?' Alex asked. 'There's no age limit on learning.'

She wrinkled her nose. 'I'm so broke at the moment. I just need a job.'

And she needed to regain her confidence. Otherwise there was no way she could go to university and face the pressures of deadlines and having her work judged.

'Things are tough right now,' he said. 'Lots of people are struggling to find work. And some are being forced into jobs when they shouldn't be.'

'I keep hearing the stories. People with disabilities being declared fit for work and the stress of it killing them. I wish we could get rid of this dreadful government,' Kerry said with fervour, then she stopped. Where the hell had *that* come from? Her hand fluttered to her throat.

'Sorry. I don't usually rush straight into politics with people I don't know.'

'Oh, it's fine. I completely agree. They're a nest of snakes.' He returned her smile. 'I'm getting the impression we're on the same wavelength.'

The tension between them was becoming intolerable. She broke their eye contact and gestured over at the books. 'I might have a quick browse through those, if that's all right.'

'Please. Let me show you.' Alex led her over to the bookshelves. 'They're categorised by genre, then the name of the author. The thrillers, fantasy and sci-fi are here. Then there's poetry, classics and literary fiction.' He pointed to the opposite side. 'Along here, we have the non-fiction titles, and some old annuals I've collected over the years. And these are the children's books. I have to admit, I love reading them. Some of the stories and illustrations are wonderful.'

'Do you have children of your own?'

'Somehow I never got round to getting married and having a family. How about you?'

'I did get married. But we never had kids, and now we're separated.'

Alex looked straight into her eyes. 'I'm sorry it didn't work out for you.'

'Thanks.'

This time he retreated from the intimacy of their conversation by changing the subject. 'Was there a particular type of book you were looking for?'

He stood beside her as she perused the poetry section and selected a volume of Keats, bound in forest-green leather with a gold leaf pattern.

'I shouldn't really be buying more books. I haven't got space for them. But I love this.'

She held it up to him. He took his reading glasses from his shirt pocket and put them on to examine it.

'Yes, it's a beautiful edition.' He opened it and flicked through the pages, then handed it back. 'You'd better take it. I'll be distracted all day if I start reading Keats.'

'I'll never understand how he could write like that in his early twenties.'

'That's genius for you. Do you want to pay for it now or leave it behind the counter to collect?'

'I'll fetch it later, if that's okay. I left my purse downstairs.'

And it would give her a reason to come up and see him again.

'I'd better go.' Kerry gave him the book to leave with Ruth. 'Sue will be wondering where I've got to.'

'Yes, she will. Don't get me in trouble, will you?'

'I'll try not to.' She grinned, then forced herself to turn and make her way downstairs.

As Kerry brushed through the bamboo curtain and entered the corridor, Sue peered up from the pile on the bench.

'Get lost up there, did you?'

'Sorry I was so long. I got waylaid by the books.'

Sue tagged a label onto an itchy-looking fake mohair cardigan.

'I bet Alex insisted on showing you around, didn't he? Loves an audience, bless his heart. Especially one who's too polite to say when she's had enough.'

'He wasn't boring me. He's an interesting person.'

Sue clucked her tongue. 'He's that all right. By the way, Dan's in the staffroom, if you want to say hello. He's just come back from taking his daughter to the doctor's.'

Another new person to face. Before she could dwell on her fears Kerry went into the staffroom where Dan sat stirring a teabag in hot water, which gave off the scent of peppermint. He looked no more than thirty-five. He had an angular jaw and a neat dark beard, and was dressed in a blazer, a crisp white shirt and jeans.

'You must be Kerry. Have a seat,' he said, pulling out a chair. She sat down nervously next to him, catching the citrus notes of his cologne. 'How are you doing?'

'Fine thanks. Sue's been teaching me to sort the clothes.'

Dan's light-blue eyes crinkled at the corners. 'Going through those bags can be interesting. The other week one of the lads tipped out a load of old-fashioned nylon nighties, and underneath were two complete sets of false teeth.'

She laughed. 'I assume someone left them in there by accident?'

'I wouldn't count on it. People have bizarre ideas about what we can sell.'

46

Dan was still grinning at the memory of the teeth. Already Kerry had decided she liked him. Her tension eased.

'Sue tells me you have a daughter,' she said.

'Yeah. Libby.' He removed his phone from his pocket and swiped the screen to reveal a photo of a strawberry-blonde freckled girl of six or seven.

'She's adorable.'

'She's a little angel,' he said. 'My boyfriend and I adopted her a year ago. Libby has autism. Her birth mother wasn't really equipped to cope with her.'

'That's an amazing thing to do.'

'We feel we've been so blessed in our lives, we wanted to give something back by supporting a kid who hasn't been so lucky.'

Kerry chatted to Dan for a while before she returned to the sorting bench, anticipating another disapproving look, but this time Sue smiled.

'What did you think of him?'

'He's lovely. He told me all about Libby. I really admire people who adopt children.'

'Aye, they're a sweet couple.' Sue bundled a bulky threadbare overcoat into the recycling bag. 'His other half is a software developer, so they're not short of cash. Dan looks after Libby and comes in here while she's at school. He's an absolute godsend. Don't know what I'd do if he left.'

Sue held up a black kimono embroidered with white silken birds.

'Now that's smart, that is. I might keep it to one side for a special promotion.' She turned to Kerry. 'By the way love, have you thought about which days you'd like to work?'

Kerry screwed up her eyes, as if thinking about it for the first time.

'The beginning of the week is good for me. How about Monday, Tuesday and Wednesday? I could do a half-day on Saturday too,' she added, to make it less obvious she'd chosen the same days Alex worked. But Sue didn't seem to have noticed.

'That'd be smashing. We're always in need of extra bodies on Saturdays. Are you sure it's not too much?'

'It leaves me three full days and the evenings to look for jobs. And it'll do me good to get out more.'

She spent the rest of the day working with Sue. Before the shop closed she ventured upstairs to collect her book. To her disappointment Ruth told her Alex had left for the day.

'He goes home at four. But he left this for you.'

She handed Kerry her book wrapped in a bag. Kerry unzipped her purse and drew out a five-pound note but Ruth waved it away.

'Alex has already paid for it. He said it was a present.'

Kerry squinted at her in surprise. 'Has he? That's very kind of him.'

Ruth's expression was unreadable. 'He likes giving books to people.

It was only when Kerry got home and opened the book that she saw what was inscribed in looping handwriting on the inside of the cover.

'A small gift from one Keats fan to another. Happy reading and best wishes, Alex.'

She sank onto her sofa with the volume of poetry clutched in both hands and told herself sternly she was too old to be starry-eyed over someone she barely knew.

# 6

On Kerry's third morning Sue took her onto the shop floor to train her on the till.

'If you have any problems press the buzzer and I'll come out.' Sue indicated a button on the underside of the counter.

'Okay.' Kerry's throat was dry and her knees shook at the thought of serving customers for the first time. She wasn't ready for this level of social contact yet, not by a long way. But now she was here she'd have to face it.

Her thoughts turned to Alex. Was she just imagining he was attracted to her? Ruth had been quick to tell her he liked giving people books. Was she hinting that Kerry shouldn't assume too much from the present? No, there was definitely a spark between them. Even her inner critic couldn't persuade her otherwise.

'Are you listening to me?' Sue said, nudging her elbow. 'You look miles away.'

'You were saying we never give discounts to customers.'

'Not unless there's something wrong with the item. Then we might knock a few quid off. But it has to be approved by Dan or me. Sometimes you have to be firm. People will try all sorts of hard luck stories.' She leaned closer. 'And keep an eye on how many garments they take into the changing room. We've had problems with theft before.'

When she'd completed the training Sue hovered beside Kerry, who struggled to concentrate under Sue's beady gaze.

After fumbling her way through her first sale she gave her second customer the wrong change.

'I'm so sorry,' she said, red-faced, as she opened the till to correct her mistake. When the queue died down Sue checked her watch.

'Can I leave you for a bit? I've got things to do.'

'I'll be fine,' Kerry said, relieved to be free of scrutiny. Sure enough her next few transactions went smoothly.

A lull followed, with the shop empty except for a young woman carrying a rucksack, who looked like a student. She kept touching her face and twisting the ends of her chestnut hair in her fingers as she replaced garments on the rails. Kerry watched her, feeling too shy to strike up a conversation. But when the woman finally gave a groan of despair Kerry came out from behind the counter.

'Is there anything I can help you with?'

The customer explained she had an interview tomorrow at a legal firm in London.

'I tried on my best suit last night and it's too tight, but I can't afford a new one as well as the train fare. I thought I'd see what you've got in here, but I can't find anything. I'm getting a bit panicky.'

Kerry recalled a tailored navy suit she'd priced yesterday, which she estimated would be the right size. It was still in the corridor waiting to go out. She fetched it and gave it to the customer, who took it into the changing room. The young woman emerged with an air of confidence and status: a different person from the anxious student in jeans and a hoodie. Such was the transformative power of clothing.

'What do you think?' the customer asked, pirouetting around to view herself in the full-length mirror.

'You look very smart and professional.'

'Thanks.' She examined the price tag. 'I'll take it. I won't get a bargain like this anywhere else.'

The young woman changed out of the suit and came up to pay. As she got out her credit card doubt crept over her face. 'You don't think they'll be able to tell it's second hand?'

'I don't see how. It's in perfect condition.' Kerry handed her the bag. 'I hope you get the job.'

'Me too.' She crossed her fingers for luck. 'My parents aren't thrilled about me stacking shelves in a supermarket after all the debt I racked up on my degree. Thanks for helping me. You're a star.'

As the customer left Kerry experienced a rush of elation. The shop not only raised funds for a charity but also provided a service to the community. Despite her nerves she realised she was enjoying herself.

Her next visitor was a man in his seventies with beetling eyebrows and deep pouches below his eyes. On the counter he placed a pair of khaki trousers and a book on fly-fishing. Kerry opened the cover to find the price. With its elegant loops the handwriting was unmistakeably Alex's.

'What's this shop in aid of then?' the man asked. 'There's so many of them on the high street these days, I can't keep up.'

'We're a mental health charity,' Kerry said. 'We raise funds to provide a helpline and a counselling service for people with anxiety and depression.' She took a leaflet from the stack beside her. 'There's more information in here if you're interested.'

'You hang onto that, love,' he said. 'I'll never get round to reading it.' He counted out the coins for his purchases. 'You hear a lot about folk being depressed these days, don't you? Makes me wonder what's wrong with us all.'

'People have a lot to be unhappy about.'

'Oh for sure. But they always have. Life's never been easy for most folk. In my day, we never took pills or anything like that.'

'Medication can be helpful for some people,' she said, trying not to sound defensive.

The old man made a face. 'I don't know, love. I don't hold with it myself. Better to get outdoors and take your mind off it, if you ask me.'

She glanced at his book. 'Is that what the fishing is for?'

'Got me through fifty years of marriage, didn't it?' He grinned, revealing crooked, brown-edged teeth; then his mouth drooped at the corners. 'Though she's passed on now, God rest her soul.'

'Sorry to hear that.'

'Comes to us all in the end, doesn't it? Would you mind cutting the tag off those trousers for me? I can never find my scissors at home.'

When he'd gone Kerry circled the shop, tidying the clothes that customers had left on the wrong rails or crumpled on the floor. She was admiring a dress with a stiff net skirt and cherries embroidered on its elasticated bodice when two well-dressed women with feathered pixie haircuts entered the shop.

'This place is better than most,' one said. 'I've found a few pieces in the vintage section before. And they sometimes have antiques upstairs.'

'I'm not sure I can be arsed to wade through the junk,' her friend said. She rifled through the tops, curling her upper lip. 'Look at the price of this. That's more than it would cost new.'

'That's charities for you. Always trying to squeeze more money out of people.'

Had they not noticed Kerry standing near them, or hadn't they realised she worked there? But they must have, because one of them swung round to face her.

'Excuse me,' she said in a peremptory voice. 'When are you next putting out new stock?'

'We restock on Wednesday evenings,' Kerry said.

'Let's come back on Thursday, shall we?' the woman said to her friend. 'I'm dying for a coffee.'

As they left, one remarked without bothering to lower her voice, 'Of course, you know these volunteers pick out the best stuff and keep it for themselves.'

Kerry was still feeling annoyed several minutes later when she saw Alex padding down the stairs.

'How's it going?' he asked as he approached her.

She placed her hands below the counter so he couldn't see how unsteady they were. As she was about to reply Alex saw someone struggling with the front door. He strode over and held it open.

The tiniest old woman Kerry had ever seen entered the shop on spindly legs, pushing a shabby tartan shopping trolley. Her thinning hair was wispy white and enormous pink plastic-framed glasses dominated her face.

'Good morning Gladys,' Alex said as he closed the door and turned to face her.

'Hello Alex. How are you today?'

'Very well, thank you. A pleasure to see you as always.' He led her over to the till. 'Can I introduce you to Kerry? It's her first day in the shop.'

'What's happened to Elspeth?' Gladys said in a tremulous voice. 'She's not poorly, is she?'

'No, no. Elspeth's fine. It's not one of her days today.'

'Oh good. Well, it's always nice to see a new face,' she said to Kerry. She turned back to Alex. 'Have you got any more detective stories?'

'I found one this morning and put it to one side for you.'

'Alex looks out for books especially for me,' Gladys said to Kerry. 'He's such a nice man, isn't he?'

Kerry mumbled something that could have passed for yes. Alex turned on his heel. 'I'll go upstairs and fetch it.'

Gladys pottered over to examine the bric-a-brac, picking up and replacing a brass paperweight in the shape of a sewing machine, an owl candle-holder and a lacquered wooden pot. Alex returned with the crime novel. The gleaming knife and pool of blood on the cover suggested a more lurid thriller than Kerry would have chosen but she supposed he knew what he was doing.

'I can only read for a little while, because it strains my eyes,' Gladys told Kerry. 'But I like to get through a few pages before I go to sleep.'

'Don't those stories give you nightmares?' Kerry asked as she rang up the price on the till.

'Oh no.' Gladys gave her a wicked grin, her eyes twinkling behind her thick glasses. 'I love a good murder, me.'

She hunted through the loose change in her purse.

'Oh dear.' Gladys became downcast. 'I'm a little short of cash today. I'll have to put it back.' She replaced the book on the counter but Alex returned it to her.

'Bring the money next time you're in. I trust you,' he said with a smile.

Gladys looked up at him gratefully. 'Thank you ever so much. I promise I'll pay you first thing tomorrow morning.'

He helped her stow her purchase in her trolley and wheeled it to the door, which he held open for her. Then he returned to the counter and withdrew a note from his wallet.

'She'll never remember. She's got no money anyway. She can barely afford to heat her house.'

'How old do you think she is?' Kerry asked as she handed Alex his change.

'She's eighty-nine. As far as I know she's completely on her own, and she gets very confused. I think she needs a carer, but with all the cuts to social care I expect she doesn't qualify for one yet.'

'Poor thing. I hope she enjoys the book. She's got adventurous taste in reading.'

'Oh, Gladys isn't easily shocked. I get the impression she's been through a lot in her lifetime. Anyway, I'm off to have lunch now.' He gave her a meaningful look. 'Do come up and look at the books later if you want a break.'

He left, and Kerry composed herself just in time as Sue bustled onto the shop floor.

'How's it been?'

'Everything's fine,' she said, proud her first morning had been a success.

They both looked round the shop. A woman in a scruffy leather coat and boots splitting at the seams was rooting through the clothes, plucking at the labels with thin agitated fingers. Her grey hair hung in snaky tangles round her face.

'That's Mo,' Sue said in a low voice. 'She's schizophrenic, like my Ian. Don't be scared of her; she's a harmless soul, bless her. Comes in here most days.'

'Does she ever buy anything?' Kerry asked as Mo held a satin ballgown up against her chest and muttered something.

'She only browses. She spends all day in charity shops and cafes. Everyone round here knows her.'

As Mo passed them Kerry gave her a shy smile but she didn't appear to notice. The smell of unwashed clothes lingered behind her.

'How is Ian these days?' Kerry asked Sue when Mo had gone.

'He's doing well, thanks love. Been stable for a while now. He's learning to play the guitar and making new friends.'

'That's great he's enjoying his life. It must have been a shock for you when he was diagnosed.'

Sue exhaled a sigh. 'D'you know what really hurt? How our friends avoided us. When my other son had childhood leukaemia, everyone rallied round with hot meals and lifts to the hospital. When Ian got sick, no one wanted to know about my poor boy who was hearing voices in his head.'

'That's awful. Stigma's such a terrible thing.' Kerry paused. 'Did your son with leukaemia make a good recovery?'

'No. Sadly we lost him.'

'I'm so sorry,' she said, shocked. Sue really had been through the mill.

'My ex couldn't handle the stress of it,' Sue said. 'Our marriage broke up and he left me on my own to deal with Ian's problems.'

'Jesus. That must have been hard.'

'He was never the world's best dad, if I'm honest. Always off out getting pissed. Got married too young, that was our trouble. But that was what people like us did in those days.'

'When did you meet your second husband?' Kerry asked.

'About five years ago. He's a real gentleman. Not like my ex at all.' She nudged Kerry's elbow. 'You see, love. It's never too late to start again.'

'Not sure I'm ready for that.'

'Get yourself divorced and sorted with a job first. And if I was you, I'd go out and have some fun while you still can.' Sue wagged a finger. 'But don't go getting involved with any bad apples. Wait for the right one to come along.'

At mid-afternoon an influx of customers led to a queue building in front of Kerry's counter. Next in line was a mum with a toddler in a pushchair, clutching a pair of trainers. She was in her twenties, pale and harassed, her hair scrunched into a ponytail. An older girl stood beside them, looking bored.

'Mummy, I need to go *now*,' the child in the pushchair said.

'Can my little boy use your loo, please?' the mum asked Kerry. 'He's desperate.'

Sue had told her under no circumstances were customers allowed to use the toilet at the back of the shop.

'If we start making exceptions, we'll have them traipsing in and out all day,' she'd said. 'It's against health and safety regulations. There's stuff in the corridor they could trip over.'

'Sorry,' Kerry said, 'but it's for staff only. I think there's one in the café over the road.'

The young mum let out an exasperated sigh.

'All right.' She crouched down next to her son. 'You'll have to hold it in while I pay for these shoes.'

'I can't,' the little boy said, wriggling and crossing his legs in distress. Kerry was tempted to let him use the toilet but Sue would be lurking in the corridor, and then there'd be trouble. The mum plonked the trainers onto the counter. They were pure white with no signs of wear.

'That's seven pounds, please,' Kerry said as she keyed in the price.

The woman looked up in surprise. 'They're one pound. It says so here.'

She pointed to the sticky label on which the number was scrawled. Kerry hunched over to inspect it closer.

'I'm sorry, but it's a seven, not a one. I know it looks unclear. Someone must have written it in a hurry.'

The young mum scowled. 'You're charging me seven quid for shoes someone else has worn? You're kidding me, right?'

Kerry's insides tensed at her tone. 'They'd be very expensive if they were new.'

'But they're *not* new, are they? Second hand stuff's supposed to be cheap. That's the whole point of it.'

'I understand how you feel. But I'm afraid we don't give discounts unless there's actually a fault.'

'Well, I haven't got seven quid, have I? So you'll have to put them back.' The woman flung the trainers across the counter and they tumbled onto the floor at Kerry's feet.

'It's a disgrace,' she continued. 'People in this country can't afford to feed their kids, and here you are, ripping us off. I bet *you've* never had to wear the same pair of shoes till they fell apart, have you?' Her eyes were hard. She jabbed her finger at Kerry. 'Hey. I asked you a question. Have you?'

'No, I haven't,' she said apologetically, conscious that other customers were waiting to be served. She needed to do something to take control of the situation but panic had paralysed her brain. All she could focus on was the threat in front of her. She felt herself starting to hyperventilate.

'I suppose you think you're special because you work for a charity?' The woman was yelling at her now. 'Do you tell all your friends what a good person you are?'

'Come on, there's no need to be like that,' the man next in line said. 'She's only doing her job.'

The mum spun round, her eyes bulging. 'Who asked *your* opinion?'

The child in the pushchair burst into howls. The older girl leaned over him.

'Mum, he's peed his pants,' she said with a smirk.

'Great,' the mum snapped. 'Now I've got to go home on the bus with him soaking wet and whining.'

Sue appeared from the back and stood surveying the chaotic scene. A damp patch was spreading across the carpet below the pushchair. The child was still crying.

'What the heck's going on?'

'The little boy's had an accident,' Kerry said, her voice shaking. 'And this lady's not happy about the cost of our shoes.'

'Are you the manager?' the woman said to Sue. 'Because you ought to be ashamed of yourself.'

Sue stood with her arms folded and her lips pursed.

'If you've got a complaint about our prices, you can send it in to our head office,' she said in a voice of iron. 'Now if you're not going to buy anything, I suggest you get your kids home.'

The mum glowered. 'You haven't heard the last of this. It's disgusting, that's what it is,' she said, and she swung the pushchair around and barged out of the shop.

'Sorry to keep you waiting,' Kerry said to the man next in the queue. She took his purchases but her hands were trembling too much to operate the till.

'I'll serve these customers, Kerry,' Sue said. 'You make yourself a brew. Alex will be down for his break any minute. I'll ask him to cover the rest of your shift. It's as quiet as a graveyard up there and he's only sitting around reading.'

Kerry retreated into the staffroom where she put the kettle on. She was drinking tea and beginning to calm down when Alex came in and drew up a chair, next to her but not close enough to invade her space.

'Sue told me what happened,' he said. 'I wanted to check you were all right.'

'I'm fine, thanks.' Her voice still sounded unsteady. She was suddenly mortified. What must he think of her, getting herself in such a state over a difficult customer? She put down her mug.

'The thing was I felt awful for the woman, even though she was shouting at me. She was obviously struggling to bring up those children, and she was right, our stuff isn't cheap. On the other hand, Sue's right too: if we charged less, the charity's income would suffer.'

'I understand,' he said. 'But we can't help everyone all of the time, however much we'd like to. And you're doing a wonderful job here. You've nothing to feel guilty about.'

'Thank you. I'm sorry.'

'Kerry, you don't need to apologise to me for being compassionate.'

She stared at him until their eye contact became unbearable.

'Her little lad made a mess on the carpet. I ought to go and clean it up,' she said, and the spell was broken.

'You finish your tea. I'll do it,' Alex said, getting to his feet. 'Is there a cloth or something around?'

Kerry searched under the sink and discovered a dishcloth and a bucket, which she filled with hot water and disinfectant. She handed them to him and he left. Later, Sue returned with the bucket swinging from one hand. She tipped the dirty water down the sink, sat down and got out a monthly sales report Dan had prepared for her. Kerry cleared her throat.

'Sorry about before. I wasn't sure how to deal with her.'

Sue was absorbed in the figures. 'It's all right, love. It's a shame it happened on your first day. But I'm sure you'll toughen up in time.'

'Do you think she'll make a complaint?'

'I don't give a monkey's if she does. I'm more concerned that our takings were down again last month.'

'We'll do well this month with Christmas coming up, surely?'

'Aye, but it may not be enough to make up the deficit. The rent on this place is exorbitant. If things don't improve, head office could start making noises about shutting us down.'

'They won't do that, will they?' Kerry asked, alarmed.

'Not if I've got anything to do with it.' Sue tossed the report onto a shelf, then she smiled. 'I was thinking about Alex out there on his hands and knees, scrubbing piss off the carpet. It's a shame really, when you consider who he used to be.'

Kerry awaited an explanation, but none came. Was Sue expecting her to prompt her with questions? As the silence lengthened Sue glanced at the clock.

'Is that the time already? You may as well get off home.'

The moment to ask had passed. Kerry took her jacket and went onto the shop floor. The wet patch on the carpet had increased in size and the acrid smell of disinfectant irritated her throat. Alex was behind the counter. She hoped he might look up but he was busy serving.

Outside it was freezing and she hurried along the darkened streets to get home. Questions crowded into her mind. What was she going to do about the situation developing between her and Alex? And what had Sue meant by her reference to who he used to be?

# 7

After her third day at the shop Kerry had the rest of the week to herself. She spent the time searching for jobs online, taking long walks through the streets and visiting the library. When her anxiety had been at its worst she'd been unable to read: as she tried to focus on the page, terrifying images of accidents and death flooded her mind.

Now her concentration was improving it was a delight to return to the world of her imagination, though when she was feeling vulnerable she still gained more comfort from re-reading beloved authors than venturing into unfamiliar territory.

On library visits she usually used the self-service checkout so as to avoid human contact. But this week she decided to sign her books out at the desk. She imagined the grey-haired librarian was a customer in the shop and approached her with a smile.

'Morning. Can I take these out please? I've read *Rebecca* so many times, but I feel like going back to it again.'

'I loved it too. And the Hitchcock film,' the librarian said, and for a few minutes they bonded over their sympathy for the shy young Mrs de Winter.

Kerry left the library elated. She'd done it. She'd initiated small talk while completing a transaction, like other people did. Despite its challenges the volunteering was already having a positive impact on her mental state.

The week after, she was due to sign on at the job centre before her shift in the shop, a prospect that filled her with dread. She left in good time to catch the bus but it got stuck in traffic. Panic seized her at the thought of being late, which could mean her benefits would be sanctioned.

She raced down the road from the bus stop and charged in through the glass doors, breathless but on time. The security guard directed her to a seat in the waiting area alongside a gaunt black man with dreadlocks, an elegant ash-haired woman and a teenage girl in a tracksuit.

Kerry waited, her anxiety mounting, until someone shouted her name. She perched on the edge of her seat opposite the advisor, who wasn't her usual one but a burly man with a ruddy complexion. He sat scrolling through her records before he turned his attention to her.

'I see you've been on jobseekers a few months now.'

She detected a note of accusation in his voice. 'I'm sure something will turn up soon. I'm very IT literate and I've got plenty of experience.'

'How many jobs have you applied for in the last two weeks?'

She showed him the diary sheet that detailed her extensive search. The companies she'd sent her CV to. The interviews she'd attended. The agencies she'd signed up with and the websites she visited every day.

The advisor flicked through the papers with a bemused expression. 'Blimey. And you got nothing from all that?'

'It seems not.'

'You say you can use computers, right? What about something in telesales? We've got a couple of vacancies on the database at the moment.'

Her cheeks grew hot. The thought of cold-calling an irritable stranger she'd disturbed at home made her panicky inside.

'I'm not sure I'd be very good at that. I'm not much of a salesperson,' she said with a nervous laugh.

The advisor evidently didn't find it amusing. He leaned forward and raised his voice, causing her to shrink back in her seat.

'Thing is, right, you've had a chance now to find something that suits you. You know your payments can be stopped if you refuse to apply for a job we tell you about?'

Her palms prickled. Should she tell him she'd been diagnosed with an anxiety disorder? Looking at his face, what was the point? He'd only see it as another excuse to get out of working. In the opposite corner the girl in the tracksuit was sitting in front of a similar desk, shaking and in tears.

'I'm only warning you how the system works nowadays,' he said in a more conciliatory tone. 'Wouldn't be doing my job if I didn't.'

'Okay. I'll apply for the telesales position,' she said in a resigned voice.

'We should get you registered on a work programme too.'

From what she'd heard these placements consisted of little more than stacking shelves without getting paid.

'Do I really need to do that? I'm already volunteering in a charity shop. I'm learning a lot about retail there.'

The advisor sat fiddling with his pen. Then he yawned. He turned to his computer and entered something in her records.

'All right. You've shown us you're looking for work. But we expect to see you broadening your search. Don't forget, you have to be willing to travel up to ninety minutes each way.'

In her haste to escape the building she ran into a lad outside the door coming in. As she began to apologise she recognised him.

'Hello Shaun.'

Shaun seemed unable to place her, and she remembered he'd only met her a couple of times before.

'It's Kerry from the shop.'

'Oh yeah. Course it is.' He gave her a rare smile. 'I never knew you was signing on here too.'

'Yep. I've just finished.'

There was a faint smell of weed coming from Shaun's hooded top. 'Did the bastards give you a hard time?' he asked.

'He wasn't very nice or helpful. But he let me sign on, so that's good.'

'Sorted. All right mate, I'd better go in. You know what this place is like, innit? They dock your payments if you're late, but they're happy to make *you* wait to see them. There's nowhere to have a piss and they won't even let you bring in a fucking drink.' He gave a bitter laugh. 'And there's no jobs anyway. They've got some fucking nerve, calling themselves a fucking job centre, when they've got no fucking jobs.'

As Shaun concluded his tirade Kerry sensed the powerless rage that consumed him.

'It's dire, isn't it? Good luck anyway. I'll see you in the shop.'

Shaun hunched his shoulders. As he slouched into the job centre, hands in pockets, the security guard gave him a hard look.

Kerry walked to the bus stop, her relief that the interview was over now tainted by her growing worry. They were clearly going to get tough if she didn't find something soon. But it could be worse. She'd be offered something in the end, even if it had to be in a call centre. Shaun was a convicted criminal, unskilled, inarticulate and treated with suspicion wherever he went. If she was struggling, what chance did he have?

At the shop Kerry was introduced to a volunteer who came in once a week to change the window display and help Sue with the clothes. Yasmeen was a twenty-year-old student with long dark hair and lustrous eyes rimmed with liquid liner. She wore tight black pants, a loose gauzy top and a stack of gold bangles on her wrist.

'Yasmeen's studying fashion design, aren't you, love?' Sue said. 'Got a real eye for style, she has.'

The three women sorted the stock, chatting as they worked. Kerry learned that Yasmeen was in the second year of her degree and that her ambition was to start up her own clothing company.

'There's some amazing things tucked away in the stockroom,' Yasmeen said. 'I love going through the boxes to find quirky stuff for the displays.'

'Yasmeen's helping us appeal to the hipsters,' Sue told Kerry. 'Not just middle-aged folk like you and me.'

'What are you working on at college?' Kerry asked Yasmeen, ignoring Sue's remark.

'I'm designing a set of wedding outfits with a contemporary twist. I'm arranging a photo shoot for my portfolio. I've got a few friends lined up as models. I just need to find a photographer who won't charge me a fortune.'

'You should ask Alex to do it,' Sue said.

Kerry's insides leapt at the mention of his name. 'Of course, Alex used to be a wedding photographer, didn't he?'

Sue gave a snort. 'Is that what he told you?'

'You mean he wasn't?' Kerry said, frowning.

'No, technically he was. But it's a bit of an understatement, to say the least.'

Sue paused to rub her nose. Kerry sensed she was longing to gossip and yet reluctant to begin.

'Alex doesn't like to talk about his past,' Sue said at last. 'But he used to be one of the top photographers in the country. Did portraits for models and celebrities, and even royalty sometimes. As well as photography for high society weddings and big events down in London.'

'Seriously?' Yasmeen said. 'Alex was famous?'

'In his own field, he was. Won loads of awards. I've got a book of his photos at home. Alexander Bowland, his name is. Sounds posh, doesn't it?'

So that was what Sue had meant by who he used to be. Someone of importance. Now Kerry knew his full name too. There was so much more she wanted to know but she didn't dare show too much curiosity. She'd have to rely on Yasmeen to ask the questions.

'So why's he working in a charity shop in Manchester?' Yasmeen said, as if on cue.

Sue pursed her lips. 'That's not for me to say. And I don't recommend you ask him either,' she added, as if regretting now what she'd divulged.

Kerry had been wondering for some time whether Alex had been ill, like her. Now she was almost certain. It made sense of why he'd given up a high-profile career to volunteer for a mental health charity, and why Sue was reluctant to disclose anything further. How bad had he been? She hated to imagine him suffering.

Yasmeen was buffing one of her shellac fingernails. 'How old is he anyway? I'm guessing he's in his mid-forties.'

'Closer to fifty, I reckon,' Kerry said.

Sue laughed out loud. 'You girls are way off. Alex is older than me. He'll be sixty in May next year. Though he says we're not to make a fuss about his birthday.'

Kerry dropped her pricing gun into the heap of clothes. There was a seventeen-year age gap between them? How could she not have realised? She retrieved the gun, hoping the others hadn't noticed her reaction.

Yasmeen seemed equally astonished. 'I can't believe he's so old.'

'Sixty's not *that* old,' Sue said with a scowl. 'He's lucky he's still got all his hair, and he's kept himself very trim. But you can see his age in his face.'

'He's not married, is he? Has he got a girlfriend?' Yasmeen asked.

The knot of tension inside Kerry's chest expanded like a balloon.

'I don't think so,' Sue said, and Kerry breathed again. 'He's dated a few women since I've known him, but nothing seems to work out for him, bless him.'

'That's a shame. He seems like a nice guy,' Yasmeen said. 'Do you think he'd do my fashion shoot for a reasonable price?'

Sue chuckled. 'He'll probably do it for nothing, love, if you flutter your eyelashes at him.'

'I'll ask him what his rates are. But I don't "flutter my eyelashes" at anyone,' Yasmeen said firmly, and she marched out of the corridor on her way upstairs.

'What's she got the hump about?' Sue asked.

'I don't think she liked the idea that she'd have to use her sexuality to get what she wanted,' Kerry said carefully.

'It was only a joke. You feminists these days are so uptight.'

Yasmeen was gone for ages. Kerry felt a stab of envy as she imagined the stylish young student chatting to Alex about photography and fashion. At last Yasmeen returned.

'He insisted on doing it as a favour, like you said,' she told Sue. 'And you were right about him being secretive. I was dying to know about all the celebrities he photographed, but he wasn't up for talking about it at all.'

'That's Alex for you,' Sue said with a superior smile. 'I did warn you.'

Kerry attached a tag to a cable-knit cardigan, the last item of clothing on the table.

'We seem to have cleared the mountain,' she remarked. 'What do you want us to do now?'

'Have a rummage through the bric-a-brac,' Sue said. 'Make sure you chuck away anything tatty. I don't want any crap going out on the shop floor.'

In the staffroom Kerry balanced on a rickety stool to lift down two cardboard boxes from the top shelf. She opened the first box and gave the other to Yasmeen. Inside hers was an assortment of cut-crystal sugar bowls, blue-and-white decorative plates rimmed with gold, cat ornaments and a landscape painting in a splintered wooden frame.

In the other box Yasmeen unearthed a pair of silver filigree serving tongs, a glass lamp with a cracked shade and a paper fan with a shiny black edge, which she opened to reveal a pattern of birds and delicate cherry blossoms.

'That's pretty,' Kerry said as Yasmeen fanned herself with it. 'Sue found a kimono the other day in a similar style. I don't know what she did with it.'

'We should put them together for a window display,' Yasmeen said.

'Good idea.' Kerry gave Yasmeen a smile. 'So how long have you volunteered here?'

'Since last year,' Yasmeen said. 'I wanted to do it partly because of the fashion. But I also wanted to help the charity because some of my friends have got mental health issues.'

'I know university can be very stressful, with all the debt and pressure to do well.'

'The demand for the counselling service is huge,' Yasmeen said.

Had counselling even been available in Kerry's day? She couldn't remember. It wasn't a service she'd have considered using.

'I guess I'm lucky,' Yasmeen continued, 'that I'm a very positive person. And my family are so supportive. I can talk to them about anything.'

Kerry was about to ask her more when a man's voice she didn't recognise spoke to Sue outside. They heard slow heavy footsteps and laboured breathing as he came down the corridor.

'That'll be Pete,' Yasmeen whispered to Kerry.

'The guy who does the furniture?'

'Yeah.' She pulled a face. 'He's kind of a creep.'

The door swung open and Pete lumbered in. He was short and balding and wore low-slung jeans and a T-shirt stretched over the expanse of his stomach. When he saw the two women he stopped.

'Morning ladies.' His eyes rested on Yasmeen, who ignored him as she checked her phone, before they flickered over to Kerry.

'I haven't seen *you* before. Are you new?' His gaze travelled down to her chest and back up to her face.

'Quite new, I suppose,' she said.

Pete drew up a chair, too close to Kerry for comfort, and sat down with a wheezing sigh. He drew an inhaler from his pocket and took a couple of puffs. 'So what's a nice girl like you doing in a dump like this?'

Yasmeen looked up, scowling. 'It's not a dump, Pete.'

He held up his hands. 'All right, petal. It was a joke. Keep your hair on.'

'And stop calling me petal. I've told you about that before.'

Pete moved closer to Kerry until she felt his hot breath on her ear. 'She's a right spitfire, that Yasmeen. I wouldn't like to get on the wrong side of her, would you?'

Kerry said nothing, but edged gradually away from him.

'I see you're more the shy retiring type,' Pete observed.

'Leave Kerry alone. She doesn't need any grief from you,' Yasmeen said.

'Which of you girls is going to put the kettle on and make me a brew?' Pete said.

Their wall of silence greeted him.

'Suit yourselves. I'll make my own.' He rose ponderously to his feet. Kerry took the opportunity to move her chair further away.

She and Yasmeen continued to sort through the bric-a-brac, talking in a subdued manner. Pete slurped his tea and flicked through the newspaper and pretended he wasn't listening.

Later, Dan joined them to eat his lunch before his shift. Then the door opened again and Kerry inhaled sharply, because it was Alex.

'Hello everyone,' he said, surprised to be confronted with such a crowded room. As there were no chairs left he perched on the rickety stool opposite Kerry.

She tried to picture him taking photos at a glamorous event, instead of sorting through dusty old books. In fact, it wasn't difficult to imagine. He was the archetypal artist: an unconventional figure who belonged nowhere and as a result was able to infiltrate any social scene.

Kerry returned her attention to the bric-a-brac, lifting out a box sealed with parcel tape. She was picking at the tape with her fingernails when Yasmeen handed her a penknife she'd found among the detritus on the shelves.

As she was slitting along the length of the tape, her hand slipped. The knife ripped into the cardboard, narrowly missing her fingers. She winced and knocked the box off the table. It thudded onto the lino floor. Something cracked.

Before anyone else had time to react Alex leaned forward. 'Are you all right?'

'I'm fine. I didn't cut myself. But I think I've broken whatever's in there.'

She retrieved the box and opened it. Inside was a layer of tissue paper, which parted to reveal a flash of gold. She removed the paper and lifted out the object.

'What is it?' Yasmeen asked.

'Some kind of ornament,' Kerry said, holding it up.

It was a ten-inch ceramic figurine of a winged cherub playing a harp. Its legs and cheeks were overly chubby, the snub nose was wonky and pig-like and its glass eyes were too close-set, giving it the appearance more of a devious gargoyle than of an angelic baby. Scuffs and scratches marred its gold coating.

'That is one of the most hideous things I've seen in my life,' Dan said in delight.

'Let's have a gander.' Pete took the figurine from Kerry and read the inscription running along the base. 'Omnia Vincit Amor. What does that mean when it's at home?'

'Love conquers all,' Alex said, making Dan snigger. 'Could I see him please?'

Kerry watched, bewitched, as Alex took the cherub from Pete, found his glasses in his shirt pocket and placed them on. He held the figurine up to the light.

'He's very shoddily made,' he said. 'The facial and body proportions are all wrong. If he's meant to be a cupid, as the inscription suggests, he should have a bow and arrow, not a harp. And one of his eyes is smashed.'

'That's from when I dropped him, I'm afraid,' Kerry said. 'I suppose we'd better throw him away. Sue won't want him on the shop floor.'

'Let's put it out and have a bet on whether anyone will buy it,' Dan said.

'I'll bet you a pint we won't sell it. No one in their right mind's going to shell out for that,' Pete said.

'Does anyone else reckon we'll sell a one-eyed cherub that's possibly the ugliest thing on the planet?' Dan said.

Alex raised his hand. 'I bet we will. I say someone will fall in love with him and take him home.'

'You said yourself it was a piece of tat,' Dan said.

'I know,' Alex said. 'But art is subjective.'

'You can't call that *art*,' Yasmeen said, regarding the thing with distaste.

'Let's give him a chance, shall we? Here you are, Kerry,' Alex said, handing the figurine back to her. Their fingers touched and the shot of electricity almost made her drop the cherub again.

'Put today's date on it,' Dan said as Kerry stuck a price label on the base. If we haven't sold it in six months, Alex loses and owes Pete a pint.'

'And no cheating, Alex, all right?' Pete said. 'You're not allowed to hide it or get one of your mates to buy it.'

'Don't worry. I won't need to,' he said with an assured smile.

Kerry wrote the date on the label. For some reason the cherub made her feel sad. Dan and the others thought it was funny but there was something forlorn about how misconceived and unlovable he was. She went into the shop with the rest of the goods she'd priced. Dan accompanied her, bearing the cherub.

'There you go, my precious,' he said as he placed it high on a shelf, next to a twisted bronze lamp stand.

Later, Sue bustled into the staffroom with a frown on her face.

'Who put that naff gold thing on display? I told you, we don't sell crap in here.'

'Come on Sue, it's a joke. Does it matter if it stays there a while?' Dan explained about the bet.

Sue huffed, but because she liked Dan she let the cherub stay. And there he remained for weeks, until Kerry stopped noticing him any more.

# 8

On Monday Kerry went into the shop expecting Alex to be there as usual. During the morning Sue asked her to take some change upstairs and she ascended the stairs with anticipation. But there was no sign of him. A crate of books sat unopened next to the shelves.

She handed Ruth her coins and affected an air of nonchalance. 'Is Alex not in today?'

'He's off sick.'

'Nothing serious, I hope?'

Ruth's face remained impassive. 'The usual, I think.'

Kerry raised her eyebrows.

'One of his low moods,' Ruth said.

So it was true. 'I didn't know he was depressed.'

Ruth responded with a slight shrug, as if to say, 'then you don't know him very well, do you?'

Kerry didn't feel comfortable enough with Ruth to ask her any more questions. She went down to the staffroom where Sue sat at the table, a biro gripped in her teeth, going through the stock list.

'Ruth told me Alex is feeling down today.'

Sue removed the pen from her mouth. 'I know. I spoke to him on the phone earlier. He'll be all right, bless him. He's not in one of his bad phases at the moment. Just needs a day to himself.'

Kerry drew up a chair opposite, sensing Sue trusted her enough now to tell her more.

'Does he have severe depression?'

'Oh aye. He can be laid low for months. He had a complete mental breakdown when he was about your age. His brain's never really recovered.'

'And that's why he works here?'

Sue put the stock list to one side and nodded.

'I was in two minds whether to say it in front of Yasmeen the other day, but Alex hasn't done paid work in years. He gets tired too easily and can't handle any kind of stress. He's okay here, but it's dead quiet upstairs, and we don't put any pressure on him. Even so he's had more days off than I can count. That's not an issue for us, because we're a mental health charity and he's a volunteer. We're grateful for anything he can do.'

'But employers would expect more.'

'He'd need a very supportive boss in order to cope. And there aren't many of them around. As he's found out in the past.'

'Does he get state support?'

'Yes, but he lives in fear that the Department of Work and Pensions will send him for an assessment and declare him fit for work.' Sue exhaled a sigh. 'I don't know who they think would hire him now, given his age and the fact he's got no recent employment history.'

'And he doesn't earn any money as a photographer?'

'He still tells people that's what he does, but he's just trying to keep some pride. The work's too stressful for him. I doubt he makes a penny from it any more.'

Kerry twisted her nose ring as she gazed down at the table. 'It must be hard. I feel bad for him.'

'We all do, love. It's a pity, especially when he was so brilliant. But he's doing all right. He's found a lifeline in this place.'

'I'm glad about that.'

Sue gave her a smile. 'Bless you. You're a caring little soul.'

It was true Kerry would feel empathy for anyone in Alex's situation, but it was more poignant when she was already halfway in love with him.

'What about Ruth?' she said, to deflect Sue's attention from her interest in Alex. 'She's here all week. Is she unemployed too?'

'Ruth doesn't need to work. Inherited a fortune from a relative. Comes in here for something to do. She lives on her own out in Cheshire with her dog. That's all we know about her. I've tried probing further, but she just clams up.'


The next day Alex returned. Kerry waited until Ruth was on her break and went upstairs. She found him rearranging books, keeping an eye on the till as he worked. When he saw her, he stood up.

'Morning Kerry. Lovely to see you.'

There was nothing in his appearance to suggest he was suffering today; in fact he was clean-shaven and his eyes looked bright, as if he were better rested than usual. He wore a shirt in a sky-blue colour, which complemented the sandy tones of his hair and skin.

'Thought I'd come up and say hello,' Kerry said. 'I hope you're feeling better now?'

'Oh much better, thanks. I'd just worn myself out and needed a rest.'

Alex noticed a book out of line on the shelves and bent over to tuck it in. He turned back to her.

'I expect they've told you all about me, haven't they? I know there's no such thing as confidentiality here.'

'I asked Sue if you were okay and she explained,' Kerry said. 'I hope you don't mind?'

'Not at all. I've learned not to be ashamed any more. Do ask me about it if you want. No really, don't be embarrassed. I don't go into detail with most people. But I'll make an exception for you.'

'Is there anything that helps?'

'A stable routine. Knowing people who understand and care. And of course, the medication. I'm on loads of it, because I've got a heart condition as well.' He gave a wry laugh. 'Just to keep things interesting.'

Her fingers crept to her lips. 'Is it serious?'

'Well, heart disease usually is. Don't worry though; I'm not about to drop dead. I stick to a low-fat diet and don't drink too much. I exercise every day, which helps with the mood swings too. I know it sounds boring, but I'm used to it now.'

'You're in very good shape as a result,' Kerry said, looking up at him from lowered lashes, then she flushed at her boldness. Had she gone too far and made him uncomfortable? But he was smiling.

'Thank you,' he said, arching his eyebrows. 'It's rare anyone gives me a compliment these days.'

Her pulse was racing. She needed to slow things down. Talk to him about something else. On impulse she blurted out the thing she'd been meaning to tell him.

'I've got a mental health problem too. That's why I wanted to volunteer here. I'm on medication for anxiety.'

Without a trace of hesitation, and in a more serious voice, Alex said, 'I'm sorry about that. If you ever need a friend to talk to, I'm always here.'

'Thanks.' Did his lack of surprise suggest he'd suspected as much?

'I mean it,' he said. 'I suffer from anxiety myself sometimes. I know how difficult it is to live with.'

'I get so nervous about silly things,' she admitted. 'Then I feel ashamed of being so weak.'

Alex took a step closer to her. 'Kerry,' he said, 'please, never think of yourself as weak. I see you here every day, pushing yourself to do things that scare you. That makes you incredibly strong. Not everyone understands the battles we have to fight to function in the world. But I do understand. And I respect your courage.'

He smiled, then he moved away again, as if fearful of encroaching on her space.

'Thank you,' was all she could say, clenching her hands into fists to stop them from shaking. Never in her life had anyone said anything that had made her feel so accepted.

A sound behind them made her jump. A man was standing at the counter, tapping his fingers on the pile of vinyl records he was waiting to pay for.

'Don't fret about me, will you love?' he said to Kerry as she caught his eye. 'I've got all day to hang about, me.'

'Sorry,' she called over to him. She turned back. 'Alex, you've got a customer.'

'Oops. I forgot about the till.' He ran his hands through his hair. 'Better go. I'll talk to you soon.'

Back on the ground floor she found Joe and Shaun sorting clothes at the bench. The radio played softly in the background. Sue hovered beside them.

'There you are,' Sue said as Kerry came in. 'Was wondering where the heck you'd got to. I need to bob out to the bank. Can you start pricing this lot?' She indicated the mound of clothing the boys had laid to one side.

Sue left, and Kerry remained with the two lads. For a few awkward minutes they all struggled for something to talk about.

'Are you a local girl, Kerry?' Joe asked her at last.

'I grew up near here. How about you? You live with your family, don't you?'

'Yeah. Me, my mum, my auntie and my two sisters.'

'That's a big household.'

'Yeah. S'all right though, innit. Except when there's a fight for the bathroom with all the ladies wanting to do their make-up before a night out.' Joe smiled as he heaved a new bin bag off the floor onto the table. 'So d'you go out much in town?'

'Not any more. I used to go clubbing when I was your age.'

'Did you go to the Hacienda?'

'Oh yes.' Happy memories flooded back to her of dancing under the glow of red and blue lights, surrounded by a sea of ecstatic faces. As well as the clubs there'd been the bands: The Smiths, The Stone Roses, Happy Mondays and so many others. 'Those were the days. Manchester was so cool back then.'

'So you were a proper little raver?' Joe said, amused.

'I guess. It seems such a long time ago now.' She turned to Shaun. 'Do you go out in the city centre at weekends?'

Shaun hunched his shoulders. 'Town's full of wankers on a Saturday night, innit?'

'Shaun sits in his room all night smoking weed and watching porn,' Joe said, grinning.

'Yeah, and you're a cunt,' Shaun said.

'Oi,' Joe said, raising his hands in mock-horror. 'That's no way to speak in front of Kerry.'

Shaun shrugged. 'I doubt she cares.'

He ripped open an overstuffed bag and tipped out the contents. A voluminous cotton dress caught his attention.

'Whoever wore this must have been a right fat-arse,' he said, holding it up. 'Look, there's loads of them.' He rifled through similar dresses in plain colours.

'They're hand-made,' Kerry said, examining the rough stitching on the hems.

Their owner must have been too large for the clothes in the shops. Why had she given the dresses away? Had she found a diet that worked and cheerily cast off her outsized wardrobe? Or had her health failed, and her grieving relatives cleared out her stuff? Kerry tried to imagine it had been a happy story.

'Put them in the recycling,' she said, observing the sweat stains around the arm holes. 'We can't sell them.'

'Why not? Some other fat fucker could wear them,' Shaun said.

'Don't be a twat, Shaun,' Joe said. 'My Nana's a big lady. She can't help it. It's genetic, innit?'

'No, it isn't. It's from sitting on your fucking arse eating lard all day, innit?' Shaun said.

'She doesn't eat fucking lard, all right?'

'All right. Calm the fuck down, will you?'

Kerry's shoulders tensed as she tried to figure out whether their exchanges were banter or genuine hostility. Since they were both grinning, she concluded it was the former. She took the dresses and bundled them into the blue recycling bag.

'Who's on the shop floor this afternoon?' she asked. 'I know it's not me.'

'I'm on the downstairs till,' Joe said.

She'd noticed that Sue never let Shaun serve on the shop floor. She was sure he'd have picked up on it too.

The boys began exchanging stories about their neighbourhoods.

'The police was down our way this morning,' Shaun said. 'They raided a dealer's house and arrested him. My sister took her chair out onto the street to smoke a fag and watch.'

'How old's your sister?' Kerry asked.

'Twenty-one. She's just had another baby. All that fucking screaming does my head in, d'you know what I mean? I wish I could get my own place, but there's no fucking chance of that.'

Joe was delving into a bag when he froze and sharply withdrew his hand. He took a second peek and a grin spread across his face.

'Oh man,' he said, shaking his head, 'now I really *have* seen everything.'

'What is it?' Shaun asked with sudden interest. 'Come on; get it out.'

'I'm not *touching* it,' Joe said with a shudder. He glanced at Kerry doubtfully. 'Are you sure you want to see this?'

She took a step back from the bench. 'It's not an animal, is it?'

He laughed. 'No. Well, not exactly.'

Joe tipped the bag upside down. Onto the table fell a lacy thong and a large purple vibrator with rabbit ears on the top and rhinestone studs around the handle.

'Jesus.' Kerry covered her mouth with her hand as she laughed. 'Someone donated *that* to charity?'

Shaun snatched the vibrator off the bench and inspected it.

'Gross. How can you touch it?' Joe said, cringing. 'You don't know if it's been washed or not.'

'This is fucking brilliant,' Shaun said, ignoring him as he tweaked the rubber ears. 'Is Dan coming in today? He thought them false teeth was funny; wait till he sees *this*.'

'I can't imagine what they were thinking,' Kerry said. 'Who's going to buy a second hand sex toy?'

'They've given us the instructions too,' Joe said, his face creasing with mirth as he emptied the remaining contents of the bag. 'And some sachets of lube. Strawberry flavour.'

'Let's leave it out for Pete,' Shaun suggested with a cackle. 'He's supposed to test the electrical stuff to make sure it's safe.'

'Oh don't,' Kerry said, dreading to imagine the crude remarks Pete would make when he saw it. 'Anyway, Sue won't like it.'

'What won't I like?' Sue said grimly as she pushed her way through the bamboo curtain into the corridor. When she saw what Shaun held in his hands, she flinched.

'Ugh. What the heck's that doing in here?' She glared at Shaun, as though he'd brought it in himself.

'It was in one of the bags, wasn't it?' he said.

Shaun pressed a button on the side. The rabbit ears quivered and emitted a low buzzing noise. He tried another button and the device began to throb and pulsate. Kerry had to fight to suppress her giggles.

'Turn it off,' Sue snapped.

'I was only seeing if the batteries worked,' Shaun said, scowling as he switched it off.

'No, you weren't. You were trying to be funny. Well, you're not. Chuck that filthy thing in the bin outside. And those panties too. Then wash your hands, grow up and get back to work.'

Still wearing a revolted expression Sue huffed her way down the corridor to the staffroom. Shaun made a face behind her back. The beads parted again and to Kerry's dismay, Alex came into the corridor.

At once she began to blush, praying the lads wouldn't share their latest discovery with him. But Shaun waved the toy in front of him.

'Look at this,' he said. 'Nice, eh?'

This was beyond embarrassing. Suddenly all she could think about was sex. She averted her eyes from the vibrator and tipped her head to one side until her hair concealed her face. Her cheeks flamed.

'I see,' Alex said in a wry voice. 'What a charming gift.'

From behind her shield of hair, Kerry cast a darting glance at him. It didn't help that he looked intolerably attractive today. How had she not noticed earlier that the top buttons of his shirt were undone, revealing a glimpse of his chest? She had to lock her knees together to stop them giving way as she imagined undressing him for the first time.

'D'you reckon it would be illegal to sell it?' Joe asked.

'I can't imagine it would do our reputation much good,' Alex said. He was avoiding Kerry too. As she stole another glance at him, a hot flush crept down the front of his neck. He put a hand to his open shirt collar and then raked it through his hair.

'I need to have a word with Sue. I'll see you later,' he said, and he turned towards the staffroom.

Still trembling, Kerry let out the breath she'd been holding, wishing she could sit down. When was the last time she'd wanted anyone so badly it made her weak? She couldn't recall.

She excused herself and hid in the toilet until she was sure Alex would have gone back upstairs. Then she ventured into the staffroom, where Sue sat alone reading the newspaper, and informed her she was taking an early lunch break.

As Kerry was about to leave Sue looked up from the paper. 'You know love, you don't have to put up with Shaun clowning around. You're twice his age. You can tell him to shut up.'

'He wasn't doing anything to offend me. He's all right, once you get past the attitude.'

'Well, you're the type to see the best in everyone,' Sue said dismissively. 'Me on the other hand, I've met too many lads like Shaun. They try to make out they're just misunderstood, but it's all bullshit.'

Kerry tried to persuade Sue to see the amusing side of the incident. 'People bring in some weird things, don't they? I always wonder what the story behind it is.'

'There's nowt as queer as folk, as my dad used to say,' Sue said, though it seemed to Kerry she showed little curiosity about human nature. She folded up the newspaper and peered at Kerry over her spectacles. 'By the way, how's the job hunting going?'

'I've applied for loads. But I'm competing against so many people who are better qualified.'

Sue tutted. 'What *you* need is more belief in yourself. There's nothing wrong with you, apart from your confidence issues.'

# 9

On Saturday morning Kerry took the bus to attend her therapy session. The counselling service was above a church hall in a draughty room with peeling paintwork and bare floorboards. Her therapist Magda had done her best to brighten the space by covering the walls with posters of rainbows and sunsets with inspirational quotes.

'How are you this week?' Magda asked as she switched the kettle on.

'Well, thank you.' Kerry removed her fur-trimmed jacket and settled into the creaky old armchair. The fabric on its arm was ripped open and the foam stuffing poked out. She resisted the temptation to pull at it.

'You look well today.' Magda set their mugs on the table, next to a plastic alarm clock and a box of tissues. She sat in the chair opposite, draped a crocheted blanket over her legs and tucked a strand of her thick treacle-brown hair behind her ears.

'Tell me what's been going on for you.' Magda spoke fluent English with a trace of a Dutch accent.

Kerry stared at the yellow smiley faces on one of the posters. They reminded her of the acid-house badges she'd worn at raves. What would her high-as-a-kite eighteen-year-old self have said if she'd known she'd be seeing smiley faces again when she was in her forties, unemployed and sitting in a therapist's room?

'I've been in the shop half the week,' she said. 'And I've done some job applications. Apart from reading books, that's about it.'

'You seem to be enjoying your voluntary work,' Magda said. 'I'm glad it's working out for you.'

'It was a good idea. It's helping with the anxiety.'

'That's excellent news. Anything else?'

Kerry couldn't resist picking at the foam any longer. 'I've met a man I like. As in really, really like. I can't stop thinking about him. And he's single, and I'm pretty sure he likes me too, but…'

She detached a piece of the stuffing from the armchair and twiddled it in her fingers.

'There's a problem?' As the silence lengthened Magda leaned forward. 'Perhaps you have doubts about starting a new relationship while you're going through all this upheaval?'

'The timing could be better, it's true. But it's not just that. It's frightening me how much I want him.'

'I see.'

What did Magda see? Her expression was pensive but it was difficult to know what she was thinking most of the time.

'Don't you think it's a bad sign that I'm so obsessed with this guy when I hardly know him?' Kerry asked.

'What makes you think it is?'

'I don't know. I'm scared I could be making a fool of myself. Love at first sight is an illusion, isn't it?'

'It can be.' Magda picked up her mug of chamomile tea and used a teaspoon to extract the bag and deposit it on a saucer.

'I haven't had a crush like this since my teens,' Kerry continued. 'I assumed I was past it now. It's so different from what happened with Stuart.'

'That reminds me,' Magda said, 'do you remember we talked about your husband in the last session? Something you said at the end struck me. In fact, I made a note to bring it up with you again today. You told me you were never madly in love with him, but he made you feel *safe*.'

As guilt washed over her Kerry tugged another clump of foam out of the chair. 'Most people compromise in long-term relationships, don't they? I thought I was doing the right thing, settling for someone I liked and cared about. I never set out to hurt him the way I did.'

'I wasn't judging you. What I'm interested in is the word "safe." Immediately, it made me wonder why you felt *un*safe to begin with.'

Kerry flicked her fringe out of her eyes and sighed. They'd been over this several times before. 'You still think something happened to me as a child that caused my anxiety?'

'I don't know. Did it?'

'No. I'd never had an anxiety attack before last year.' She stopped and bit her lip. 'Having said that, all my life people have told me I worry too much. But nothing happened to cause it. Honestly Magda, I'm not hiding anything from you. I was an ordinary girl with an ordinary life.'

Magda glanced at the clock, leaned back and rearranged the crocheted blanket over her legs. 'Okay. So why don't you tell me about your ordinary life?'

She was always the good child. The one who could be trusted to behave in adult company. The dreamy little girl who kept her feelings locked inside, instead of yelling or stamping her feet like Fran did when she failed to get what she wanted.

Her family lived in a modest terraced house in Chorlton, long before the South Manchester suburb became gentrified with teashops and health food stores. Her mum worked part-time in a nursery; her dad was a clerk in the council's town planning department.

Since the house had only two bedrooms Kerry and Fran had to share, though Kerry often had the room to herself to read or play with her dolls while Fran was out on her bike or kicking a ball round Longford Park with the boys. When she wasn't lost in a story Kerry adored dressing up in costumes and jewellery that her mum bought from jumble sales. In her imagination the cheap glass beads were strings of emeralds and rubies. She also loved to write plays and act them out, and in that Fran shared her enthusiasm.

Both girls went to their local comprehensive. Although Kerry wasn't the star of her class, she was conscientious and her marks usually placed her somewhere near the top, particularly in English, her favourite subject. She was neither gregarious nor especially popular but had a circle of close friends, and as far as she could recall she was happy.

At the age of thirteen her body began to transform alarmingly fast. In contrast to the straight torsos and lithe limbs of her classmates she developed rounded breasts, sturdy thighs and wide hips, which she soon learned to despise.

As they reached puberty too, the boys would comment on the girls' assets as they passed them in the playground.

'Check out the tits on that,' a boy said one day, leaning against the wall with his friend, as Kerry was heading to a lesson.

'Not a bad pair of melons. She's too fat though. Look at those legs,' the other said.

'Yeah. They're like tree trunks,' the first boy said, sniggering. 'She's got a huge arse too.'

'I bet you'd still do her.'

'Piss off. I'm not that desperate.'

Even her family made observations about her figure.

'Your Kerry's a strapping young lass, isn't she?' her uncle George said to her mum as they stood beside the buffet table at a family gathering. 'She's twice the size of when I last saw her.'

'She takes after me, I'm afraid,' her mum said. 'The same child-bearing hips.'

Kerry, who was helping herself to a slice of chocolate cake, overheard them. She wished, as she often did in those days, that she could be invisible.

'I see you've got a healthy appetite,' her uncle George shouted over to her.

Her face burned. She replaced the untouched cake on the plate and quietly went to sit on a chair in the corner.

'I was only teasing her,' she heard Uncle George say to her mum.

'She's a bit shy at the moment. I expect it's just a phase.'

'Where's my other niece?' George said, looking round for Fran. '*You're* not shy, are you, love?' he said as Fran grinned at him through a mouthful of chocolate.

Kerry recalled vividly an incident when she was fifteen and on her way to meet her friends for pizza and the cinema. A boy she fancied like crazy was going to be there, and she'd dressed with great care in a denim miniskirt, stripy legwarmers over tights and patent high heels. Her hair was cut short with a feathered fringe and scrunched into spikes with mousse. Although her mum forbade her from wearing make-up, she'd managed to apply eyeshadow and blusher, and avoided scrutiny as she shouted goodbye and sneaked out of the back door.

She walked along the main road, past the elegant Carnegie library where she was a regular, and boarded the bus. She took a seat near the back and got her book out of her bag. Soon she was absorbed in *Jane Eyre*, which had captivated her romantic teenage imagination. Also in the bag was a chocolate bar, which she began to eat.

A group of lads in their twenties stomped up the stairs, carrying cans of beer. Her heart sank as they headed towards where she sat. She turned her face to the window but one of them noticed her as he passed.

'All right love?' he said, stopping in the aisle to stare.

She focused her attention laser-like on the page in front of her, in the vain hope he'd sense her longing to be left alone. But he sat down next to her, reeking of booze and cigarette smoke. The others occupied the back row and leaned in to listen.

'What's your name?' the lad said.

'It's Kerry.'

'And where are you off to all dressed up, Kerry?'

'Just to meet some friends.'

'What's that you've got?' He snatched her book and scanned a few lines. 'Looks like bollocks to me. Why are you reading this crap?'

Her heart pounded. 'Why shouldn't I?'

He flung the book on the floor and put his arm around her shoulder. She pulled away but he moved in closer. His fingertips encircled one of her breasts.

'There you go. Isn't that more fun? Nice boobs, by the way.'

Her unease flared into fury.

'Get lost,' she said loudly, wriggling in her seat as she struggled to push him away.

His friends on the row behind whooped and whistled. 'Don't reckon you're going to score there tonight, mate.'

His mocking smile faded. 'Not good enough for you, am I?'

'Please,' she said, 'I just want to be left alone, okay?'

The man got to his feet and stood over her.

'Listen slag,' he said. 'I was doing you a favour by even talking to you. You're not *that* good-looking.' He noticed the chocolate wrapper that had fallen into her lap. 'What are you eating that for, you fucking fat cow?'

Her face burned with shame. She looked around the bus for support, but the other passengers were resolutely staring out of the window. The young males owned the space and now she'd made one of them angry.

The lad sat behind her, opened a can and began kicking her chair. She pretended to read her book as his foot dug into her back. The group commenced a loud conversation that she knew was for her benefit. They bragged about the bitches they were going to fuck. The slags they'd like to rape.

Waves of fear washed over her. These weren't boys showing off in the playground. They were adult men, out of control and dangerous. Kerry sat rigid in her seat, praying they'd get off soon. She felt an urgent need to go to the toilet.

To her immense relief the bus arrived at their stop and they got up and lurched along the aisle. The lad who'd groped her leaned over as he passed.

'You're a fucking dog, d'you know that?' he said in a low voice, and slapped the back of her head. He caught up with his friends and they were gone.

Kerry sank back into her chair, trembling. A woman a few rows in front turned around.

'You all right love?'

'I'm fine thanks.'

It was nothing, she told herself. Lone girls got harassed on the buses all the time. Everyone knew that. She was lucky it hadn't been worse. At least they hadn't followed her home and attacked her, like in the stories she read in the papers.

But something changed in her. After that she carried around a new tension, starting at sudden noises and loud male voices, always anticipating negative remarks about her appearance. Then one day a few months later she found herself crouched over the toilet bowl, sweat-soaked and shaky, the sourness of bile in her mouth and her throat sore where her fingernails had scraped it in order to rid her stomach of her last meal.

She was never diagnosed with an eating disorder; in fact no one ever found out, but the habit continued on and off during the rest of her teens, especially when she felt stressed or hurt. She became withdrawn, spending hours alone in her room. She chose black and flowing clothes to hide her figure. Her sexuality had become a source of shame.

After A-levels she applied to study English at Manchester Metropolitan University. She had no idea what she wanted to do with her life but the idea of spending three years absorbed in literature appealed. To her and her parents' delight she was accepted. The first person in her family to go to university.

When she arrived at the university campus near the city centre, although she'd only travelled a few miles, she entered a different world. The other students were overwhelmingly middle-class, more self-assured than Kerry, but also laid-back party lovers. She was soon introduced to Manchester's thriving clubbing and ecstasy scene.

Dancing all night on pills proved more effective than any diet, although even when she was so thin that her ribs showed she couldn't do anything about the width of her pelvis. Within a term she'd cast off her black clothes and replaced them with tiny hotpants and neon vest tops. She got her nose and ears pierced and reinvented herself as a raver.

The drugs and her new figure gave her a semblance of confidence, which men were drawn to, and she had several flings and one-night stands. Sometimes she'd wake up with a guy she'd chatted to all night in the club and found that once sober, she was too shy to look him in the eyes.

'You're not the same person I met last night,' one of them said to her as he got dressed. He still took her phone number, though she didn't answer his calls. After these encounters she could never rid herself of a sense of guilt. It wasn't what nice girls were supposed to do.

Her parents were dismayed at the changes in her. They'd been so proud of their clever little girl, and now she'd become a strange young woman: someone they couldn't understand or respect. They didn't know about the pills of course, but they hated her piercings and skimpy clothes and the numerous phone calls from men she received at home in the holidays.

It didn't help that Fran was going through a wholesome phase as captain of her netball team and lead actress in the school play. And then Fran acquired a string of perfect grades and a place at Oxford, throwing all Kerry's academic achievements into the shade.

In her final year she realised she'd have to work hard to pass her degree. Her people-pleasing instincts went into overdrive and she spent her nights studying instead of raving, which by then was losing its appeal. She realised she'd always felt most at peace when lost in a book.

On graduating from Manchester Met with a second-class degree Kerry entered the job market but found little on offer. After a few aimless months working in a supermarket she went on a computer skills course and signed up with a temping agency. Her first job was for a marketing agency in a city centre office where she answered the phone, made tea and entered client billing details into spreadsheets.

While Fran was submitting her first articles to national newspapers, Kerry worked her way through a series of similar admin jobs in PR, marketing or design. Her reliability and her literacy meant she was often given tasks outside her job description but her tendency to avoid the limelight meant she was never considered for promotion.

Life drifted on. Like so many city dwellers she daydreamed her way through the tedium of the week and lived for the weekends when she went out to gigs and galleries or drank in bars with her friends. Then she met Stuart. A year later she removed her nose stud and put on a white dress for her church wedding, much to her parents' relief. After a long absence their good daughter had returned.

After that everything was set for a conventional happy ending. Until the dark terror emerged from the depths of her subconscious and ripped apart the life she'd built for herself, forcing her to start it over again.

It was true what she'd said to Magda. It *was* an ordinary life. If you changed a few of the details it could be any one of a million people's narratives. The story of a woman growing up in the western world.

# 10

'I want you and Joe to sort through these ties,' Sue said to Kerry as she lugged a crate off a shelf. 'We've been collecting them for donkey's years.'

Kerry followed her to the sorting area. Sue poured the ties onto the bench where they lay entangled like snakes. Joe stood nearby waiting for instructions.

'First off, get rid of any that are fraying or stained,' Sue said. 'Then split them into two piles: silk and synthetic. It says which is which on the label. Silk gets priced at six or seven quid. Put three or four on the others.'

Kerry and Joe began to work their way through the ties.

'Where's Shaun today?' she asked him.

'Got an interview at the job centre,' Joe said with a grin. 'He was having a right old bitch about it yesterday.'

'I can sympathise. It's hard looking for work.'

'It's mad, innit? That'll be me when I finish college this summer.'

She fished out a tie with a university crest and placed it on the silk pile. 'Do you know what you want to do?'

'I figure I'll take whatever I can get.'

'You must be getting good experience here.'

'It'd be better if I was paid though,' Joe said. 'My sisters take the piss out of me for working for nothing. They think charity shops are for smelly tramps and mad old ladies.'

His grin broadened as he held up a wide orange-and-brown striped kipper tie against his white T-shirt. 'Check this out. Who wears this shit?'

'That's vintage,' Kerry said. 'Put it to one side and we'll ask Sue what to do with it.'

Joe laid down the tie. 'So you're divorced, aren't you? What went wrong with you and your husband?'

Taken aback by the abruptness of the question, Kerry shuffled her feet. 'It's hard to say. It didn't work out.'

'Did you fight? My sister argues with her boyfriend on the phone every day.'

'That sounds exhausting. No, we didn't really fight. We grew apart.'

'But you must have liked each other a lot to get married, right?'

'Sure. But people change.' How could she explain the baffling nature of marriage to a lad of eighteen when she barely understood it herself? 'Do you have a girlfriend?'

'Sort of. But it's complicated.'

'Exactly. Relationships are. Even when you're over forty with a wedding ring on your finger.'

'And you're not dating anyone else?' Joe laughed at her expression. 'Sorry. I ask too many questions. I'll shut up if you like.'

Kerry turned her attention to the ties. The more she looked at them the more bizarre they seemed. Thin strips of material with no function other than to convey the wearer's social status or personality.

She examined one patterned with frothing beer mugs, the store tag still attached. Did anyone wear these things to the office? Or were they last-minute gifts for dads and uncles, accepted with feigned gratitude and stuffed in a drawer, to be consigned to charity once a decent amount of time had elapsed?

The bamboo curtain parted and Alex came in for his coffee break. As he stopped at the bench to greet her, she held up a paisley tie and put on a posh accent.

'Can I interest you, sir, in this pure silk tie from Harrods of London?'

'No thank you, madam. I would have no use for that whatsoever,' Alex said with a smile. 'You've got a lot of those to get through, haven't you? I'd offer to help, but the books can't be left alone for very long.'

'I'll bet they can't,' she said. 'It's so unfair that you get to read them all day.'

'It's a shame you can't help me upstairs. Maybe I'll ask Sue again.'

'You know she'll say no. There's not enough work for two of us.'

'I don't think we'd get bored though, do you?' Alex said quietly, and he gave her one of his intimate looks. Her throat swelled. She glanced at Joe to see if he'd overheard but he was engrossed in a message on his phone.

'Are you staying this evening to restock?' Alex asked her.

Every other Wednesday a few of them stayed behind after closing time to remove the clothes that hadn't sold and replace them with new ones.

'I am. Are you?' She'd never known him to work late before.

'I thought I might for once. The book display needs changing and I want to have a think about what theme to go with.'

Later that evening Kerry helped Sue wheel the big rail out onto the floor and they loaded on the clothes that had failed to appeal to buyers. Then they started pricing the new stock to go out. Kerry longed to chat to Alex but she couldn't think of an excuse to go upstairs.

After twenty minutes Sue provided her with one.

'Kerry love,' she said, retrieving a label she'd dropped on the floor, 'could you bob upstairs and ask Alex to come down here? The phone's not working and I've got some boxes I need him to help me take up.'

Kerry mounted the stairs. Before she reached the landing she brushed her hands through her hair, hoping her eye make-up was still intact. Alex was sitting on a small metal stool, his legs crossed and a book balanced on one knee. He looked up, startled, as she approached.

'Hello. I didn't hear you coming.'

'You must have been absorbed in your reading,' she said. 'I came to say Sue wants you.'

'Okay.' Alex took off his glasses, folded them up and tucked them into his shirt pocket. 'I'll come down with you.'

She remained where she stood. 'Have you decided on a theme for this week?'

'Travel guides. I've got loads. I've been trying to select the best ones, but I keep reading them instead. Look at this.'

He passed her his book, which was a collection of photographs of Rome. She flicked through images of pale marble statues, the city at sunrise wreathed in mist, the celestial blue on the walls of the Sistine Chapel.

'It looks stunning,' she said. 'Have you been?'

'A couple of times. When I left university, I travelled round Europe for a year taking photographs. That was the first time I saw Rome. It's a long time ago now, but I remember how the city literally took my breath away.'

'I'd love to see it one day.'

'Then I hope you do.'

They looked at each other, and suddenly she knew it was time.

Alex rose from the stool and approached until he was standing closer to her than ever before.

'Kerry,' he began, then stopped. 'Maybe I shouldn't say this, but I think you're amazing. And very beautiful. But of course I can't expect you to…'

He faltered again. The harsh strip lighting overhead made his lined face pallid and emphasised his sunken cheeks and the shadows below his eyes.

'Go on,' she said, and the dryness of her throat made her voice crack. Slowly, he reached out and stroked her cheek. At the touch of his fingers, she trembled.

He was about to speak when a voice behind interrupted them.

'Don't mind me, will you?'

Kerry flinched and spun around. Sue was standing at the top of the stairs, a large box precariously balanced on her arms. Alex stepped back and gave Kerry a quick grimace. He turned to Sue.

'I was about to come and find you. Do you need a hand with that?'

Sue huffed. 'If you're not too busy, Alex, that would be nice.'

He took the box from her and carried it to the stockroom. Sue followed him.

'I'd better get on with pricing the clothes,' Kerry said to no one in particular. She scurried downstairs, almost tripping on the carpet. In the corridor she leaned against the wall to catch her breath.

Alex had touched her face. He'd called her beautiful. Everything she'd dreamed of was happening for real. She wasn't going to let Sue's interruption spoil her triumph. She picked up the labelling gun, her mind in a whirl, and tried to focus on her work.

Sue took her time returning but at last she bustled in and retrieved her gun. An uneasy silence fell, punctuated by the sound of tags crunching into labels.

'So,' Sue said as she held up a sleeveless dress to check for faults. 'I'll be honest, Kerry, you gave me quite a shock up there. I'd no idea there was something going on between you two.'

'There isn't.'

Sue gave a snort. 'Come off it. I wasn't born yesterday.'

'We're not in a relationship. Not yet, anyway.'

'Look love,' Sue said briskly, 'I'm sure you think this is none of my business. But I can't let you carry on like this in my shop and sit back and say nothing.'

Kerry twisted a loop of her hair in her fingers. This was beyond embarrassing. She was in her forties and she felt like a schoolgirl hauled in front of the headmistress for kissing a boy behind the bike sheds.

'I'm sorry it happened while we were here. But I'm not sure we were doing anything wrong. We're both single.'

'But you *know* Alex's background.'

'I know he's older than me and he's unemployed and he has depression and heart disease. None of that stops me liking him.'

'Well, it should.'

Kerry frowned. 'Why?'

Sue put her gun down. 'Okay. I'm going to tell you something in strict confidence. A few years ago Alex started seeing one of our volunteers. A girl a lot younger than him. I didn't like it at the time and I said so, but he told me off for meddling. He doesn't appreciate being given advice, Alex. So I drew in my horns and let them get on with it.'

She paused and rubbed her nose.

'It was all moonlight and roses for a few months. Until he hit one of his bad patches and she saw what she was up against. One day he let her down over something and she dropped him like a shot. And do you know where he ended up after that?'

Kerry shook her head, though cold dread was settling in her stomach.

'In a psychiatric unit,' Sue said. 'It was me who called the mental health crisis team out to him. He was so suicidal I was terrified. He pulled through in the end, but I can't stand by and watch him make the same mistake again. As long as I'm his manager, I've got a duty of care to him.'

Kerry struggled to collect her thoughts. 'I do see why you're concerned. But that's what happened on *that* occasion. It doesn't mean all his relationships will end the same way.'

'Most of these romances come to nothing. But Alex can't handle pain like most folk can. He might act strong, but he's like a little child inside.' Her eyes grew stern. 'I'm warning you, Kerry. You're playing with fire if you think you can fool around with a man as sick as he is.'

As guilty fear stole through her, Kerry's ears burned. Then she recalled the touch of his hand on her face. The erotic energy still flowing through her body shifted into defiance. Sue was being awfully patronising about him. And she didn't like the implication she was 'fooling around'.

'But Sue, Alex is an adult. Isn't it up to *him* to decide what risks he takes? Or do you want him to be alone for the rest of his life?'

Her heart pounded as she finished speaking.

Sue pursed her lips. 'I never said I wanted him to be on his own. I'd like to see him settle down one day with the right woman. But with all due respect, love, I'm not sure that's you.'

'Why shouldn't it be me?'

Sue puffed out her cheeks and exhaled noisily. 'All right, I'll be honest with you. You're very sweet, but you're very insecure for someone your age. And no woman's going to survive with Alex unless she's down-to-earth and mature and as tough as old boots. I know what it's like to live with someone with a serious mental illness. You've got to be a rock for them without going under yourself.'

She peered over her spectacles. 'Do you think you can be a rock, Kerry?'

Her words struck a nerve. Kerry couldn't endure the scrutiny of Sue's gaze any longer. She picked up a crumpled satin skirt and examined it intently as she chewed the inside of her lip.

'Are you all right?' Sue said. 'Sorry if I was a bit sharp. Why don't we have a cuppa? Go on, forget the clothes. I'll put the kettle on.'

She followed Sue into the staffroom, where she sank into a chair. In the last few minutes her euphoria had evaporated. Sue filled the kettle, made their tea and drew up a seat opposite Kerry.

'I shouldn't have been so blunt,' she said. 'I can see you're a sensitive little thing. But it shows why the two of you are wrong for each other. You've both got too many needs. You'll burn each other out. It's a disaster waiting to happen.'

Kerry stared at her mug, concentrating on a chip on the rim of the china. She'd already ruined one man's life through her inability to stick at a relationship. Did Sue have a point? That it wasn't fair to do the same to someone so vulnerable?

'I don't want to hurt him,' she said.

Sue patted Kerry's arm. 'I know you don't. You're a nice girl. You know, there are plenty more fish in the sea. Men your own age who are less… damaged.'

Kerry's voice became choked. 'I don't want to meet anyone else.'

'Oh dear,' Sue said, clucking her tongue. 'You've really fallen for him, haven't you? I'm sure you'll get over it. Why don't we change your shifts so you don't have to see him every day?'

Panic seized her. 'Oh no. There's no need for that.'

'All right. But I'll tell you this for nothing: it won't help.'

'I like him as a friend. He's been very kind to me.'

'Alex has a good soul, bless him,' Sue said. 'But he's not the answer to your prayers, far from it. He can't fix you, any more than you can fix him. You need to trust me on that.' Her voice turned stern again. 'And don't let *him* persuade you otherwise.'

Kerry didn't trust herself to speak. When she'd finished her drink, Sue looked up at the clock. 'I'll let you get off home now. I'm sure you've had enough of me for one day. Alex and I can lock up.'

Clearly Sue didn't want them to see each other again tonight. When Sue had returned to her work, Kerry cleared away the mugs, put on her coat and left. Outside she glanced up at the first floor window. What had Sue said to Alex upstairs? What was he thinking now? Shaking her head, she hurried down the cold street towards her flat where she lay awake in misery until dawn.


After that Alex wasn't due to work in the shop until next week. Since she didn't have his phone number, and her previous search had revealed that he had no online profiles, she had no way of contacting him. On Monday morning they exchanged awkward smiles when they passed on the stairs but there were too many people around for them to talk. It was mid-afternoon by the time he found her drinking tea alone in the staffroom.

'How have you been?' he said, drawing up a chair near her.

'Not bad, thanks. And you?'

'Oh, I'm fine.'

She fiddled with one of her earrings while he examined the button on the cuff of his shirt. Then he clasped his hands together and looked up at her.

'I've been thinking about what happened the other night. I've no doubt Sue had words with you.'

'Yep. She sure did.'

'I'm sorry about that. I do wish she'd stop interfering in my life. She's a pathological busybody.'

She couldn't help smiling at his turn of phrase. 'It's only because she cares about you.'

'Yes, yes. I know that too.' He sighed. 'Anyway, there's something I wanted to say to you. I bet Sue told you all about my last relationship, didn't she?'

'She did mention it.'

'I can imagine the picture she'll have painted. That I was a victim, badly treated by a flaky woman. But it wasn't like that. I had a lot of stresses in my life and I was on the wrong medication. Our relationship didn't work out, and that made me sad. But my girlfriend wasn't responsible for my illness, and I never blamed her for it. That's all I want to you know.'

'I understand. Thanks for telling me.'

He leaned forward and gave her an earnest look. The sunlight stealing in through the window illuminated his tawny eyes.

'Kerry, will you come out for a drink with me tonight? There's so much I want to talk to you about.'

She held her breath as her feelings threatened to overwhelm her. But this time she was going to do the right thing.

'I don't know,' she said, hunching her shoulders and inspecting her fingernails. 'Maybe it's not such a good idea.'

The veins in his clenched hands stood out. 'I was afraid you were going to say that.'

'It's not because I don't like you. I do, very much. It's just that…'

'It's all right. You don't owe me an explanation. I shouldn't have asked you in the first place. It's too much to expect of you.'

She swallowed hard. 'We can still be friends, can't we?'

He gazed out of the window, and then he sat up and squared his shoulders. 'Yes. Yes, of course we can.'

After a pause he got to his feet. 'I'd better get back to work,' he said, and already a cool distance had crept into his voice. 'I'll see you later.'

'See you soon,' she said in the brightest voice she could muster. As soon as he'd gone she rested her head on her arms on the table, reflecting that she'd undoubtedly turned down the love of her life.

# 11

Alex took the next two days off sick. Nauseous guilt plagued Kerry as she wondered if her rejection was the cause of his absence. The degree of stress it caused her convinced her Sue was right. She simply wasn't calm enough herself to deal with someone else's ups and downs.

When he returned he remained scrupulously polite but his manner towards her had altered. He'd put up a barrier to protect himself and no more lingering looks or flirtatious remarks passed between them.

As Christmas drew closer the shop became hectic and Kerry found herself rushed off her feet. She had an interview at a publishing company, which went reasonably well, but she heard nothing further from them. After steeling herself to chase them several times she was told the position had gone to an internal candidate.

'I hate it when they don't even let you know,' she told Sue as they sat trawling through bric-a-brac. She'd discovered a set of old hairbrushes with long polished enamel handles. Despite a thin crack on one of the handles, she thought they merited a place in the display cabinet. 'It's so much work preparing for an interview and travelling there. I don't think it's very considerate to leave you waiting forever.'

'It's downright rude, that's what it is,' Sue said as she slit open a box with vigour. From it she lifted a red vinyl vanity case and a set of canvases printed with large monochrome dahlias. 'But that's the way society is these days. Although from my own selfish point of view I'm glad to keep you a bit longer. We're more short-staffed than ever this year. Having said that, I've got a new chap coming in later. Bit of a drip, to be honest. He'll be no use on the shop floor. But he could help Pete out with the furniture.'

That afternoon the new volunteer Colin arrived. He was a timid little man with unkempt stringy hair. Kerry felt immediate empathy toward him. Sue adopted her frosty manner.

'All right Colin,' she said, 'you're going to be working with Pete, but he's not here yet. Kerry here will look after you until he shows up.' She turned to Kerry. 'That all right with you, love? Just show him where the loo is and make him a brew. I need to go to the bank.'

Kerry led Colin into the staffroom and offered him a seat. He was wearing cord trousers too large around his waist, which he had to keep hitching up.

'What made you decide to volunteer here?' she asked as they settled down with their drinks.

'I'm on the work experience programme,' he said. 'If I don't come in here, I don't get my benefits no more.'

'I'm unemployed too. It's not easy finding work, is it?'

'I used to be a postman, but I got sacked,' Colin said. 'Do you want to know why?' He sounded hopeful, as if longing to share his story.

'If you don't mind telling me.'

'Well, it was raining, right? And I was delivering the mail on my bike like normal, when I realised the mailbag wasn't zipped up properly and the rain had got inside. You can't give people their post all wet and soggy, can you?'

'I suppose not. So what did you do?'

'I had one of my bright ideas, didn't I? I thought if I took the mail home with me, I could dry the letters off on the radiator. That makes sense, right? Problem was, the ink had smudged and I couldn't read the addresses no more.'

'Didn't you open them to find out who'd sent them?'

'It's illegal to open someone else's post, isn't it? But I had no way of delivering them to the right houses. So I put the bag in the cupboard under the stairs while I thought what to do. And then I forgot about it altogether.'

'And people reported their missing mail?'

'They got complaints at head office. They knew those houses was on my route, so they brought me in for questioning. One of my mates said I should pretend I didn't know anything about it. But I've never been much of a liar, and they saw through it. Then they sacked me. Thirty-six years I'd worked there. Now no one wants me, what with my age and all.'

Kerry could see all too clearly how the hapless Colin would fare at a job interview. Even Sue had barely given him the time of day, and she was benefiting from his free labour.

When Pete arrived for his shift Kerry introduced Colin, noticing how he shrank and grew reticent in the presence of another man. Pete carted him off in the van to help collect a sofa from a house.

Only a few minutes later, when Kerry was emptying a bag of clothes onto the bench, Pete returned.

'Forgot the bloody van keys, didn't I?' he said as he barged down the corridor. 'Scuse me petal. Can I shove past you?'

Before Kerry had time to move he was already forcing his way past. She held her breath and pressed herself against the edge of the bench as his stomach touched her back.

And then he stopped and placed both hands quite deliberately on her hips. She drew in a gasp. His hot hands fondled her haunches and buttocks, his stubby fingers digging into her flesh. His breath tickled the back of her neck. Alarm and revulsion rooted her where she stood. She wanted to protest but her tongue had gone numb.

'Bit of a tight squeeze, isn't it?' Pete said as he let go.

Kerry brushed her leggings down with her palms as if to get rid of all traces of his touch. He carried on through to the staffroom and returned with the keys, by which time she'd edged round the bench to avoid him.

'See you later alligator.' He disappeared through the curtain.

Shame swept over her. She should have said something the instant he'd touched her. But she'd been too shocked to react, and now it was too late. Next time she'd be ready to deal with him. She wasn't going to let him think he could get away with it twice.

When Sue returned from the bank Kerry wondered whether to broach the issue. Perhaps it would be better to confront Pete privately first.

'Anything happen while I was away?' Sue could never quite believe she was able to leave the shop without disaster ensuing.

'Pete went off to fetch a sofa.'

'Did he take Colin?'

'Yep.' Kerry adopted a neutral tone of voice. 'Has Pete worked here a long time?'

'As long as I have. He's an old friend of mine. Why do you ask?'

'Just wondering if he's ever had a job.'

'Not a regular nine-to-five. He does odd jobs and a bit of painting and decorating. It's very good of him to help out here for nothing.' Sue changed the subject. 'By the way, are you coming to the Christmas meal? I need to confirm the table booking.'

Kerry cringed inside. Thanks to the accepting atmosphere in the shop she'd grown comfortable there and had no problem chatting to the other volunteers. But going to a restaurant and making small talk was a different matter.

'It's on Friday, isn't it?' she said, to stall for time. 'Who else is going?'

'That's what I'm trying to establish,' Sue said. 'I know I can count Ruth out: she never comes to anything social. Pete neither. Dan can't make it this year, unfortunately. Yasmeen, Elspeth and Joe said they'd be there. Alex did too, though he may bail out at the last minute. Come on Kerry love, it'll be fun. We'll have a couple of drinks and let our hair down for once.'

She couldn't think of a reason not to. Maybe it would be good for her to confront her fears instead of avoiding them. It was what her therapist Magda was always encouraging her to do. A knot of tension formed in her stomach at the prospect. But she'd conquer it. She'd dress up and show up for the party, and tell the anxiety it wasn't going to control her life.

# 12

The secret to surviving a social event when you suffered from anxiety was to be prepared for it, Kerry thought as she clambered dripping wet out of the bath. Wrapping a towel around her she returned to the bedroom where she'd laid her outfit out on her bed.

It was a glittering green dress with thin shoulder straps, a staple in her wardrobe from the days when she used to go out regularly. Luckily it still fitted. She dried herself and slipped it on. Then she added stilettos, dangling earrings and a diamante clutch bag she'd bought in the shop.

Perched on her bed she squeezed foundation from a tube into her hand. She pressed too hard and the creamy beige liquid squirted onto her dress.

*Jesus.* What an idiot. Why the hell hadn't she done her make-up *before* she put on the dress? She raced to the bathroom and scrubbed at the dress with a flannel. The stuff had to come off. It had to because she had nothing else to wear.

So much for being prepared.

She sat on the edge of the bath and put her head in her hands as dizziness came over her. She could still ring Sue and make an excuse. But what could she say at this late stage that Sue would believe? Instead she inhaled and exhaled to a count of five and willed herself to calm down.

After drying the wet patch on the dress, she applied a layer of powder to hold her foundation in place. She swept dark eyeshadow liberally across her eyelids and completed the look with a flick of eyeliner and a burgundy lipstick that matched her newly-dyed hair.

By the time she was halfway down the road to Didsbury where they were meeting in the bar of the Metropolitan, not far from where she'd first lived with Stuart, she'd remembered why she favoured her sturdy boots over stilettos. The back of her foot was already blistering. She hobbled past boutiques and bars, arriving at a building resplendent with black-and-white mock Tudor panelling. Laughter resounded through the open door.

As she'd feared it was stiflingly hot and crowded inside. Where was everyone? Disorientated, she peered around at leather-backed armchairs and ferns trailing from pots on the windowsills until she heard voices bellowing.

'Kerry! We're behind you.'

She spun around. Seated at the table were Yasmeen, Colin, Joe, Elspeth, Sue and Sue's husband. How could she not have noticed them? She slid into an empty seat next to Sue.

'We were shouting at you for ages,' Joe said, grinning.

'It's hard to hear in here.'

She removed her leather jacket and all eyes were on her sleeveless shimmery dress.

'You look very glam,' Yasmeen said in a tone of surprise.

The men were in jeans and shirts, except for Colin, who was clad in his cords and a reindeer jumper. Yasmeen wore a midnight-blue tunic over yoga pants. Sue had chosen a velvet top to go with her wide-legged trousers. Elspeth was buttoned into a knitted cardigan. Kerry was the only one who'd arrived dressed for a ball.

'Are you going somewhere else later?' Joe asked.

'No. Just here,' she said as the heat in her cheeks mounted. On the wall to her left hung a mirror. She froze at the sight of herself. What the hell had she been thinking?

The make-up that had seemed alluring in the dim light of her bedroom was now clownish and absurd. The powder made her skin colourless and her eyes looked more bruised than smoky. Not only was the dress too dressy, but it was also revealing and too young for her. And now she was stuck in it all evening. She hitched the neckline up to hide her exposed chest.

Sue's husband leaned across to shake Kerry's hand.

'I'm Mike. Nice to meet you.'

Mike had silver hair and a large bent nose. Kerry knew from Sue that he'd worked his way up from labourer to managing director of a construction firm.

'I'm off to the bar,' he said. 'Can I get you a drink?'

She rooted in her purse for cash.

'It's my treat,' Mike said. 'I've got so much respect for you volunteers.'

Mike headed off. Kerry sat twisting her hands in her lap, wishing the men in suits on the other side of the bar would stop staring at her. She hoped Alex wouldn't assume she'd got dolled up in this ridiculous outfit to impress him. Where was he anyway?

'Are we expecting anyone else this evening?' she asked.

'Alex texted to say he's on his way,' Sue said. 'Joe reckons Shaun's coming, but I suspect he'll be a no-show.'

Not long afterwards however Shaun slouched in, hands in pockets. Heads turned to regard his shaved head and tattoos with suspicion as he slumped into a seat at the end of the table. Kerry guessed they must seem an odd little group, so different in ages and backgrounds.

'This is my Christmas jumper, this is,' Colin explained to her, pointing to the reindeer.

'I can see that. It's very nice.'

'I like your dress,' he said, blinking rapidly. 'You look like one of those models in the magazines.'

Colin began to tell Kerry one of his anecdotes from when he worked at the post office. She was straining to hear him when the door swung open and she glimpsed Alex's tall figure and grey-streaked hair. Her chest tightened but she continued listening to Colin's story. Alex approached the table and sat in the remaining seat opposite her.

'Sorry I'm late,' he said to Sue. 'The bus didn't turn up and I ended up having to walk. Then it started raining.'

He swept his wet hair out of his eyes. He was wearing a long wool coat with the collar turned up, which made him look sophisticated and slightly disreputable, like a detective in a film noir. Kerry was sure she'd put that coat out on the shop floor the other week.

Sue tutted. 'You're soaking, Alex. Don't you own an umbrella?'

He draped his coat over the chair. 'I forgot it.'

'Did you bring your camera?'

'No.'

Sue huffed. 'I suppose it was too much to ask.'

'I thought professional photographers took their gear with them everywhere,' Mike said.

Alex's voice became stiff. 'Then perhaps you can deduce that I'm not a professional photographer any more.'

Kerry had never known him to be so brusque. Perhaps he hated social gatherings too.

'Alex is awesome,' Yasmeen said to Mike, her dark eyes shining. 'He did a brilliant job of my fashion shoot.'

'Yet he won't take a few snaps of a Christmas night out,' Sue said.

Exasperated, Alex shook his head. He looked at Kerry but seemed stuck for words.

'Are you okay?' she asked.

He gave her a wry smile. 'In a vile mood, I'm afraid. I probably should have cancelled tonight. I'm going to have to snap out of it and get in the spirit.' He took a deep breath and exhaled, as if trying to expel his irritation. 'That's a beautiful dress you're wearing.'

'Thanks. I feel really self-conscious in it. No one else has got dressed up.'

'Then that means you outshine them all, doesn't it?' he said. 'Really, you look fabulous. That colour suits you.'

It was the first time in ages he'd spoken to her in such an intimate tone. Kerry returned his smile, reminding herself it was unfair to flirt with him. She sat turning the cocktail stirrer around in the ice at the bottom of her glass until a waitress informed them their dinner table was ready. They trooped into the relative quietness of the restaurant at the back. In the corner a Christmas tree glistened with silver baubles and white fairy lights.

To Kerry's disappointment Alex chose a seat at the other end of the table. She picked up her menu and scanned the choices. Perhaps she was relieved he wasn't near her, since her dread of eating in front of people was beginning to kick in. Yasmeen and Sue were already talking about calories and saturated fat.

'Come off it, you don't need to worry about your weight,' Sue said to Yasmeen.

'I don't,' Yasmeen said. 'I eat healthily and look after myself, that's all.'

'What about you, Kerry?' Sue said. 'Do you ever go on diets?'

'Not really.' She felt like they were all looking at her in her skimpy dress, judging her imperfect body.

'Why should she go on a diet?' Yasmeen gave Kerry a thumbs-up. 'You rock those curves, girl.'

'Men prefer real women anyway, not stick insects,' Mike said.

Yasmeen looked up from her menu. 'That's not the point though, is it? We don't make choices about our bodies just to please men.'

'I only meant it as a compliment,' Mike said, taken aback.

'You know love, you don't have to be on your feminist high horse all the time,' Sue said.

Yasmeen didn't reply but she flicked back her long hair, got out her phone and began scrolling.

The conversation froze into stillness as Mike reflected on his *faux pas*. As a peace offering he held up the wine bottle to Yasmeen, forgetting she'd already told them she was teetotal. Mike filled Kerry's glass instead. She drank in the hope of numbing the anxiety washing over her in waves. Her rigid posture was making her neck and shoulders ache. Why did she feel so uncomfortable when other people weren't getting on?

From behind her hair she stole a glance at Alex, who'd put on his black-framed glasses to read the menu. He was sitting with Colin and Shaun. She couldn't imagine what the three of them were finding in common either. Indeed, the awkwardness between them was palpable. When she looked again Alex was yawning and fiddling with the buttons on his cuff.

Sue and the others fell to chatting about safe topics such as restaurants and holidays. Kerry drank her wine too fast, picked at her cuticles and picked at her food. The smells of garlic, fish, turkey and sage-and-onion stuffing mingled in the air, making her queasy.

After the main course Alex got up. As he passed along Kerry's side of the table, he bent to whisper in her ear.

'Are you all right?'

She gave him a grateful smile. 'I think so. Just… you know.'

He nodded. 'Let me know if I can help.'

For a brief instant he rested his hand on her shoulder, then he sauntered out to the bar.

Mike was watching him with an expression of dislike mixed with pity. Suddenly Kerry saw Alex as he must appear in Mike's eyes. Old, poor, broken and alone: a failure by every conventional measure. Someone like Mike could never perceive the depth of soul and the ragged, leonine grace that made Alex more mesmerising than anyone in the room. Despite her resolve, she couldn't deny how much she still wanted him. Desire after all was an appetite: a gnawing hunger that could be satisfied by one person alone.

Her head was spinning from the wine. She gave up on her dessert and put down her fork. The waitress took her plate away. As she was thanking the waitress she caught a glimpse of Sue, who was also watching Alex as he returned from the bar with a drink. There was something unusually thoughtful in her eyes.

*What if Sue was in love with him too?*

It was possible, wasn't it? It would explain why she'd made sure Alex and Kerry never got together. Her protectiveness of him could be genuine, but it could also be a way to get rid of rivals. And Kerry had fallen for it.

Or had she misinterpreted that wistful look?

By the time they'd had coffee and paid the bill it was half-past ten and she'd had as much as she could stand of socialising. To drink any more would be a mistake. Elspeth and Colin had gone home. Joe, Yasmeen and Shaun were discussing moving on to another bar.

'I ought to get going,' Kerry said, slipping on her jacket. 'There's a bus that leaves in five minutes.'

Mike was shocked. 'You can't get the bus alone at *this* time of night.'

'I'll be fine,' she protested. 'It's not that late. Cabs are expensive. Anyway, I fancy some fresh air.'

'We can't have you wandering the streets alone in the dark,' Sue said. 'It's too dangerous.'

Clearly they were determined not to allow her to make her own decisions with regard to her safety. Alex, overhearing their conversation, came over.

'You live in Fallowfield, don't you, Kerry?' he said, sitting down next to her. 'I'm going that way too. I could walk back with you. But only if you want me to,' he added.

Her heart leapt. Was this her moment to ignore Sue's advice? To take a risk and see where their feelings led them?

'That would be lovely, if it's no trouble.'

'Don't be daft.' Sue peered over her spectacles at Alex. 'I suppose neither of you's noticed it's raining? Kerry's not got a proper coat. And you've got no umbrella.'

'A drop of rain won't kill me,' Kerry said.

'She can borrow my coat if she wants to,' Alex said.

'I'll sort out a cab,' Mike said. 'I'm more than happy to pay for Kerry to get home safely.'

His emphasis on her name made it clear his offer didn't extend to Alex accompanying her. Without waiting for her assent, Mike booked Kerry's taxi, as well as one for himself and Sue.

'There you go. It's been charged to my account,' he told Kerry.

Visibly annoyed, Alex stood up and walked out. An uncomfortable few minutes passed. Kerry sat twisting the strap of her handbag until Mike's phone beeped to announce that her taxi had arrived.

'Thanks for dinner,' Kerry said as graciously as she could manage, and headed towards the door. Outside, the car was waiting at the kerbside. Alex stood beside the stone steps leading up to the entrance, staring at the reflections of the streetlights on the wet pavement. The street echoed with the shouts of revellers.

'Are you going?' he asked her.

'Sorry about what happened in there. It was nice of you to offer to walk me home.'

'It wasn't your fault. Sometimes everyone else thinks they know what's best for you,' he said, with bitterness in his voice.

'I know what you mean.'

Alex swung round to face her, his arms held open, as if inviting an embrace. 'Goodnight Kerry.'

She was on the brink of approaching him when a second car drew up and she heard voices behind her as Mike and Sue emerged from the building. Her driver tooted his horn. Her heart fluttered in her rib cage like a panicky little bird.

'I'd better go. Goodnight.'

She clattered across the pavement to the car, pulled open the door and clambered into the back seat. As the taxi sped away she glanced back along the street. Alex was still standing there, watching the glowing city lights.

In her flat she kicked off her shoes to find the backs of her heels raw and bleeding. When she looked in the mirror her eyes were shining.

'I love him,' she said out loud.

That night a dream troubled her. She was standing on a rocky beach below a luminous full moon, watching waves ride onto the shore. One wave reared into the darkness until it was taller than her, then higher than a house, then bigger than a mountain.

The wave hung motionless, waiting to break, and she knew she had to run away to survive. Instead she remained still and waited for the force of the seawater to crash down over her. And just as the wave collapsed she awoke, shaking.

# 13

After the party Alex went off on holiday, and he wasn't due back in until the second week of January. Kerry worked in the shop until the morning of Christmas Eve. In the afternoon she caught a train from Manchester out to Buxton, a picturesque spa town in the heart of the Peak District.

Her mum picked her up at the station and drove her to their stone cottage outside the town, with a view of green hills through the windows. Although they'd never earned much her parents had scrimped and saved, and after retirement had been able to buy the little place in the countryside they'd hankered after.

In the cosy living room Kerry curled up on the sofa on a woollen blanket and petted the golden retriever while her mum made tea. On the mantelpiece below the holly wreath and tinsel sat framed photographs of Fran's wedding and of both girls' graduations. There'd been one of Kerry and Stuart's wedding too, but that had gone. Although she was still married to him, her parents rarely talked about Stuart any more, as though he'd died. Kerry suspected they kept silent for fear of upsetting her with their disappointment.

On the walls hung a selection of their childhood photos, over-exposed and blurry. Two little girls in their dressing-up clothes, acting and singing. Later on, Fran as Ophelia in the school play.

A holiday snap featured a sixteen-year-old Kerry with a chubby face and mud-brown hair, sitting on a pebbly beach and swathed in a cardigan and baggy jeans. She was smiling for the camera but there was tension in the way she held herself. She remembered that day: her mum had tried to persuade her to put on shorts like all the other kids. But although she was sweltering, the thought of the other beach-goers observing her body had caused her far greater discomfort than the heat.

It was only since her sessions with Magda that she'd begun to realise how low her self-esteem had been from childhood onwards. As an adult she'd drifted into a less-than-fulfilling relationship with Stuart because her anxiety gave her a craving for security. And having acquired it, her lack of self-worth had convinced her she had no right to expect anything more.

So many years of unhappiness that could have been avoided. It felt like a waste. Yet understanding her past wasn't enough. How was she supposed to change how she felt? There was no magic wand that could undo decades of conditioning.

'How's the job hunting going?' her mum asked as she ambled into the room with tea and fruit cake on a tray. Since she'd moved to the country she'd taken to dressing in rustic tweed skirts and was finally letting her hair go grey. Kerry wondered how her mum felt about ageing. It wasn't the kind of thing they were in the habit of discussing.

'No luck yet,' she replied.

Her mum tutted as she laid down the tray. 'And with all your education and experience. Why aren't they jumping at the chance to employ you?'

'I guess you'd have to ask them that.' Kerry tugged at a loose thread of wool on the blanket. 'Anyway, how are you?'

'We're fine. You know love, if you don't find something soon, you're welcome to come and live here. You must be struggling to pay all that rent on that place of yours.'

'Thanks, but I'll be okay. I'm getting some housing benefit and I can use my credit card for anything else.'

Mum frowned at the mention of credit. 'I don't like the thought of you getting in debt. You don't owe them a lot, do you?'

'Not too much,' Kerry said, trying not to think of the interest accumulating on the thousands she'd borrowed.

'I'll give you the money for your rail ticket here.'

'You don't need to do that,' Kerry said, but Mum insisted.

Her dad, who despite the freezing cold had been walking in the hills, came in grinning as he saw her, and took off his checked cap and overcoat.

'Kerry's *still* not got a job,' Mum said to Dad as he settled in his armchair and opened the newspaper.

'I blame the bloody government, me,' he said. 'We should never have voted to leave Europe, that's what I reckon. It's buggering up the whole economy.'

Mum rolled her eyes. 'He talks about nothing other than Brexit these days.'

In the evening Fran arrived in her car alone, as her consultant husband was on call. After she'd informed them in a doleful manner that there was still no sign of any pregnancy, the conversation turned to her recent achievements in journalism.

'The things I write about are trivial compared to what our war correspondent friend does,' Fran told them as she kicked off her shoes and nestled on the sofa next to Kerry, holding a glass of the chilled Prosecco she'd brought with her. 'Some of the horrors he's witnessed in Syria are beyond imagining. It makes me so impatient when we moan about our lives in this country and get upset over little things. We've no idea what real suffering is.'

That night Kerry lay awake and restless in her parents' overheated spare room, guilt washing over her. What would Fran say if she knew of the struggles Kerry faced just to cope with her daily life? Would she show impatience, or contempt for her weakness, as Stuart had done?

It was probably better that her sister never knew.

The rest of the holiday passed pleasantly enough but it was an effort for Kerry to join in the festivities, hiding her frequent spells of anxiety and acting as if nothing was wrong. She was relieved when the decorations were packed away and she was able to return to the shop. Although she'd tried her best not to, she'd missed Alex every moment they'd been apart.

# 14

One gloomy grey January morning Kerry entered the shop and encountered Alex, back from holiday and on his way upstairs. He was wearing his wool coat with the collar turned up. He leaned over the stairs, elbows resting on the banisters, and smiled. His hair was rain-laced and windswept.

'Morning.' She attempted to keep her voice steady. 'Did you have a nice break?'

'Lovely, thanks. I went to stay with a friend. She's an artist and she's just come back from overseas to live in North Wales. We spent hours walking across the beach with her dogs and taking photos. It was very relaxing.'

Kerry's throat tightened as she listened. Were he and this woman really just friends?

'Vanessa and I have known each other over twenty years,' Alex said, as if reading her thoughts. 'She's like a sister to me.'

She closed her eyes. 'Sounds like you had a good time. I'll catch up with you later,' she said, and retreated into the back of the shop.

Later, Sue asked Kerry to take a box of board games upstairs. When she arrived on the first floor Alex was chatting to a customer. Kerry lingered to see if he'd be finished with the customer soon but he'd been drawn into listening to a long story. She couldn't think of anything to say to Ruth, who was watching her from behind the counter, so she returned downstairs and went into the toilet. She was repairing her eye make-up in the cracked mirror when she heard Dan and Sue in the corridor.

'He claims she's a friend. But I'd bet my bottom dollar there's more to it. A man doesn't spend Christmas alone with a woman unless there's something going on,' Sue said.

'That's good news, isn't it?' Dan said. 'The poor guy's been on his own most of his life. He deserves some happiness.'

Sue whistled through her teeth. 'I'd feel more reassured if I knew her. He doesn't make the most sensible choices when it comes to women, bless him.'

'You worry too much,' Dan said. 'He knows what he's doing. He's older and wiser than any of us.'

'Alex isn't *wise*. Brainy, aye, but he's got no common sense.' Sue lowered her voice. 'Did you know there was something between him and Kerry not long ago?'

Inside the toilet, Kerry froze.

'I never knew *that*,' Dan said, intrigued. 'What happened?'

'I found out and nipped it in the bud. Warned her to leave him alone.'

'Oh Sue,' Dan said with an audible wince. 'That's so mean. How could you?'

Sue's tone grew defensive. 'Don't look at me like that. It was for his own good. It would've been a disaster. She'd have bailed out at the first sign of trouble and it would've broken his heart.'

'Why would you think that about Kerry?' Dan sounded astonished. 'She seems lovely and kind to me. I can imagine her being just what he needs. You should have let them get on with it.'

Sue huffed. 'Well, that's your opinion. I don't happen to agree with you. Anyway, it's in the past now. I just hope this latest one doesn't end in tears too.'

'You should try to have more faith in people,' Dan said. 'I'd better get going. I've got a meeting with Libby's head teacher at twelve.'

'I'll head out with you. Elspeth's on the till and Kerry's floating around somewhere, so it should be okay if I bob out for a while.'

When they'd gone, Kerry came out of the toilet and stood by the bench, mulling over what they'd said. A rush of boldness seized her. To hell with what Sue thought of her. She marched towards the curtain, not looking where she was going, and crashed straight into Alex coming in. She gasped.

'Jesus. I'm sorry.'

He gripped her arms to steady her. 'Kerry. Where are you off to in such a hurry?'

She'd come to a halt pressed right up against him. Neither of them moved. Seconds passed. She thought her heart might stop. Alex looked down at her face.

'So this is nice,' he said.

Somehow she found her voice. 'I was on my way to find you.'

'It seems like you *have* found me.' He was still holding onto her arms.

'I was coming to ask if I could change my mind about that drink.'

'That makes me happier than you can imagine.'

She put her hands around his neck, touching his hair. He drew his arms around her and held her closer. She rested her head against his chest, feeling the softness of his cotton shirt, inhaling sandalwood soap mingled with the faint scent of his skin. Then she glanced at the curtain through which Sue could return any minute, and pulled away with reluctance.

'Let's save this for later, shall we?' she said.

Alex leaned against the wall opposite. His warm eyes glowed and a flush was creeping down the front of his neck. He took her trembling hand and pressed her fingers. 'How about tonight? Do you know the Friendship Inn in Fallowfield?'

'Sure. It's not far from where I live.'

'I could meet you there at eight.'

Behind them the phone rang. Alex ran his hands through his hair and picked up the receiver. 'I'll be up in a second.'

He turned back to Kerry. 'That was Ruth. She needs help with a customer. I'll see you soon,' he said in a low voice. With a light press of his hand on her arm he left.

Kerry remained where she was, running the light and dark bamboo beads through her hand, feeling their cool sensuousness. A minute ago she'd been in Alex's arms. There, in a dingy corridor full of musty clothes and cracked old shoes. It couldn't have been a less erotic setting, yet every nerve in her body tingled from his touch.

She retreated into the staffroom and sat in a daze of emotion until she heard wheezing and shuffling in the corridor. Pete came in, clutching a foil parcel in one hand and a newspaper in the other. He positioned his chair close to hers and unwrapped a large kebab.

The smell of the doner meat made her feel sick. Pete chewed noisily, breathing through his nose. Fragments of raw onion and green chilli dropped onto the table. He scooped them up in his grubby fingers and shoved them back inside the pitta bread.

Kerry shut her eyes and thought about Alex instead.

'Have you had your dinner?' Pete asked her.

'Yes,' she lied, trying not to watch the food glistening in his mouth.

'What did you have?'

'Just a salad.'

'You can't survive on rabbit food, you know.'

Sue marched in, frowning. 'Pete, whatever that is, it stinks. I've told you before not to bring takeaways in here. Poor Kerry has to sit in here too.'

'She hasn't complained. Have you petal?'

Desperate to escape him, Kerry stood up. 'I'd better get on with the clothes.'

'Actually love, I'd rather you sorted out the shop floor,' Sue said. 'It's in a right old state.'

'I'll do it now.' She hurried out. Elspeth was on the till.

'I'm going to tidy up,' she said, gesturing at the garments lying crumpled on the floor.

Elspeth appeared to take it as a criticism, as the corners of her mouth turned down. 'I do my best to keep it in order, but I'm busy serving customers. I can't do two things at once.'

'I know. It's not your fault.'

Kerry wandered around picking up clothes, brushing them down to remove dust and replacing them on their hangers. A top in a delicate silky material with a lilac floral pattern caught her eye. It had a low neckline and gathered-in waist. She held it up against herself in front of the mirror.

'That would look pretty on you,' Elspeth said.

'Do you think so? I'm going out tonight and I've got nothing to wear.'

'Why don't you try it on?' Elspeth said. 'It won't take you a minute.'

She entered the changing cubicle and drew the curtain around her. As she removed the tunic she was wearing over her leggings, she flinched as she always did at her unclothed reflection. She really should start swimming again. She pulled the top over her head, fearing it would be too small, but it fitted as if it had been made for her.

The neckline revealed just a hint of cleavage and the nipped-in waist gave her a shapely silhouette. All she needed to go with it were her best jeans and heeled boots, instead of the flat slip-on shoes she wore around the shop.

As she slipped it back over her head, she heard Alex's voice. She'd assumed he'd be occupied upstairs.

'Kerry's here too,' Elspeth was saying to him. 'She's trying on a blouse.' Her voice grew louder as she approached the changing room. 'How are you getting on in there?'

Inside, Kerry cringed. 'I won't be a second.'

Flustered, she pulled her tunic back on and attempted to smooth down her hair, which was crackling with static. She opened the curtain and emerged with the top draped over one arm. Alex was standing beside the counter.

'Did it fit?' Elspeth asked.

'Yes. Could you put it to one side for me and I'll pay for it later?' Kerry said.

Elspeth took it from her and held it up. 'It's a dainty wee thing. Don't you think?' she said to Alex.

'It's beautiful,' he said, looking at the top and then at Kerry. Elspeth folded it fussily and put it in a bag.

'You'll look very pretty when you go out tonight,' she said. 'Have you got a date with a nice young man?'

Kerry blushed to the roots of her hair. 'No,' she said, too emphatically.

Alex's face twitched and he began to smile. Kerry saw the amusing side of it too and she cupped her hand to her chin to hide her giggles.

'I'm sure the nice young man will appreciate the effort,' Alex said, 'whoever he is.'

Elspeth's lips set in a thin line. 'What's so funny? Is it something I said?'

At once Alex became serious. He put a reassuring hand on Elspeth's shoulder.

'We weren't laughing at you. It was a joke about something Kerry told me earlier.' He turned away. 'I ought to get back upstairs.'

As he left, he looked Kerry straight in the eyes. 'Have fun tonight. And make sure he's worthy of you.'

'I will.' She gave him a grin.

He went upstairs, still shaking his head and smiling.

'He's a peculiar chap, that Alex,' Elspeth said to Kerry. 'Nice but odd. Don't you think?'

She was still watching him as he ascended the stairs. 'He's not like anyone else I've met before.'


That evening as she was getting ready in her flat Kerry rummaged through her drawers for her best set of underwear. She fastened the clasp on a lace bra she hadn't worn in a decade. It was only to help her feel more confident. It wasn't as if things were going to go far tonight. They'd have a few drinks and a goodnight kiss, and then she'd return home alone.

When she emerged into the street wearing the new top under her leather jacket, students were heading to bars or to catch the bus into the city centre. For once they didn't make her feel old. Tonight she was as energised as they were by the adventures life still had to offer.

The pub was a red-brick building with hanging baskets on the walls and benches outside. Inside, the clientele were a mixture of students and elderly locals watching sports on the big screen. Painfully self-conscious, she looked around for

Alex, but she couldn't see him. She ordered a gin and tonic and had just paid for it when a hand touched her shoulder.

'Kerry. There you are.'

She turned to face him. He was wearing the sky-blue shirt she liked.

'You look gorgeous,' he said, and he kissed her on the cheek. 'I found a seat over there in the corner, so we can hear each other speak.'

She followed him into the corner beside a window. A pint of beer sat on the table.

'Are you all right?' he said as she fumbled to get her jacket off.

'A little nervous.'

As she sat down, he reached for her hand and caressed her fingers. 'I couldn't believe it when you literally ran into me and told me you'd changed your mind. It was so wonderful.'

'I'm glad you thought so. And then there was the thing with Elspeth and the top. I could have died, only it was so funny.'

'Yes, wasn't it? It looks lovely on you, by the way. I knew it would as soon as I saw it.'

'How?'

'I've done a lot of fashion photography. And it's an instinct.' He leaned across the table and his voice became confiding. 'I've been thinking about you all afternoon. I was so distracted Sue thought there was something wrong with me.'

'She'd be fuming if she knew we were meeting like this.'

His smile faded and a muscle twitched in his jaw. 'It's none of her business.'

'Should we keep it a secret then?'

'I think that would be best for now. Because I'm in danger of losing my temper with her, and I don't want to do that. She's been good to me in so many ways.'

Kerry took a sip of her gin, suddenly unable to think of anything to say.

'So, Kerry,' he said. 'There's so much I want to know about you. I remember when we first met you told me you were interested in studying literature.'

'Yes, but it was only a crazy daydream. I don't have the time or the money.'

'What would you study if you could?'

'I'd love to write something on Charlotte Bronte. *Jane Eyre* has been my favourite book since I was a girl. But she's been studied to death already. I'm not sure what I could add of value.'

'I'm sure you could think of an original angle.'

They discussed it for some time, until she felt like she was commanding an unfair share of the attention.

'How about you?' she said, following a natural pause in the conversation. 'Do you have any family close by?'

'My dad passed away ten years ago. My mum's in a nursing home in Hampshire where I grew up. She's in the advanced stages of dementia.'

'I'm sorry. Do you see much of her?'

'I visit her as often as I can scrape together or borrow the train fare. But she doesn't really understand who I am anymore.' He looked down at his fingers. 'She was such a character. She loved to read and had strong opinions on everything. It's very distressing to witness her suffering. It takes me days to recover from a visit and I have to be careful of my own health. But of course I can't abandon her.'

'That sounds hard. Do you have any brothers or sisters?'

'No, there's just me.'

'And your dad? What was he like?'

'He was a decent man. Very conservative and never approved of my choices. He went to a lot of trouble to get me into a highly regarded Catholic school so I could have a good education and go into a traditional profession. When I told him I wanted to study art at university, he was very disappointed. He thought I was going to be poor all my life, and it wasn't what he'd had in mind for me.'

'Wasn't he proud of you once you were doing so well?'

'Possibly, although he never showed it. But it was too late by then anyway. I'd long since internalised the idea that I was no good. When I had to give up my photography because of the depression, my dad didn't get it at all. He said I should be a man and snap out of it.'

'Oh, love.' She squeezed his arm. 'That must have hurt.'

'It wasn't the most helpful thing he could have said. I didn't talk to him for a long time after that. And then he died of heart failure. So that was that.'

A silence. Then Alex gave her a guilty smile. 'I didn't mean to get us into such a miserable conversation. Let's talk about you again. You were born and bred in Manchester, weren't you?'

She told him about her family and the places she'd lived. 'I've lost touch with most of my friends now. I haven't been out much socially since I split up with my husband.'

'How long were you married, if you don't mind me asking?'

'Twelve years.'

'I've never had a relationship even half as long as that.' He paused and tension came into his voice. 'Kerry, I wanted to check: you do know how old I am, don't you?'

'Yep. Sue told me.'

He laughed. 'Of course she did. I should have anticipated that.'

She looked up at him through lowered lashes. 'Do you know how old *I* am?'

'No, but I'd say you're in your early to mid-forties.'

'Well done. I'm forty-three,' she said, although she couldn't help being disappointed. He sensed it at once.

'I'm sorry. It's something I'm good at noticing. I know it's the custom to tell women they look younger than they are. But I don't want to be insincere with you; and there's nothing wrong with being the age you are. You're a very beautiful forty-three-year-old woman. That's the truth as I see it.'

'Thank you.' It felt more flattering than if he'd told her she looked thirty. 'I genuinely *did* think you were ten years younger than you are, until Sue set me straight.'

'That's nice to know. Because most days I wake up feeling more like ninety.'

She took his hands in hers. More than anything else, they betrayed his age. His fingers were bony and gnarled and the loose skin on the back of his hands was mottled with brown. As she examined them, fierce affection seized her. She leaned over the table and kissed him on the lips.

When she moved away he stared at her, and then he cupped both his hands around her face and pulled her towards him, kissing her more deeply. She closed her eyes, tasting the beer he'd drunk, feeling his warm tongue exploring hers.

'I can hardly believe this is happening,' he said as he broke away at last, regarding her in awe. He sat back in his chair, as if requiring a break from the intensity of what had passed between them. 'Can I get you another drink?'

When he returned from the bar he asked her about her taste in films, books and music, all the time holding her hand and gazing into her eyes with rapt attention.

'We could visit the galleries in town one day if you'd like that,' he said when they discovered a mutual interest in art.

'I'd love to,' she said.

He bent his head and pressed his forehead close to hers. 'I'm very much looking forward to getting to know you better,' he said in a low, tight voice.

'You too. You know, you really are gorgeous,' she said, running her fingers lightly along his forearms.

'God, so are you,' he said, and he kissed her again.

When she turned in her seat, she saw the old men at the bar muttering and giving them curious stares.

'Alex, I think we're attracting attention.'

'Ignore them. They're just jealous,' he said, but he glanced in their direction too. 'Maybe we should go somewhere more private. How about my house? I'd love you to stay the night.'

Kerry squinted at him in surprise. She hadn't anticipated him being so impetuous.

'Sorry,' he said with a grimace. 'That was way too soon, wasn't it? Please forgive me. I'll walk you back to your flat instead.'

There was something so endearing about the awkwardness he couldn't quite hide. If he'd been supremely confident as well as intelligent and attractive, he'd have been too much. Too intimidating for her.

She stared at him through half-lidded eyes. Was it so wrong that she wanted to sleep with him tonight? She knew the rules: self-respecting girls were supposed to say no, at least the first few times. But what was the point in playing those conventional games with him?

She made up her mind. 'I don't want to go back to my flat. I want to go home with you.'

It was his turn to be surprised. 'Are you sure?'

She leaned across the table and kissed him. 'Totally.'

He clasped both her hands. 'Then let me know when you're ready to go.'

# 15

As soon as Kerry had finished her drink, she retrieved her jacket from the back of her chair. 'Let's get out of here, shall we?'

They left the pub and wandered along the street. Alex's arm was draped around her shoulder, hers around his waist. She was feeling the effects of several gin and tonics and her long-suppressed desire for him. She slipped her hand under his coat, and then under his shirt, touching his bare skin. He winced.

'Sorry. Are my hands cold?'

'No. It just felt so good, I'm going to have to stop and kiss you again.'

They halted on the pavement, locked in an embrace, until they were whistled and jeered at by a group of drunks. A police car screamed down the street.

'Let's get home, before we get arrested,' Alex said.

They proceeded past neon signs glowing above takeaways and homeless people huddled in doorways. The smells of fried chicken, pizza and falafel drifted out of the shops and dispersed into the cold night air.

Kerry knew this was the moment she should mention contraception. She was working up to the subject when they reached the traffic lights at the junction and he stopped.

'There's a late-night pharmacy up the road,' he said. 'Perhaps I should stop on the way?'

His eyelids flickered as he spoke, which she knew by now signified his discomfort with the topic under discussion.

'I was thinking the same thing,' she said, glad he'd raised the issue first, and a little relieved he hadn't been so presumptuous as to plan in advance.

'Do you mind if I wait outside?' Kerry said when they reached the pharmacy, not wanting to face the scrutiny of the woman behind the counter.

'Of course not. I won't be a minute.'

While she waited, a male student came out of a nearby bar and stopped in the shelter of the doorway beside her to light a cigarette. As he extracted his lighter from his pocket, he stole a furtive glance at her. Kerry took out her phone and pretended to check her messages. The student inhaled several times on his cigarette and flicked his dark curly hair out of his eyes.

'Had a good night so far?' he asked her.

'Yes thanks. How about you?'

'Been to a couple of bars. Now I'm meeting some mates at a club in town.' He paused, shuffling his feet. 'Don't suppose you fancy coming along?'

She gave an astonished laugh. 'Thanks, but no. I'm on my way home.'

Alex had emerged from the pharmacy and was leaning against the doorway watching them. He arched an amused eyebrow.

'Oh Kerry. I see you've had a much better offer.'

The student's hand jerked to his throat. 'Sorry mate. I didn't realise she was with you.'

Alex grinned at the young man as he edged away and escaped towards the bus stop.

'Enjoy the rest of your night,' he called out. He draped his arm around Kerry's shoulders again. 'You see, you're so beautiful, I can't leave you alone for a second without someone else trying their luck.'

She was still bemused. 'I'm old enough to be his mum. I bet he'd have been horrified if he knew.'

'Trust me,' Alex said quietly, 'he wouldn't have minded.'

'How do you know?'

'Because I was nineteen myself once. If you can believe that.'

Holding hands, they left the lively student zone and wandered through the quiet residential streets of Fallowfield until they arrived at an estate: a grid of small box-like modern houses with white pebble-dashed walls, satellite dishes and plastic windows. A group of teenagers with bikes stared silently at them as they entered the estate.

Alex grew quiet too as they walked along the path and arrived at his house at the end of the row.

'It's nothing special, I'm afraid,' he said as he got his keys out of his pocket. 'I rent it from a housing association. When you're disabled and reliant on the state, you have to be grateful for what you can get.'

'I live in a tiny attic flat. A house of any size is luxury to me. Anyway, it looks fine.' She squeezed his hand.

'You're so kind. It's one of the many things I adore about you,' he said, and he slipped his arm around her waist and kissed her before he unlocked his front door.

A cramped chilly hallway led into a small living room with laminate wood flooring. On each side stretched a pair of narrow couches in chocolate leather, showing signs of wear. There was also a cherry red desk, two lamps with stained-glass shades, a gilt-edged mirror and an oak bookcase filled with leather-bound books. The classy antique style contrasted sharply with the soulless exterior of the house.

'I love what you've done to this place,' she said.

'Thank you. It's all quality furniture, but I paid next to nothing for it,' he told her. 'I searched in skips and rubbish tips or Pete brought things back for me from house clearances that were too damaged to sell in the shop, and I restored them myself.'

The television in the corner was a large widescreen. Alex noticed her looking at it.

'That was my one expensive purchase. It took me forever to pay off the loan. But my eyesight's not as good as it used to be, and I do like to watch films on a big screen.'

He switched on the lamps and turned off the main light. 'I have to get the lighting exactly right or it affects my mood. Too much gloom gets me down but too much brightness makes me irritable and then I can't sleep.'

Kerry's attention was drawn to a photograph on the wall above the mantelpiece, of a dark night sky with fireworks exploding in showers of colour.

'I took that last Bonfire Night in Platt Fields Park,' he said.

'It's amazing. I was at the fireworks that night too. We might have been near each other.'

'Perhaps, though I don't go near the crowds if I can help it.'

Another image caught her eye: the stark outline of Manchester Cathedral rising into the violet light of a winter dawn.

'That's stunning. The colour of the sky is so intense.'

'It really was that exact shade. I didn't alter it at all afterwards. Now this is one of my favourites,' he said, showing her a grimy brick archway near Piccadilly Station, under which glamorous young people queued outside a former air raid shelter to get into a rave. 'I love the urban setting and the anticipation on their faces.'

'Did they mind you taking their photos?' she asked.

'Not at all. They were all drunk or high and we had quite a good chat. One of them was a photography student. He was thrilled when I told him who I was, because he'd learned about me on his course.' He smiled. 'I have to admit, that gave me a moment of pleasure. That my work hadn't been completely forgotten.'

'Why don't you sell or exhibit any of these?'

He seemed surprised she'd asked. 'Because I can't cope with going back into that whole business again. It wouldn't be good for me.'

'Do you have a website?'

'God no. Nothing like that. They've got no commercial value anyway. I take them purely for pleasure.'

It seemed a waste that he couldn't do anything to promote his art. But she sensed that as well as incapacitating him, the depression had robbed him of his faith in his talent.

Alex showed her the kitchen, which was clean and tidy, though the cooker was pitted with rust and the tiles were webbed with cracks. A patio door led onto a small fenced garden. Peering through the glass, Kerry made out the dim shapes of a tree and a table.

'It's nice sitting outside in the summer,' he said, 'except when my neighbours have noisy parties. We've been fighting about it for years.' He turned away from the door and put his arm around her shoulder. 'Shall we go upstairs? Or would you like a drink?'

'I'm fine, thanks.' She was feeling unexpectedly shy in his presence. The tipsiness and uninhibited lust she'd experienced outside the pub had diminished on the walk home. Now her nerves were building at the prospect of undressing in front of him.

He led her up the narrow stairs. On the landing were more of his photographs and several framed art prints, including Van Gogh's self-portrait with his bandaged ear.

'That's a sad picture,' she remarked.

Alex stood back to look at it. 'I'd say it was contemplative. I think he's reassessing his life, wondering how he came to lose his sanity, and where he goes from here.'

He gestured at the first door on the landing. 'That's the spare room.'

'Have you been affected by the bedroom tax?'

A flash of annoyance crossed his face. 'My housing benefit was reduced because of the extra room. It made me furious, not just on my account, but for all the poor families living on this estate. The council said that if I didn't like it, I'd have to move to a smaller flat. And I wasn't well enough to cope with the stress of that.'

She peeped through the open door at piles of scattered clothes and shoes, and an exercise bike.

'It's a complete tip, I'm afraid,' he said. 'I try to keep the house uncluttered but all the junk ends up in there.'

'Do you use the bike a lot?'

'I do half an hour on it most days. It bores me to tears but it helps me stay well. Though when I'm feeling low the good habits tend to slip.'

'I should probably do more exercise,' she said guiltily.

'You walk everywhere, like me. Not owning a car is good for staying active.'

'Do you have a driving license?'

'I had to give it up the last time I was admitted to a psychiatric hospital. I might be able to reapply for it but I don't want a car. I can't afford the petrol, and also…'

'What?'

'Oh, it was nothing.'

Something in his manner dissuaded her from pursuing the subject. Instead she pointed at a photo of the singer Amy Winehouse among a collection of old bands she didn't recognise. 'I take it you're an Amy fan?'

She was asking him a lot of questions. As if she was delaying the inevitable, even though it was what she'd wanted.

'One of my favourite musicians,' he said. 'I was devastated when she died so young. If only I'd had the chance to photograph her myself. It would have been the highlight of my career.'

Alex turned away and opened the second door.

'This is my bedroom,' he said, and they went inside. It was spotless and simply furnished with a pine cupboard and a double bed. The walls were plain white except for a mirror and a wide photograph of a tranquil bluebell wood opposite the bed. Black-out curtains hung from the windows.

'I have to block out any light at night,' he told her. 'Even then, I'm a very light sleeper.'

'I can relate to that. I am too.'

He perched on the edge of his bed. She placed her bag on the chair, removed her jacket and her boots and sat next to him on the white quilt. He gave her a kiss but it was soft and tentative, and she guessed nerves had seized him too.

'Kerry,' he said, 'I'm conscious it's still very early in our relationship. But I want you to know I've been in love with you pretty much from the start.'

She gave him a smile that combined scepticism with delight. 'Do you really believe in love at first sight?'

He looked thoughtful. 'I know I trust my intuition, and it told me you were the one I'd been waiting for. And as I got to know you better you were every bit as amazing as I thought you'd be. Only I was so afraid you wouldn't want me, with all my disadvantages. And when you didn't, it was…'

'I always wanted you, Alex. It was just…'

'It's all right.' He kissed her forehead. 'It doesn't matter any more.'

Alex took her in his arms and they fell back onto the bed. He rolled on top of her, kissing her deeply. As desire swooped through her insides once more, Kerry began to unbutton his shirt. He pulled off his jeans and soon he was lying next to her, naked apart from a pair of black shorts.

He had a figure some men half his age would have envied, with toned muscular limbs. Close up, however, it was apparent he was no longer young. Blue knotted veins stood out on his calves and forearms, the flesh around his midriff sagged a little and the strip of hair that ran down his chest was patchy and streaked with silver.

He was the most beautiful man she'd ever seen in her life.

'Wow. You are *gorgeous*,' she said, running her hands across his chest and stomach.

He gave her a self-conscious smile and caressed her hands, and then he rolled over on top of her and kissed her neck.

'Now it's your turn,' he said, and his hands moved over the curve of her breasts and down to her waist to lift her top. Instinctively she flinched.

He removed his hand and sat up, and she did too.

'What's wrong, darling?' he said, kissing the side of her face. 'Have you changed your mind?'

'No.' She hesitated. 'I'm just embarrassed because I'm in my forties now and I've never exactly been skinny.'

The instant the words were out she regretted them. Everyone knew how unattractive it was to have low self-esteem. Why the hell had she confessed her insecurities to him at this crucial moment?

He put his arm around her shoulders. 'Actually, Kerry, I've noticed you have a true hourglass figure.' He traced his fingers slowly down her side. 'Like the shape of a violin. It's rarer than you'd think, and absolutely sublime. And young women don't have a monopoly on beauty,' he added gently, and he kissed her face again.

Slowly she stripped off her top, thankful she'd decided to wear her best underwear. Had her subconscious mind known all along this was bound to happen?

Alex unhooked her bra and removed it.

'You're even more beautiful than I'd imagined,' he said, regarding her bare breasts with awe. He caressed her, and then he lay back on the bed and pulled her on top of him, laughing. 'Come here, you divine goddess. Christ, I want you so much.'

She unbuttoned her jeans and wriggled out of them, and he removed her scanty lace knickers, and there she was, pale and naked and imperfect in front of him.

For a few seconds he stared at her, and then suddenly he was all over her, his hands and mouth exploring her body. Her fears melted away as she responded to his touch, arching her back and wrapping her legs around him as she plastered his shoulders and neck with kisses.

It wasn't long before she was aroused enough to allow him to enter her. When he did, she gasped and closed her eyes as her inner nerves contracted and pulsed, sending waves of electricity rushing through her.

'I love you,' she whispered in his ear.

She opened her eyes. Alex was looking down at her, his face flushed and his pupils dilated.

'My God,' he said in a breathless voice as he moved inside her, 'I love you so much, I can't bear it.'

Afterwards he lay collapsed on top of her, his face buried on her chest. She stroked his damp dishevelled hair and they talked in hushed voices, until he confessed he was tired and needed to sleep.

In the middle of the night Kerry woke with a jolt.

Why was it so dark? And so hot?

As her brain dragged itself from sleep, she became aware of Alex's arm around her shoulder. It felt strange to have someone else in bed with her again after she'd got used to sleeping alone. The inkiness of the room was unnerving, like being trapped in the bottom of a deep pit. She had no idea what time it was.

It was stiflingly warm. She wriggled free of him and pulled back the covers. Alex remained fast asleep, breathing with a rattle as he exhaled. He was very noisy for a supposed light sleeper. She tried to get back to sleep but she was too uncomfortable and restless. At last she got up and groped her way along the wall until she located the door.

On the landing a faint light crept in from the window. Van Gogh loomed out of the wall like a wraith. Kerry tiptoed to the bathroom, switched on the light and closed the door. The paintwork was scuffed and the side of the bath was cracked but he'd done his best to make it look nice by scattering seashells on the surfaces and mounting seaside images on the walls. On the shelf sat numerous bottles: prescription pills, vitamins and herbal supplements, as if he was desperately seeking something to cure his ailments.

A toothbrush still in its wrapper that he'd bought her from the pharmacy rested on the sink. She used it to clean her teeth and removed part of her make-up with a wet tissue, leaving on her eyeliner as she wasn't ready yet to let him see her completely bare-faced. Then she sat on the edge of the bath and rested her head in her hands.

Perhaps she *had* rushed into it sooner than was wise. Only this morning she'd been dithering over asking him out. A few hours later she'd slept with him and told him she loved him. But he hadn't coerced her into anything. She'd followed her heart and left herself vulnerable.

It would kill her now to give him up.

She sat thinking until tiredness overwhelmed her and she crept back into the darkened bedroom, where she fumbled her way towards the bed and slipped in beside him, only now he was awake.

'Are you all right?' he asked, rolling over and pulling her close to him. 'You were gone a long time.'

'I'm fine. Sorry I woke you up.'

'Don't worry about it,' Alex said sleepily, and he kissed her nose. 'I love you.'

'You too,' she said, reassured by his warm affectionate presence. Love would make it work. All they had to do was love each other, and everything would be fine.

# 16

In the morning she woke early and found Alex awake too. She rolled into his arms and they made love again in the darkness. Afterwards, exhausted, they curled up together and slept in late, until at last he sat up and opened the curtains. Sunlight danced on the white walls and rippled over the bed.

'Those bluebells are so calming,' she said, indicating the photograph.

'Yes, aren't they?' He lay back on the pillows and yawned. 'I could spend all day in bed looking at them. But I should get up and make you a coffee.'

She turned over until she was lying with her head on his chest, seeing his face in bright daylight. His sandy-grey hair was a tangled mess and he looked tired, with deep wrinkles and stretched skin below his eyes. The sunlight was giving his brown irises their amber glow.

She could spend all day in bed looking at him.

'There's no rush to get up,' she said, wrapping her arms around his waist.

'Sorry you couldn't sleep. I hope it wasn't my fault.'

'It wasn't you,' she lied. He'd kept her awake with constant fidgeting when he wasn't asleep, and breathing heavily in her ear when he was. 'I can't sleep in strange places.'

'Nor can I. It's one of the reasons I don't go away from home any more.' He sat up. 'Right. I should get up now.'

He clambered out of bed, and then he leaned over and kissed her lips.

'I adore you,' he said in her ear. He put on a dressing gown and padded downstairs, where he clattered around in the kitchen. Kerry luxuriated in the sunshine until he returned with her coffee.

She was about to get up and make a trip to the bathroom when paralysis came over her as she realised it would mean walking across the room naked in front of him. Obviously she was being ridiculous. He'd already explored every inch of her body. But he hadn't seen her standing up in the full glare of sunlight.

Perhaps Alex guessed how she was feeling because he went to his wardrobe and found a paisley satin robe, which he handed to her.

'Here you are. Something to wear around the house.'

She slipped it on, enjoying the loose softness of the fabric around her shoulders.

'You look gorgeous in that,' he said, his head tilted to one side.

'Thank you.' She smiled up at him. 'Sorry about all my hang-ups. I was bullied about my weight for years at school.'

Alex got into bed next to her with his coffee and put an arm around her.

'Sorry to hear that, darling. Children can be little sods, can't they?'

Encouraged by his sympathetic attitude, she talked to him at length about her experiences.

'So food became a source of comfort. I used to hide chocolate under my mattress and eat it when my parents had gone to bed. I hated myself for doing it, but it was…'

'A way to numb the pain. I know how that feels.' He took a sip of his coffee. 'I remember it from when I was overweight.'

'I find that hard to believe.' She slid her hands under his dressing gown, feeling the taut muscles on his upper arms and chest. 'You're in amazing shape. It's very sexy.'

Alex caressed her hands. 'That's lovely of you to say so. But I wasn't always. All right, if you don't believe me, I'll show you.'

He disappeared into the spare room and returned with a photograph album, climbed into bed beside her and retrieved his glasses from the bedside table.

'This was taken at some party or other. It was in 1995, so I'd have been about thirty-eight.'

The photograph showed a heavy-set man with a puffy face, dressed in an evening suit and starched white shirt. His short hair was expensively styled and he stood with a cigarette in one hand, the other placed possessively on the waist of a slender tanned woman with tumbling blonde curls.

Kerry almost recoiled from the page. It wasn't the shock of how unhealthy he looked so much as the way he was standing there, showing off his model girlfriend. He exuded a kind of privileged arrogance she couldn't reconcile with the Alex she knew. It wasn't at all how she'd imagined him when he was young.

'Do you recognise me?' He was watching her intently.

'You look very different.'

'I must have weighed fifteen stone there, but it's definitely me, I'm afraid.'

She looked more closely. Despite his superficial confidence, the man's light-brown eyes were full of painful confusion, as if he'd had no real clue what he was doing there. She edged closer to him in the bed until she was at his side with her arms wrapped around him and her chin resting on his bare shoulder.

'The only familiar thing about you is your eyes. But you look so lost.'

'Oh God, I was. Totally lost. I was such a mess back then.'

'What was going on?'

'I'd started to become really successful and was making a *lot* of money. And I was so depressed, and I had no idea why.'

She kissed his shoulder tenderly. 'Was it the career you'd planned to have?'

'Not really. I got into it by accident. When I left Durham, where I went to university, I went on my trip around Europe taking photos of ordinary people and street scenes. I felt like a real artist. I sold some of those images, but I couldn't make a living from it.'

'So you had to do something else to make ends meet.'

He leaned over to the bedside table to retrieve his mug. 'I did a few promotional shots to help out some aspiring musicians I knew, and that's when I got noticed for my ability to make people look their absolute best. I used the connections I made to find more work, and soon I was getting bookings from models, singers, actors, even the aristocracy.'

'Did you like working with them?'

He moved his leg so it rested on her legs. His foot caressed hers.

'I liked the challenge of producing outstanding work that made them happy. But I got so tired of the narcissism and the superficiality. Magazine editors always wanted to alter the images to make the women look younger and thinner than they were.'

'And you didn't like that?'

'I wanted to bring out the beauty and character that was naturally there.' He paused. 'I can show you some of my work from that time if you like?'

'I'd love to see it.'

He got up and returned with a larger album. 'This is one of my portfolios.'

Alex knelt beside the bed and laid the portfolio on her lap. She noticed how calloused his feet were, she guessed from walking around the city to take his photographs and being unable to afford new shoes.

She turned the pages, revealing moody monochrome images of rock bands and headshots of men and women with big hair and dramatic make-up.

'These are brilliant,' she said, and they were, though in truth she preferred the ones she'd seen on his walls.

'Thank you.' He smiled, and then he climbed back into bed and lay against her, his head against her collar bone. She smoothed his untidy hair, then turned the page to a portrait of a curvy blonde in a corset and fishnet gloves.

'You must have met a lot of people through your work,' she said. Meaning that he'd clearly been involved with a host of glamorous women.

'Oh, I was out at parties all the time. I found it draining. I'm lucky that I can be outgoing if I need to, but I'm not a social butterfly by nature. I'd rather stay in with a good book.'

'I can relate to that,' she said, and she kissed the top of his head.

'I didn't expect anyone to sympathise, considering how enviable my life was. But some nights I'd be out in the latest bar or nightclub acting like I was king of the world, and then I'd go home and cry myself to sleep because I felt so cut off from my true self.'

She slid her arms around his waist and held him close. 'It sounds awful. Did you never think about quitting and doing something else?'

'No. But it wasn't just the money that kept me there. I'd never had much faith in myself when I was growing up, and I was addicted to the recognition and praise I got for my work.'

'I can imagine being so unhappy would have affected your health.'

'Absolutely. I worked crazy hours to drown out my feelings and I was heavily into drink and drugs.'

He took off his glasses and shifted uncomfortably in the bed.

'I was into drugs too in my youth,' she said. 'I took ecstasy most weekends for three years.'

Alex regarded her with interest. 'How did it make you feel?'

'Incredible. But the person I became when I was high was never really me. I always knew that.'

'I know what you mean,' Alex said. 'Though I never tried that myself. I was too old by the time the scene got going, and the crowd I hung around with weren't the sort to be raving in a muddy field. Cocktails and cocaine were more our style.'

He gazed at the photo of him in the other album again and shuddered. 'Christ, I look awful there. I'm glad you didn't meet me back then. I doubt you'd have liked me much.'

'Although *she* did,' Kerry said, indicating the woman in the picture.

'I suppose she must have done. We were together a few months anyway. I think she liked me because I listened to her problems and took such flattering photos of her.'

He looked up from the page at her. 'Sorry. Is it tactless of me to show you this?'

She bit at her thumbnail. 'Not really. I know you've got a past. It's just that… she's stunning.'

He kissed her lips. 'So are you. And I was never really in love with her.'

She decided to change the topic. 'So how did you manage to give up your bad habits?'

'I was left with no choice. My body couldn't handle it any more. One night I was rushed to hospital with severe chest pain and breathlessness and they diagnosed me with coronary heart disease. The shock of that led to the most severe depression I'd ever experienced. And then…'

Alex stopped and glanced up at the cracked ceiling. The sun had disappeared behind a cloud and its warmth had faded. He pulled the duvet up to cover them. He took her hand in his and stroked her fingers.

'I decided I wasn't going to wait around to die from a heart attack. So I drank a lot of vodka, then I went out into my garage in the middle of the night, closed the door and got in my car. I tried to switch on the engine but nothing happened. I was so drunk, I couldn't figure out what was going on, until I realised I must have left the headlights on and the battery had drained flat.'

Kerry let out the breath she'd been holding. 'Jesus. That was lucky.'

'Yes. I'm still alive because I'm an idiot.' He laughed. 'But it's one of the reasons I'm reluctant to have a car again. In case the temptation ever came back. At the time, I was furious with myself, and yet relieved, as if I'd become two people with conflicting goals. And the half of me that wanted to survive phoned a friend, and he drove me to a hospital. When I got there I started crying and couldn't stop.'

He closed his eyes. She began to rub his shoulders with a soothing rhythm.

'It turned out I was having what in those days was called a nervous breakdown,' he said. 'I was in the hospital for weeks and it took me months longer to get better. The psychiatrist who treated me reckoned I'd been having major depressive episodes since my teens, and I'd almost certainly have more in future.'

'Was it a relief to get a diagnosis?'

He screwed up his eyes, trying to remember. 'I'm not sure it was, at the time. I'd only just turned forty and I was landed with two serious health problems, one of which had a huge amount of stigma attached to it. But I suppose it helped to give a name to the distress I'd suffered from all those years.'

'And was that when you gave up work?'

'No, I still wanted to be a photographer. But I had to escape the celebrity lifestyle. I moved to Manchester to be near a close friend who'd been through a similar experience and managed to turn his life around. He supported me while I made the transition to a healthier life.'

'He must be a very good friend.'

'He was. Sadly he's dead now, but I'll always be grateful for what he did for me.'

Alex returned to the photo album. 'This is me six months after I moved here.' His cheeks had hollowed dramatically, more lines had appeared on his face and his hair was longer and less styled. He wore a black sweater and was staring straight at the camera with an intense expression.

'You'd lost a lot of weight by then,' she said.

He had one hand on her thigh, the other on the back of her neck, playing sensuously with her hair.

'When I set out to achieve something, I tend to be pretty obsessive about it. I started work again as a wedding photographer. But the depression kept coming back. I couldn't live with the fear of letting a client down, so I gave up the business for everyone's sake. Despite all the money I'd made in London I hadn't managed to save enough to live on.'

'So you became unemployed?'

'No, I was determined not to fall into that trap. I needed a job, but one that didn't cause me too much stress. For a while I worked in a camera shop, then in low-paid jobs for various photography and print companies. But my health was still a problem. The companies all had disability discrimination policies, but they only paid lip service to them, especially when it came to mental health. Once they realised the extent of my issues and how much time off I was going to need, several managers tried to get rid of me in unpleasant and illegal ways.'

'I hear it happens a lot to people with mental illnesses. It makes me so angry,' she said, shifting her legs so she could sit up straighter.

'Me too.' He twirled a bunch of her hair around his fingers. 'I stood up for myself, but I found the conflict incredibly stressful. The third time I was sacked I overdosed on pills and ended up back in hospital. For weeks after that I couldn't move out of bed, I was so overwhelmed with despair at the trainwreck my life had become. But with my psychiatrist's help I came out of that phase. And then I tried to find another job.'

'You're such a fighter despite your problems, Alex. I love that about you.'

'Thank you.' He gave her knee an affectionate squeeze. 'But that time the economy beat me. It was 2008, the stock market had crashed and everyone was being laid off.'

'I remember. It was an awful time.'

'By then I was over fifty with a patchy CV, which meant I had zero chance of finding work. I kept trying, until it destroyed what was left of my self-esteem and I got sick again. As well as the depression I was getting a lot of angina, which meant I was at serious risk of a heart attack. That was when I gave up and applied to go on benefits. It was accepted at the time that my health was too fragile to withstand any more pressure. But I still needed something positive to do, so I decided to volunteer in the shop.'

She took his gnarled hand in hers and pressed it against her lips. How sad it was that he'd fought so hard and had had so much to offer.

'Your life hasn't been easy, has it?'

'Not always, no.' He closed the album. 'But then it hasn't been that hard compared to some. I spent years feeling bad for being in so much pain when I had so little to complain about.'

'But you don't any more?'

'I get the odd twinge of guilt now and then. But my psychiatrist convinced me I didn't need a dramatic history of trauma or abuse to justify my emotions. The truth is I struggle with my moods more than most people. I can't help that, so I refuse to be ashamed of it.'

'What do you think makes people like us different?'

He looked thoughtful. 'Possibly something to do with the way our brains process our experiences. But there's still so much we don't understand. With all the discoveries happening in neuroscience and genetics, in future we may have to radically change our view of mental illness.'

'But things are okay for you at the moment?'

'Oh, right now I couldn't be happier.' He kissed her forehead and both cheeks and finally, her lips. 'But that's because of you.'

By the time Kerry left his house it was late afternoon and they'd spent most of the day in bed together, making love and kissing and dozing and exchanging stories about their lives. She felt shattered and elated and emotionally drained and hopelessly in love. On Monday they were both due to work in the shop. How was she going to hide her feelings for him in front of the others?

# 17

When Kerry sailed into the shop on a wave of euphoria she sensed at once that Sue was under pressure. She was bustling around the shop floor, tidying up with even more vigour than usual, tutting and whistling through her teeth whenever she noticed something out of place.

'My boss Pam, the regional retail manager, is coming in for a visit,' Sue explained. 'She's a bit of a dragon, as you'll see.'

Kerry dreaded to imagine the woman who could intimidate Sue.

'The shop looks stunning today,' she said reassuringly, and indeed it did. She and Yasmeen had created their best window display yet, of 1970s clothing. In front of a spangled backdrop the centrepiece was a pair of fringed cowboy boots and a tie-dyed rainbow shirt.

'But our sales are still down,' Sue said. 'And that's not good. She'll want to know to the last detail what promotions we've done, how we're pricing and restocking and so on.'

'I'm sure you're doing all the right things. And if you need any help, I'm here. I can make tea for her and be friendly.'

Today she was so giddy with happiness that she wanted to spread her bliss like a virus to anyone who crossed her path.

'Ta love.' Sue gave her a smile. 'I nearly forgot; there's a bloke coming to replace a pane in the front window. Don't know if you noticed on your way in, but there's a crack in the glass where some bloody twerp rode their bike into it. Could have done without that today and all, but it can't be helped.'

Kerry noticed Sue's flushed cheeks. 'Are you okay?'

Sue stopped and fanned herself. She ran a hand through her glass-smooth blonde bob. 'I feel all hot all of a sudden.'

'Can I get you some water? Would you like to sit down?'

'Ta, but I'm all right. It's only half an hour now till she gets here. I'd better go upstairs and find out what Alex has done with those books. I told him to put out the best ones this week, but we sometimes have a different idea of what that means.'

Kerry restrained the automatic smile that came to her lips in response to the mention of her lover's name. 'Okay. Let me know if you need a hand.'

'See if you can sort out the mess in the staffroom.' Sue turned around and then she halted, frowning. 'What did I say I was going to do?'

'Check the book display upstairs.'

'Aye, that was it.' She pursed her lips. 'Honestly, some days I reckon I'd forget my own head if it weren't screwed on.'

Kerry had never seen Sue in such a muddle. She retreated to the staffroom where she washed dirty mugs, vacuumed the carpet and concealed chaotic piles of paperwork. None of it cost her any effort. As if she'd grown wings and learned to fly.

At ten o'clock Pam arrived, a tight-lipped, grey-haired woman in a trouser suit and heels. Sue showed her around the shop, then the three of them gathered in the staffroom. To Kerry's amazement, Sue became deferential in her manager's presence.

'Kerry here's been a godsend,' Sue said gushingly. 'She's helped me out so many times when we've been short-staffed.'

'I see.' Pam gave Kerry a searching look. 'And why do you volunteer here?'

'I'm looking for a job, but I had some time free, so I thought…'

'So you'll be off once something else comes along?'

'I'd love to stay, only I don't get paid, and I need to earn a living,' she said calmly. Today she felt invincible, as if nothing could faze her.

'Yes of course.' Pam turned back to Sue. 'Are the staff upstairs still with you?'

'Ruth and Alex? Oh aye,' Sue said. 'Neither of them two's going anywhere in a hurry.'

'Good. We like the ones who stick around.' Pam bared her teeth in a smile.

'Can I make you a drink, Pam?' Kerry asked her.

'No thanks. I grabbed a coffee on my way here. Shall we get on with the figures?' Pam said, looking pointedly at Sue.

Sue's face reddened again. 'Kerry love, could you supervise the shop while I'm busy?'

Kerry went out onto the shop floor where Joe was on the till. Seeing there was nothing that required her attention she went upstairs, excitement rising in her chest at the prospect of seeing Alex. He was crouching in the stockroom among a pile of books. He stood up as she came in.

'Morning darling. Is Pam here yet?'

She giggled. 'Don't tell me you're scared of her too.'

'I wouldn't say I was *scared* of her. I'm not fond of her company.'

'Nor is Sue. You should see how flustered she is this morning.'

'I did. She was up here earlier, fussing because I'd left a box out on the floor.'

Alex peeped out of the doorway to check Ruth wasn't hovering nearby, then drew her into his arms. 'You look absolutely gorgeous this morning.'

'I can't stay long. I just wanted to say hello.'

'Then say hello to me properly.' He kissed her on the mouth and neck. She pulled away, laughing.

'Alex, we can't do this. Kissing in the stockroom. It's like some awful clichéd office affair.'

'I don't care,' he said, but he let her go. 'Do you still want to meet up tonight? I could come to your flat this time. I'd love to see where you live.'

'You're welcome any time. But I doubt you'll get much sleep there,' she said.

'I'll take some sleeping pills.'

'I don't want you to do that on my account.'

'Let's see how it goes, shall we? I don't want you to have to make all the effort coming to see me.'

Kerry felt a stinging itchiness on the tender skin of her chest and neck where he'd touched her. She looked up at him. 'Did you forget to shave today?'

He put his hand to his chin. 'Have I scratched you? I'm sorry, darling. I was so tired this morning I didn't get round to it.'

'Are you all right?'

'I'm fine. Never been better in my life.' He gave her one of his intimate smiles.

'Good. Okay love, I ought to go.'

They came out of the stockroom and she turned to leave, and then she looked back at Alex, who was leaning against the doorframe, holding his glasses in one hand. He raised his fingers to his lips and blew her a kiss. A crazy rush of desire swept through her. She pushed him back in through the door, kicked it shut with the heel of her boot and flung her arms around his neck.

'I thought you didn't want to do this,' he said, amused, when she broke away.

'You made it impossible for me not to.'

At last she emerged and returned downstairs, still in a trance. Later, Sue finished her meeting and showed Pam out.

'How did it go?' Kerry asked when Sue came into the corridor.

Sue pulled a face. 'Not great, if I'm honest. As I expected, she said we need to be making more effort to shift the stock.'

'I don't see how you can work any harder than you do,' Kerry said.

'Me neither. But she wasn't having it.' She peered over her spectacles at Kerry. 'What the heck's happened to you? You're all red and blotchy.'

Kerry cast around for an explanation. Her glance fell on the bags piled up on the bench.

'Maybe I'm allergic to something in the clothes today. Some kind of washing powder?'

Sue continued to examine her. 'Your eyes look strange too. Sort of bright and feverish. You know, I've not been feeling so well myself this morning. I wonder if there's something going round.'

Not unless love is contagious, Kerry thought. What would Sue say if she knew? She recalled the way Sue had looked at him at the Christmas party. Would there be envy mingled with her disapproval?

'I feel fine,' she said.

'All right, but you'd better keep away from those clothes. Could you supervise Shaun on the till this afternoon instead?'

At Kerry's suggestion, Sue had reluctantly agreed to allow Shaun to serve customers. Kerry had trained him herself. She'd been impressed by how fast he'd picked everything up. Even his manner with the public was better than she'd anticipated: he'd managed not to swear for the duration of his shift. At the end when the shop was closed, he'd turned to her.

'You know what, mate? That was all right, that.'

'Glad you enjoyed it,' she'd said.

'Shaun doesn't need a lot of supervision,' she told Sue. 'He's doing fine. He's not as hopeless as everyone seems to think.'

Sue gave a snort but said nothing. She bustled into the shop to see if anything had happened while she was with Pam.

The next day Kerry, Joe and Shaun were sorting through donations when Sue came in with the coldest expression on her face Kerry had ever seen.

'I need a word with everyone,' she said. 'I'm shutting up shop for a few minutes.'

Kerry's shoulders tensed. Was this a consequence of Pam's visit yesterday? Along with the boys, she entered the staffroom. Pete and Dan were already sitting at the table. Soon Alex and Ruth joined them. Alex gave Kerry a questioning look as he sat opposite her. She shrugged and spread out her hands.

Sue stood in front of them and cleared her throat. 'I'll get straight to the point. Dan's been reconciling the sales receipts with the cash in the tills and they don't balance. Which means some money's been taken.'

A shocked silence ensued. Then Alex spoke up. 'Sue, I'm afraid that was me.'

Everyone, including Kerry, stared at him in astonishment.

'Gladys was in yesterday afternoon,' he continued, 'and I let her have a couple of books because she'd forgotten her purse. Afterwards I realised I didn't have enough money left to pay for them either. I was going to the bank at lunchtime today to check my balance.'

Sue pursed her lips and frowned. 'Alex, I've told you before, I don't like you doing that. If Gladys hasn't got her purse, she has to put the stuff back, like anyone else.'

'Sorry.' He fidgeted in his chair. 'It won't happen again.'

'It'd better not,' Sue said sternly. 'But that's a separate issue. I'm talking about more than a few quid here. Several hundred, in fact.'

She gazed around the room. For the briefest instant her eyes rested on Shaun, but it was long enough for Kerry to notice.

'You know how much trust I place in you all,' she said, 'and I'm disappointed beyond belief that one of you would betray that trust. But I can't see any other explanation. Dan's checked and re-checked the figures, haven't you love?'

'I'm afraid it's definitely gone,' Dan said.

Another disquieting silence. Kerry fiddled with an earring and avoided everyone's eyes. Why did she feel so guilty when she knew she hadn't done anything wrong?

'I know not everyone's in today,' Sue said, 'but I'll be speaking to the other volunteers too. I'm going to wait until the end of tomorrow for someone to own up and pay it back. If nobody does, then we proceed with a formal investigation.' She scrutinised them again. 'All right, that's it. You can go and open up shop again.'

Kerry was heading towards the door when Sue nudged her elbow. 'Can I have a word with you in private?'

She flinched. Surely Sue didn't think it was her?

'Okay,' she said anxiously, coming back into the room. Sue closed the door and sat down.

'When you were supervising Shaun on the till yesterday did you notice anything suspicious about his behaviour?'

'Nothing at all,' Kerry said at once. 'He was doing a great job.'

'Were you watching him all the time?'

'Well, no. I left him alone for most of his shift because he was coping fine. Why, what makes you think it was him?'

'Who else could it be?' She looked straight at Kerry. 'I know it wasn't *you*. I'd trust Dan with my life. Pete and Colin are out in the van most days.' She counted the volunteers off on her fingers. 'Yasmeen's a sweet girl, and Joe's a decent kid too. Alex is a daft sod, but an honest one. Ruth's a dark horse, but she's been here years and she doesn't need the money anyway. As for Elspeth and the other old dears, I can't see any of them being light-fingered, can you?'

'Could someone have come into the shop and taken it while one of our backs was turned?' Kerry asked.

'Nah.' Sue made a face. 'You all know better than to leave the till unattended. And they'd have to figure out how to open the cash register in a rush. No, I can feel it in my bones, it was Shaun. He's got a conviction for theft and it happened as soon as he got access to the money. You've got to admit it all fits.'

'But you can't accuse him without any evidence.'

'I know. Obviously he's not going to confess and I don't see how we can prove it if no one saw anything.' She clenched her fists. 'I'm fuming with the little scrote for showing us such disrespect after we've given him the chance to make a fresh start.'

Kerry's sense of injustice was rising. 'Sue, you don't *know* it was him. It's not very fair to make assumptions based on his past.'

'All right, love. I've not said anything to him, have I? I'm only telling you in confidence what I think.' She paused to rub her nose. 'By the way, could you go on the downstairs till this afternoon? Shaun's on the rota, but I need him to help Pete deliver a wardrobe. None of the other men can do it. Colin's at the job centre, Joe's leaving early and Alex can't lift heavy furniture because of his heart.'

After lunch Kerry returned into the corridor, where she smelt smoke drifting from under the garage door. On impulse she pushed it open and went out into the yard to find Shaun leaning against the wall, puffing moodily on a cigarette.

'Hi. Just came to let you know I'm on the rota instead of you today,' she said.

'I know. Pete said.' Shaun stared sullenly at the concrete.

'Are you okay?'

For a second he ignored her, and then he hunched his shoulders and scowled. 'I'm not fucking thick, you know? I know why she doesn't want me on that till. She thinks I pinched that money.'

'She doesn't know who took it. That's why she spoke to everyone.'

'She gave me one of her fucking looks though. She's never trusted me from the start.' Shaun took another drag on his cigarette. 'I never took it, all right? I've robbed people before, but that was when I was off my head on crack. I'm not like that now.'

'I believe you,' she said, and she did, though she couldn't have explained why.

'She'd better not try and pin it on me,' Shaun said, and a dark look came into his eyes. 'I'm not going back to jail for something I never fucking did.'

'Don't worry. Sue can't confront you without proof. She knows that.'

'But she'll treat me even more like scum from now on.' He scuffed the top of his trainer against the wall. 'You know what mate? I've half a mind to get the fuck out of this place. But then she'll think it's because I'm guilty, and I'll have my probation officer giving me grief.'

'Maybe she'll find out who did it.'

'Yeah. I wonder who it was.' He narrowed his eyes. 'Maybe it was that Ruth upstairs. They say it's always the quiet ones. What d'you reckon?'

'There's no evidence it was her either.'

'Suppose not.'

They heard laboured breathing and Pete emerged into the yard.

'Oi Shaun. I've been waiting for you in the van for bloody ages. Are you coming or what?'

Shaun hesitated, as if considering refusing to go, but then he stubbed out his cigarette, thrust his hands into his pockets and loped off after Pete.


The atmosphere in the shop remained tense for the next few days. Kerry found herself getting nervous in case she gave customers too much change or left the cash register open by mistake.

Meanwhile she was spending as much time as possible with Alex. Within days she was as intimate with him as she'd been with anyone. For the first time she felt not only loved but also understood to the extent that he often guessed what she was feeling without her needing to express it.

They were walking home from having a drink in the pub when the topic of the thief came up.

'It's not the first time this has happened,' Alex said as they wandered along the pavement, arms around each other. 'There was a volunteer years ago, before Sue's time, who used to help herself to cash and clothes. When she got caught she couldn't see what she'd done wrong. She thought she deserved the occasional treat because she wasn't getting paid.'

'That's incredible,' Kerry said. 'People are strange, aren't they?'

'It was such a shock, because I'd never have suspected this woman. She was so cheerful and willing to help out. I have better than average intuition about people, but that time I got it wrong.'

'Sue's convinced it was Shaun.'

'Maybe it *was*.'

'I don't think so. He told me he didn't, and… well, it's intuition, like you said. I feel sorry for him. I get the impression no one's ever had much faith in him.'

'You're a very kind-hearted woman. I love that about you,' he said, and he stopped to kiss her. 'It's sad to think it must be one of us.'

Kerry slipped her arm around his waist and under his shirt, delighting in the warm velvety feel of his skin beneath her fingertips. Never had she felt such an urgent longing to be in constant physical contact with another person.

'You don't think Dan could have made a mistake with the figures?' she said as they arrived at a crossing.

'Dan's smart and he's very thorough. He'll have made absolutely sure he was right before he told Sue.'

On Monday Kerry entered the shop and found Sue waiting for her in the corridor.

'We've got a problem with Shaun,' she announced before Kerry had even said hello.

They went into the staffroom, made drinks and sat down. Sue gave a heavy sigh and put her elbows on the table.

'It happened last thing on Friday. I never meant to accuse him outright. I was intending to check whether he understood our procedures for handling cash. Just to gauge his reaction, you know? But my words must have come out wrong because he lost his rag with me straightaway. Called me a stuck-up bitch and said I was going to regret it.'

Kerry put her hand to her mouth. 'Jesus. Were you okay?'

'Don't worry about me, love. I've been called worse. And he wasn't violent, just letting off steam. The problem is, now he's gone missing.'

'I can't imagine he thought he'd be welcome back after saying that to you.'

'No, not missing from the shop. He's run off. He's not supposed to leave his home address but his family haven't seen him all weekend. The parole officer called me this morning. She's worried he might be using drugs again.'

'Oh. I see. That's not good news.' Kerry cupped her hot mug in her hands, not knowing what else to say.

'I know what you're thinking, Kerry,' Sue said in a sharp voice. 'That I shouldn't have said anything to the lad. And maybe I shouldn't have. But I still think he did it, and I couldn't stand to let hundreds of pounds of charity money go into his pockets and do nothing about it.'

'I just hope he's all right.'

Sue took a swig of her tea. 'The police will be looking out for him. Let's hope they find him before he gets in any trouble.'

# 18

The front window of the shop was smashed and shards of glass glinted in the pale winter sunlight. Inside, the place was in disarray with rails tipped over and clothes strewn across the floor. Police tape was drawn across the entrance and a crime scene investigator was dusting the window frame for fingerprints.

'Mind where you step, ma'am,' she said to Kerry, who had arrived for her shift. 'The shop's closed today. As you can see, there's been a break-in.'

The hair on the nape of Kerry's neck stood on end. 'I work here.'

'You'd better go round the back and let the manager know you're here.'

Kerry went down the side alley to the rear of the building, tiptoed through the garage door and went into the storage area where she encountered another police officer taking photographs.

'Please don't touch anything,' he warned her.

In the staffroom an ashen Sue sat at the table staring into space, her chin resting on the heels of her hands.

Kerry sat down shakily next to her. 'What's been stolen?'

'Not much, as far as I can see,' Sue said. 'It's mainly damage to the stock and the windows, which our insurance should cover. All the valuables were in the safe and that's still locked, though it looks like someone tried to force it open.

But it seems like most of it was done out of anger. I'm sure I don't need to tell you who we think it was.'

'Have the police found him?'

'Not yet, but he can't survive long on his own with no money.' Her voice hardened. 'Then he'll be right back in prison where he belongs.'

'What a nightmare.' Kerry was starting to feel sick.

'It's going to take ages to get this place straight. I suppose I'd better start by phoning the glass repair people. It's maddening when we only had that pane replaced the other week.'

Sue stood up, then froze. Her eyes widened. 'Oh, shit. Oh bloody hell, no.'

'What is it?' Kerry said, alarmed.

Sue sank back into her chair. Her shoulders dropped.

'You remember the day the window man came? And Pam was visiting, and it all got a bit hectic? When he'd finished, he wanted to be paid in cash and I didn't have time to go buggering about unlocking the safe. I know it's against our policy, but I was that mithered I took the money straight out of the till and gave it to him. And then I forgot to give Dan the receipt,' she said, her face reddening.

Kerry sat still, absorbing the implications. 'Then no one stole the money after all.'

'I can't believe I didn't remember before. But I was so fixated on it being Shaun.' Sue put her head in her hands. 'What the bloody hell have I done?'

A long silence followed.

'It was a mistake,' Kerry said. But one that had had devastating consequences. She gestured towards the wreckage outside the staffroom door. 'Whatever you did wrong, you didn't force Shaun to do this.'

'I suppose that's true.' Sue whistled through her teeth. 'I can't believe what a bloody fool I am. Pam's going to hit the roof when she finds out. I could lose my job over this.'

Kerry heard Alex's voice speaking to the policeman. He came in, a muscle twitching in his jaw.

'My God. This is terrible. What can I do to help?'

'Nothing,' Sue said, stony-faced.

He sat next to Kerry. Somehow she managed to resist taking hold of his hand.

'Do the police know what happened?' he asked.

Sue reluctantly related the story.

Alex let out a low whistle. 'So it wasn't Shaun after all.' He turned to Kerry. 'Your intuition was spot on. You remember what you said on the way home the other night?'

At once Sue's head jerked upwards. 'On the way *home*?'

Kerry winced.

'I see.' Sue pursed her lips. 'I shouldn't be surprised, I suppose.'

'Sorry we didn't tell you,' Kerry said. 'We thought…'

'That I'd have something to say about it? Well, I would have. But if there's anything I've learned today, it's that I shouldn't jump to conclusions.' She peered over her spectacles. 'Good luck to the pair of you. Let's hope you won't need it.'

She stood up. 'I'd better tell the police about Shaun and the money.'

Sue went to speak to the officer. Kerry reflected on the tragic course Shaun's life had taken. Alex put his arm around her shoulders and kissed her. He looked tired.

'Did you sleep badly again?' she asked.

'Terribly. I had a nightmare that I lost you.'

'You mean we split up?'

'No, I literally lost you. One minute we were walking along together and the next minute you'd gone. I ended up somewhere deep underground searching for you, only I couldn't see in the dark.'

'Don't worry. I'm not about to disappear anywhere.' She smiled and squeezed his hand.

'Sorry I slipped up in front of Sue.'

'It's all right. She was bound to find out sooner or later. Actually I feel better now she knows.'

'Me too. Though I was surprised it didn't get more of a reaction,' Alex said.

'She's still in shock. It must have been awful coming in and finding the shop like this. And then realising what she'd done.'

He shook his head. 'How on earth did she forget about paying for the window? It's the sort of thing I could easily do, but Sue's so practical.'

'She's been kind of absent-minded lately.' She hesitated. 'I don't know this for sure, but I suspect she's starting her menopause. She often complains about feeling hot.'

Kerry wondered how long she had before she herself approached the change of life. Sue was fifty-four, but of course it could happen long before that. And how would she feel once she had physical confirmation that her child-bearing years were over?


The thought returned to her several weeks later. By then Shaun had been found by the police, shivering from withdrawal and begging in the city centre. When questioned, he'd broken down and admitted what he'd done. Kerry hoped he'd get treatment for his addiction, though she feared for his future after another spell in prison.

Sue was in trouble with her boss over the cash she'd taken from the till and the way she'd handled the situation with Shaun. However, she hadn't been sacked as she'd feared. Pam had no desire to seek a replacement prepared to put in the long hours Sue did.

The shop now resembled its former self. The boxes were back on the shelves, the windows and the rails were fixed and Sue and Kerry were busy replenishing the clothes. While she was going through the boxes Sue had discovered a stash of children's clothes she'd forgotten about at the back of the storage area.

'I don't normally bother with kids' stuff, to be honest. Most folk don't want to buy them second hand when they're so cheap new. But it's worth putting some out every now and then.'

Kerry took the labelled boxes and tipped their contents onto the bench. There was an array of sleep suits in soft fluffy pinks and blues, as well as a little frilly skirt, a tiny pair of dungarees, a dress with a lace bib and several pairs of miniature woolly mittens and booties. They were so adorable she wasn't sure she could bear to throw any of them away.

Alone in the corridor she picked up one of the sleep suits, rubbing the softness of the material against her cheeks and inhaling its fresh scent. She could almost see the infant's shining eyes and hear its gurgles and cries. How had the mum felt once her child outgrew its outfits and she had to dispose of them? Excited for the next stage, no doubt, but was there a sense of loss for the little baby she'd never hold in her arms again?

She pressed the suit to her face and took a shuddering breath. What the hell was wrong with her? Maybe her period was due. She'd chosen not to have children, so she shouldn't get upset over a few baby clothes. But everything felt different now she'd met Alex.

Sue emerged into the corridor. 'How are you getting on?'

Kerry laid the sleep suit back onto the pile. 'Just having a look through before I decide what to put out.'

'Don't waste a lot of time on them. They're not going to make us much money. I just want rid of them one way or another.'

Sue picked up the dungarees. Her face softened.

'I remember my Ian had a pair like this. That's a long time ago. He's nearly thirty-two now, bless him.'

'What was he like as a child?'

She puffed out her cheeks and exhaled. 'He was always a sensitive little lad. Got picked on a fair bit at school. His dad and I grew up in tough neighbourhoods and learned to stick up for ourselves. But it wasn't his fault. It's just the way he was.'

'And the schizophrenia? Is that genetic?'

'We don't know for sure. But my aunt spent half her life in an asylum because she heard voices. So there was family history. Mind you, it didn't stop me blaming myself for a long time.'

'Do you think Ian will ever be well enough to have a family?'

'I'm not sure that would be wise. Not everyone's cut out to be a parent. It's a shame I'll never be a grandma, but there you go.' Sue looked at Kerry. 'What about you? Any regrets over not having kids?'

'None at all,' Kerry said quickly. 'I'm not the maternal type.'

'Aye well. Not everyone is.' Sue put the dungarees down. 'I'll let you get on. Give me a shout if you need a hand.'

Once Kerry had finished pricing the children's clothes she went to hang them on the promotional rail at the front of the shop. Mo had come in for her daily visit and was making her way round, tossing her head and scratching at her tangled nest of grey hair.

When Mo saw the display of children's garments she grew intensely agitated. She rifled through the stock and pulled the frilly skirt off its hanger. As she clutched it in her trembling fingers, she poured out a stream of muttering.

Kerry watched her from a distance. Although Mo was shabby and haggard she had fine dark eyes and a delicate bone structure. At some point she'd been an attractive woman. What relationships had she had? Did she have children she no longer saw or who'd been taken from her?

At last Mo flung the little skirt onto the floor and marched out of the shop. Kerry wondered where she lived, and who, if anyone, cared for her.

# 19

Kerry was in the habit now of spending her Saturday nights at Alex's house. One Sunday they stayed in bed late until he decided he should spend some time on the exercise bike.

'Though I'd much rather stay here with you,' he said, running his hand along the curve of her hip bone as they lay under the white quilt, their warm legs entwined.

'Why don't you stay with me then?'

'Because I need to keep fit.'

She rolled on top of him and nuzzled his neck. 'I think you're fit enough.'

He laughed. 'Kerry, I need to exercise.'

He stood up, stretched and yawned, then looked back at her lying naked on the bed. He leapt onto the mattress like a cat and tumbled into her waiting arms.

'What have you done to me?' he said as he buried his face in her breasts. 'I can't resist you.'

During their love-making he attempted yet again to give her an orgasm. She wanted to tell him to stop trying. There was no chance it would happen: it never had, not with any of the multiple partners she'd had. Even Stuart had given up trying in the end and they'd stopped talking about it.

Her inner muscles relaxed and her nerves responded as they always did to the touch of his lips, tongue and fingers. But this time a new nerve, hidden deep in her core, twitched and vibrated as it was stimulated for the first time. She arched her back, her breath coming in short, sharp gasps as she rode on a rising wave of pleasure, until she wasn't sure she could bear the tension any more. Her other senses faded to black, her body became a tightly coiled spring and then she lost control entirely and screamed and writhed and dug her fingers into the flesh of his shoulders.

Afterwards she lay exhausted, her arms wrapped around him, her heart thumping and intense feelings of love pulsing and flooding through her.

'That was the first time,' she said.

He leaned up on one elbow and brushed a strand of her burgundy hair out of her eyes.

'Do you mean the first time with me? Or that you've never had an orgasm before?'

'I've never had one. I know it sounds crazy at my age. I assumed there was something wrong with me.'

To her relief his expression bore no hint of amusement or surprise. 'Oh, there's absolutely nothing wrong with you. You can be sure of that,' he said, kissing her. 'Maybe you've felt too tense in the past?'

'But how did you do it?'

'There's no particular secret. I took the trouble to learn what worked and what didn't, and I cared deeply about what I was trying to achieve. The same principles that apply to almost anything.'

'You're rather pleased with yourself, aren't you?' she teased.

'Slightly,' he admitted with a grin. 'But I'm more pleased you felt secure enough with me to relax.'

'It was amazing. I didn't know it could be so intense.'

'It certainly seemed that way from your reaction. I think I may get more respect from my neighbours in future.'

'Come on. I didn't scream *that* loudly,' she said, but she was laughing too. She put her arms around his neck and pressed her forehead against his. 'I am so in love with you right now.'

She raised her head to stare into his flushed face and glistening eyes, and then she froze, hardly able to breathe.

'What's the matter?' he asked.

'Nothing. This feeling. Sometimes it's almost too much.'

'I know what you mean. It's wonderful and frightening at the same time.' He kissed her lips and took hold of her hands. 'Kerry, I realise it's too soon to be making commitments, but I'm getting the impression this is for the long term. Are you?'

'Definitely,' she said at once. 'Though of course, I need to get divorced first.' She noticed the slight downturn of his lips. 'Does it bother you that I'm still married?'

'A little bit.' He traced his finger along the length of her collarbone and regarded her thoughtfully. 'Not that it's a problem. It just feels strange. Perhaps it's my Catholic upbringing.'

She smiled. 'You think you'll burn in hell for sleeping with a married woman?'

'Of course I don't *really* believe that. I suppose I'd rather there weren't any obstacles to prevent us being together. But I know that's not how life works.'

'It's only a legal thing. Stuart and I were over long ago. I don't have any regrets about leaving him.'

His shoulders stiffened. 'I hope you'd tell me if you did.'

'Sure. But I don't.' She kissed him hard on the mouth and he relaxed again. A thought occurred to her.

'Isn't it funny to imagine ourselves in ten years' time? I can't believe I'll love you any less than I do now.'

'Well, I'll be seventy by then. Assuming my heart lasts that long, which is doubtful.'

Kerry shuddered as if a bucket of ice had been tipped down her spine.

'Jesus, Alex. Don't say that. Of course you'll still be alive at seventy.'

He caressed her hands. 'I'm sorry, darling. I didn't mean to upset you. I'm a terrible pessimist, I'm afraid. Let's talk about something else.'

But she couldn't forget. Now he'd said it, all she could think was that he was seventeen years older than her and they might not have much time left together.

'I wish we'd met when we were younger,' she said.

'Yes. Things might have been very different.'

What would their child have looked like, she wondered. Her and Alex's baby. Would it have had his mesmerising eyes?

'Are you wondering what it would have been like to have a family?' he asked, reading her mind as usual.

She pulled herself together. 'I know I shouldn't dwell on it.'

'It's all right. I understand.' He stroked her hair, pensive. 'It may not be too late for you. But I'm afraid it's not something I can give you in my situation,' he said gently.

'It's all right. I'm probably too old anyway. I just can't help thinking...'

'About the little person we could have created? I know. I feel regretful too. We've missed what could have been an amazing experience.'

She slid her arms around him and hugged him tight. 'I'm so lucky to have met you; I've no right to be sad about anything.'

'Sadness doesn't work like that though, does it?'

'No.' Kerry changed the subject. 'What shall we do today once you've finished on the bike?'

They ended up visiting a café attached to a second hand bookshop, one of Alex's favourite places. As Kerry sat watching him stir milk into his coffee (she never took her eyes off him for long), she reflected on how much she'd learned about him in the seven weeks they'd been together.

She knew he felt other people's emotions almost as intensely as his own, and that watching the news upset him. Certain pieces of music brought tears to his eyes. He was blessed with a near-photographic visual memory yet he was forever forgetting to return library books or to put the bins out for collection. A lifelong learner, he was fascinated by a wide range of subjects, as well as by the people he met. He adored Italian food, especially if it contained cream or cheese, but he avoided eating it for the sake of his heart.

Although she would never describe him as lazy, he liked to take life at a leisurely pace and have few specific plans. Once engaged in an activity he devoted his whole attention to it and hated to be interrupted or rushed. Although he tired easily, she sensed he'd once been more energetic than his health now allowed him to be. His fears included large dogs, crowds, being trapped underground and losing his sanity. He loathed superficiality and being lied to. And he needed a lot of physical affection in order to feel loved.

Alex put down the milk jug to reach for her hand then leaned across the rickety table to kiss her. 'You look beautiful today.'

'No I don't,' she said, flicking her fringe out of her eyes. 'My hair's a state and these jeans were obviously designed for skinny women. I should have known better than to buy them.'

Why was she always doing this? Putting herself down in front of a man who adored her despite her flaws? It was such an ingrained habit that the words were out of her mouth before she'd had time to consider them. She glanced at him to see whether he was annoyed but he seemed merely thoughtful.

'Kerry,' he said, 'can I ask you something? If I told you a hundred times a day you're beautiful, would you ever believe me?'

'I don't know,' she said slowly. 'I mean, it's always nice to hear. But I'm not sure I'd ever feel the truth of it.'

'That's what I suspected.' He rested his cup on the table. 'Then if I can't convince you by telling you, maybe I can show you instead.'

'What do you mean?'

'Well, I was once an award-winning professional photographer.' He arched his eyebrows at her and smiled.

'You want to take photos of me?' Suspicion knotted her forehead. 'You don't mean nude pictures, do you?'

'No,' he said. 'Of course, you'd look fabulous in those too, but you'd have to trust me completely for that. I meant with clothes on. Do you remember the dress you wore for the Christmas party? You looked amazing in that.'

She pulled a face at the memory. 'I thought I looked awful.'

'Perhaps if I could show you how you looked to *me*, it might change your mind.'

She picked at her thumbnail. 'I don't know, love. You've photographed some of the most beautiful women in the world. I'd feel so…inadequate in comparison.'

'Do you know what almost all of those women had in common?'

'What?'

'They were full of insecurities. They begged me not to shoot from any angle that made them look fat. They complained their noses were too big or they hated their legs or whatever. It rarely bore any relationship to what they actually looked like.'

'Did you find it frustrating?'

Alex returned to his coffee and stirred it. 'Sometimes, but I understood how society made them feel that way. And I hated my body then too, though with better reason. But I realised I couldn't alter their perception of themselves with words. So I let the camera do the talking instead.'

'And they felt better when they saw the photos?'

'There were some who could never be pleased. But more often than not, they went away with a new-found confidence. It's the reason I got so wealthy. Celebrities would pay whatever I charged to give them that.'

Kerry put her elbows on the table. 'But they were gorgeous women, regardless of what they thought of themselves. I know you're talented, but even you can't make a silk purse out of a sow's ear.'

She was testing his patience, she knew, but she couldn't help herself. What the hell was wrong with her?

'Do I have to do it?' she asked miserably, biting on a fragment of thumbnail.

'Of course you don't *have* to.' For the first time Alex sounded irritated. 'Do you really think I'd force you into something you didn't want to do?'

'I suppose not.'

'All I'm saying is that it hurts me when you talk about yourself that way. You're being cruel to someone I love, and it cuts me up inside.'

She took hold of his hand as she considered the idea again. What was the worst that could happen? The photos would be awful and they'd both politely pretend she looked amazing and that would be the end of it.

'Okay. I'll give it a try.'

'Great. I think you'll be pleased when you see the results. We could take them in my garden just before sunset when the light's best. I don't have all the equipment I used to have, but I've got a decent camera. It was a present from my friend Vanessa.'

She arrived at his house for the shoot with her dress and make-up in a bag and her enthusiasm at rock-bottom, but she didn't want to disappoint him now. By the time she was ready the sun was setting and a soft golden light bathed the small garden. Beside the fence the lone cherry tree was in full blossom.

In the next garden cannabis smoke drifted from the open patio door. A man inside the house answered his phone and began a loud, expletive-laden conversation.

'Ignore my charming neighbours,' Alex said in a low voice. 'Would you like a glass of white wine? I feel it ought to be champagne, only I can't stretch to that.'

Kerry sat at the cast-iron table as he went inside and returned with her wine in a thin-stemmed glass. He moved around a few of the plant pots and set up a tripod.

'Are you warm enough?' he asked her.

'I'm a northern girl. I'm bred to tolerate the cold.' In fact it was warm for early spring and the sun was radiating a gentle heat across her bare shoulders.

'Shall we start with a few informal shots? You don't need to pose,' he added as her shoulders tensed. 'Relax and enjoy your drink.'

He crossed to the other side of the garden with his camera.

'What do you think of it out here?' he asked as he peered at the screen and altered the settings. 'I know I'm not much of a gardener.'

She gazed around at the overgrown lawn and the wild plants emerging from the cracks in the patio. 'I like the hanging baskets. The ones with the violets in.'

The camera whirred as he took a series of photos.

'That's not fair,' she protested. 'I wasn't ready for that.'

'It was perfect,' he said, examining the images. 'You're smiling and looking natural. Right, now this time look at the camera. Not at me, at the lens. That's lovely.' He took some more shots. 'How about you have a wander round? I want to experiment with some different backgrounds.'

Kerry rose and strolled around the garden. He chatted to her as she moved and took photos whenever he asked her to stop.

'Maybe you could tidy up these?' she said, gesturing at the patch of stinging nettles thriving beside the fence.

'I like them. And they stop people climbing over into the garden. Why don't you try standing under the tree?'

She halted beneath the blossom-laden canopy. He mounted the camera on the tripod opposite her and directed her where to stand.

'Am I in the right place now?'

'Not quite.' Alex glanced up from the camera. His face was alight with concentration and his voice exuded an assertive energy. 'Take a step forward, away from the tree. Then turn your shoulders slightly to your left, so you're not head-on. That's better. Now bring your chin forward a little. Down, not up. That's it. And stand up straight. Imagine there's a thread above you holding your spine straight. Like a string on a puppet.'

She forced her back into an upright position. 'That feels so uncomfortable.'

'But it makes you look great.' He put on his glasses to look at her and then he took them off again, squinting in the sunlight.

'Put your right hand on your hip. Yes, that's perfect. Now look at the camera. Have you any idea how much I love you?'

She laughed. The camera whirred. 'How much?'

'More than you can conceive of.'

'I love you too.' She put her fingers to her lips and blew him a kiss. He smiled as he captured the gesture.

The man next door emerged into the garden to continue his call and the volume of the swearing increased. Distracted from his work, Alex rolled his eyes, then he turned back to her.

'How would you like to go away with me?'

'I'd love to,' she said, imagining he meant a cheap weekend trip somewhere nearby. 'Where to?'

'I was thinking of Rome, since you said you've never been.'

She gasped in surprise. 'How are we going to afford that? I can't put it on my credit card.'

'Don't worry. I'll pay for everything. It's my gift to you.'

'I thought you were broke, Alex. How have you got the money to go abroad?'

'Something happened that I wasn't expecting. I'll tell you about it another time. But seriously, what do you think?'

As the idea sank in, she clasped her hand to her mouth.

'Wow. That would be amazing.'

He looked through the viewfinder at her. 'Take your hand away. I want to see your smile. That's nice. Now let's try something else. Look up at the cherry blossom.'

Was there a moment in her life when she'd been happier? She'd almost forgotten she was being photographed. She gazed up into the mass of fragile petals. Although she'd grown up with cherry trees lining the city streets where she lived, it was as if she was seeing them for the first time.

'They look like heaven,' she said in awe.

'Reach up to touch them. Yes, like that. Your expression is divine. Kerry, these pictures are going to be stunning. I can't wait for you to see how fantastic you look.'

When it was over she put on a cardigan and sat in the garden to finish her wine while he cooked for her. After dinner Alex loaded the images onto his laptop. When he'd finished editing them they sat together on the sofa in front of the television.

'You're not going to put them on the TV, are you?' she said in alarm.

'I want you to see them properly.'

She gritted her teeth and prepared her politest smile. On his computer, he opened the first image.

Kerry drew in a sharp breath.

On the screen was a woman, clearly not young, but still fresh-faced and pretty, her face framed by wisps of burgundy hair that glowed like flame in the light of the descending sun. She was reaching upward to the blurred cloud of blossom hanging above her. The focal point of the image was her liquid brown eyes, shining with joy.

The glittering dress emphasised her shapely breasts and the narrowness of her waist, while flowing gently over her hips and thighs. Her dark lipstick and nose stud suggested a quirkiness that prevented the portrait from being overly feminine.

Alex was watching her intently. 'What do you think?'

191

'I don't know what to say. It's amazing. I can't believe it. I mean, I can see it's me. But I hardly recognise myself.'

His face relaxed into a smile. 'It definitely is you. Because as far as I'm aware, no other gorgeous red-haired woman sneaked into the garden and placed herself in the shot.'

Suspicion dawned on her. 'Have you done something to it?'

'Only some basic post-processing. I increased the contrast a little, lightened the shadows and cropped out the fence on the left. But otherwise it's pretty much as shot.'

'But I've always looked terrible in photos.'

Alex began to laugh. 'At the risk of sounding conceited, Kerry, I doubt you've been photographed by anyone with my level of experience before.'

She stared again at the radiant woman on the screen, still unable to accept she was real. 'Even so. I don't look like that.'

'Yes, you do. Under those lighting conditions, from that angle and in that particular mood, that's exactly what you look like. What you see there is what I saw with my own eyes.'

He flicked through the remaining images. Kerry saw herself sipping white wine, laughing and standing confidently with her hand on her hip, as if she were being featured in a glamorous lifestyle magazine.

'That dress *does* suit me, doesn't it?'

'I hate to say I told you so,' Alex said, 'but I did.'

'Then why did it look horrible on me at the party?'

'Because you weren't comfortable there and you were embarrassed that no one else had dressed up. You were seeing yourself through the lens of your own anxiety.'

She moved closer to him and put her arms around his neck. 'Do you know much I adore you right now?'

'Do feel free to show me,' he said, laughing as he moved the laptop out of their way and she kissed him on the mouth.

'I wouldn't mind doing some more portraits,' she said, her hand resting on his knee.

'Great. But there's no rush. How about we open some more wine? I've got a bottle of red somewhere. I don't know about you, but I'm in the mood for getting hammered.'

'Okay,' she said, surprised. She'd never known him to want to get drunk before. He must be very pleased with himself.

She looked more closely and saw the exhaustion in his face. The controlled energy from earlier had left him. He must have been under intense pressure to ensure his experiment didn't go wrong and upset her. It occurred to her that he wasn't nearly as sure of himself as he seemed.

'I really appreciate what you did for me today,' she said once he'd returned with more wine and they were curled up on the cushions together drinking it.

'It was a pleasure.'

'And you meant what you said about the holiday?'

'Of course. Do you really think I'd make it up just to get a smile out of you?'

'And you're sure you can afford it?' she said, still curious about his sudden source of funds.

'Yes. You don't need to worry about that at all.' There was something in his tone that dissuaded her from asking a third time. After all, she reasoned, they didn't have the level of commitment yet that gave her the right to enquire about his finances.

'So we're going to Rome?' she said instead.

'If that's what you want. I know you'd love all the wonderful art and history as much as I did. But we can go wherever you like.'

'Anywhere in the world?'

A shadow crossed his face. 'Nowhere remote or dangerous, if that's okay. I'm too old for adventures now. It's hard enough getting travel insurance for Europe with my medical history.'

'I'll have to tell the job centre too.' Her spirits dipped as the reality of their lives intruded. 'If I'm not available for work, I'll have to sign off benefits and sign on again when I get back.'

Alex's tone grew sombre. 'Sorry. I never thought of that. I don't want you to go short of money or miss out on an interview.'

'I'm not giving up a trip to Rome with you because of some stupid job I probably won't get anyway.'

'We'll only be gone a week anyway. I'd better start looking into flights and hotels.'

'Sue's going to be left short-staffed.'

'She'll have to cope. We're only volunteers.'

The mention of Sue brought another memory from the party back to Kerry.

'Alex,' she said, putting her glass on the table and looking up at him, 'do you think Sue's in love with you?'

He spluttered and almost choked on his drink. 'God, no. Sue isn't in love with me. What on earth made you think that?' He dissolved into helpless laughter as he wiped wine from his mouth.

He seemed pretty tipsy already. It wasn't *that* funny.

'It's the way she's so protective of you,' she explained. 'I wondered if there was an ulterior motive.'

Alex stopped laughing at her and grew thoughtful. 'Sue feels compelled to rescue me. If I was going to play the amateur psychologist, I'd say she feels guilty that she couldn't help her sons and she's trying to make up for it by saving someone else.'

'That makes sense.'

'It's only speculation. Who knows, it may just be her personality.' He paused. 'Or maybe she *does* like me, in her own strange way. But she's happily married to a man who provides her with a comfortable life. And I doubt I'm her type at all.'

'What about Ruth? You spend a lot of time in her company. What do you talk to her about?'

'Oh, we find things to chat about. Books and art and current affairs. But her personal life is strictly off-limits. I learned to respect that a long time ago.'

She took a breath and then stopped.

'I'm curious,' he said, amused. 'Who are you going to ask me about next?'

Why was she pestering him with these silly questions? Maybe the wine was affecting her too. Or perhaps it was that no one had inspired such insanely possessive desire in her before.

'Sorry.' She reached up and touched his wrinkled face. 'I suppose I love you so much, I can't believe everyone else doesn't too.'

He took her fingers in his hand and pressed them to his lips. 'Thank you for saying that. It means a lot to me. But I can assure you most women don't see me the way you do.'

'Then they don't know what they're missing.'

After his third glass of wine Alex buried his head on the arm of the sofa. 'I feel hot and dizzy.'

'Are you all right?' Unease came over her. 'Is there anything I can get you?'

'I'll be fine. Just gone over my limit. I need to rest.'

He lay still for a minute and then raised his head and regarded her with unfocused eyes.

'Alcohol doesn't mix well with my medication. I've been advised to cut it out completely, and maybe I should. I know that's no fun for you.'

'It's okay.' She sat beside him and stroked his hair. 'I don't need you to be drunk to have a good time with you.'

'You're lovely,' he said in a slurred voice, and he closed his eyes again.

Kerry sat watching him, anxiety prickling along her spine in case he was falling unconscious. But as he breathed heavily and peacefully, she decided he was only sleeping.

'Alex love, perhaps you should go up to bed,' she said in his ear, and she gave his shoulder a shake.

He rolled over and moaned. 'Let me stay here.'

She kicked off her shoes and wriggled along the couch until she was lying beside him in the narrow space, his hair tickling her face. She removed his glasses and kissed his wine-stained lips and held his clammy hand, and a terrible fierce tenderness overwhelmed her.

Unable to persuade him to move, she fetched him some water and a blanket from upstairs to lay over him in case he got cold. Then she went outside and sat in the garden, where she finished the bottle of wine and stared up at the emerging stars.

# 20

Not long after the photo shoot Kerry was sitting at home on one of her days off, browsing through job advertisements, when a vacancy leapt out. It was in the head office of the mental health charity the shop belonged to. They were running a major campaign to reduce the stigma of mental health problems and were recruiting an assistant. The successful candidate would need experience in office administration and preferably knowledge of marketing or PR.

'It sounds perfect,' she told Alex excitedly that evening when he came over to see her. 'The pay isn't great, but I'd love to get involved in something like that.'

'I'm sure you'd be brilliant. When do you have to submit it?'

'The closing date is tomorrow. I've already filled in the application form and written the covering letter. I wouldn't mind a second opinion, if that's okay?'

He sat at the table in front of her computer, scanning the application. She'd always been told her writing skills were her best asset and she'd demonstrated such enthusiasm for the role that she couldn't imagine him having any major criticisms. But when he'd finished reading he seemed uncomfortable, as if unsure how to proceed.

'It's very well-written,' he said, looking up at her. 'But I can't help feeling you're underselling yourself. It's been a long time since I applied for a job, but the principles are still the same. You have to persuade them they'd benefit from hiring you, as well as explaining why you want to work there.'

Did he really think she didn't know that? 'I thought that's what I'd done.'

He held out his arm to her. 'Hey, don't worry, darling. We can fix it before tomorrow. Come and sit next to me and we'll go through it together.'

A frustrating two hours later she had to admit that her application was a hundred times stronger. Ever the perfectionist, Alex had been tough on almost every sentence.

'We need to eliminate these hesitant phrases,' he'd said. 'Like here, where you say you've got "some experience of social media." Change it to say you've managed social media accounts.'

They'd disagreed heatedly when she thought he was over-stating her abilities but had managed to compromise on a final version.

Later in the week she received an email informing her she had an interview. When she asked Sue if she could change her shift, Sue was so pleased that she went onto the shop floor and picked out a dark green trouser suit she'd noticed Kerry admiring, and paid for it herself.

The day before her interview she went over some practice questions with Alex.

'Do you think I should tell them about my anxiety condition?' she asked.

'Usually I'd advise against it, but in this instance I would. The job is about combating stigma, so your personal experience should count in your favour.'

In the morning Kerry left the house satisfied she looked smart and professional. It was strange, but ever since the photo shoot her mirror had reflected a different person. Instead of heavy hips and ageing skin she saw hourglass curves, flaming hair and alluring dark eyes. Alex was right: a picture had been worth a thousand words.

On the bus nerves gripped her until she recalled what he'd told her. She could do this. His reworking of her application had helped her realise she had more to offer than she'd given herself credit for in the past.

She clattered in her heels along Oxford Road and on to St Peter's Square, past the pale stone library with its Corinthian columns, through Albert Square, dominated by the grandeur of the neo-gothic Town Hall, out onto bustling Deansgate and into the business district of Spinningfield, where to her relief she located the office building.

She sat down to wait in the carpeted reception area. While she was doing her breathing exercises, a plump woman with frizzy ginger hair and a nose stud like her own came over and introduced herself cheerfully as Lisa, the campaigns manager. Kerry's potential new boss. This was going to be fine, she thought. These were the sort of people she could fit in with.

Lisa led her into a room along the corridor and introduced her to Jonathan Cartland, the managing director of the company that was providing the funding for the role, and the occupant of the plush office suite in which they now sat. He was in his sixties with sleek white hair.

'So,' Lisa said, 'we've got about half an hour. Could you tell us about yourself and why you're interested in the role? Then we'll ask you a few questions. After that you can ask us anything you want to know about the job.'

'Okay.' Kerry's voice cracked with dryness.

'Would you like some water?' Lisa indicated the jug and glass on the table. They both watched as with shaking hands she poured out the water and drank.

'I think I have lots of relevant experience to bring to this role,' she began.

Remembering to take pauses to breathe, she outlined the skills that would help her run the charity's campaigns. To her astonishment her voice remained steady and she could hear herself sounding more persuasive than ever before. Lisa was nodding and smiling.

'That all sounds great,' said Lisa when she'd finished. 'And what attracted you to our organisation in particular?'

'I've been volunteering in one of your shops while I've been looking for work. Also, I have a personal interest in the subject.'

Lisa leaned forward. 'Would you be able to tell us more about that?'

'Sure. I'm having treatment for anxiety.'

As she told them about her experiences, her speech flowed almost effortlessly.

'And that's why I was so attracted to this job,' she concluded. 'Because I want to help people like me stop feeling so ashamed and alone.'

'That's exactly what we're all about,' Lisa said with a wide grin. 'Aren't we?' she said, turning to Jonathan, who seemed absorbed in Kerry's application.

'Absolutely.' He nodded and perused the form again.

'I hope you don't mind my asking, Kerry, but I'm curious,' he said. 'I notice you graduated from Manchester Met in 1994.'

'That's right.'

'You understand this is a junior role we're offering?'

'I don't mind that. It's a good opportunity for me to learn and progress.'

'Right. I was only asking because it struck me as unusual for someone of your… with your length of time in the job market to be applying for roles like this.'

She swept her fringe from her flushed forehead. 'I'm interested in developing a new career in the charity sector.'

'Fair enough,' he said, apparently satisfied. 'I notice it's been a while since you left your last position.'

'It hasn't been easy for me to find work. I get nervous in stressful situations, as you may have noticed,' she said with a little laugh, taking a sip of water to ease her parched throat. 'It's one of the disadvantages of having anxiety.'

She could hardly believe she was being so open at an interview. But Lisa was regarding her with empathy.

'You sounded impressive when you spoke just now. And we're looking to hire someone with a genuine understanding of mental health issues. If we offered you the role we'd be able to support you in the workplace with any adjustments you needed.'

'That would be fantastic. Thank you.'

Her optimism was growing by the minute. Lisa liked her, she could tell, and that was the most crucial aspect of landing any job.

'Hopefully we'll be able to let you know later this afternoon,' Lisa said as they shook hands at the end.

Outside in the street Kerry inhaled the fresh air and savoured her relief that it had gone so well. Back at home she paced around her living room, unable to focus on anything constructive until she knew about the job. She wanted it so badly. Other elements of her life were falling into place. Why not this too?

At five o'clock her phone rang. Her stomach contracted as she picked it up.

'Is that Kerry? This is Lisa. Thanks so much for coming in earlier today. It was lovely to meet you.'

Kerry held her breath. Her life was poised at a crossroads.

'I'm just calling to let you know I'm afraid we offered the job to another candidate.'

She squeezed her eyes shut as the blow fell. So that was it. She wasn't going to be working in the job of her dreams.

'I appreciate you must be disappointed,' Lisa said. 'But in terms of feedback, you did really well. You had all the qualities we were looking for. So it was nothing you said wrong. It was just…'

Lisa broke off, as if embarrassed, and then she jettisoned her professional manner. 'Kerry, I shouldn't be telling you this, but I'd have hired you on the spot. I loved that you were so open about your anxiety. Out of everyone we saw, I got the most sense of connection to the cause from you. But Jonathan… well, he had a very fixed idea about the sort of person he wanted. And seeing as his money is funding the salary…'

'He had to have final approval. Yes, I see. What was he looking for that I didn't have?'

'He thought the other lady presented herself a bit more confidently. And she was… at an earlier stage in her career where a role like this was a natural step for her.'

Kerry bit the inside of her cheek. So essentially the other woman was young and dynamic and didn't suffer from interview nerves.

'I'm sure you'll find something else,' Lisa said.

Perhaps. But not if she was always going to be second choice.

'Thanks for letting me know,' she said, wanting Lisa to go so she could be alone. But as soon she'd ended the call she found herself phoning Alex.

'I'm so sorry, darling,' he said when she'd explained. 'I know how hard you worked for it.'

'Thanks. It's just frustrating when your future hangs on someone else's opinion of you.'

'Did they say why you didn't get it?'

She told him what Lisa had said. 'I wish now I hadn't been so honest. I feel like I made myself too vulnerable.'

'It was courageous of you. And I still think it was the right thing to do.'

Kerry twisted a strand of her hair in her fingers. 'It was weird, because they insisted they wanted someone with experience of mental health issues. And yet when it came to the crunch, he still preferred a more "normal" candidate.'

'Ironically, it's possible he doesn't understand how poor mental health affects people's lives.'

'Never mind. There's nothing I can do about it now. I'll just have to pick myself up and get on with it.' She fiddled with the tassel on the sofa cushion. 'How are you?'

'I woke up feeling shattered, so I went back to bed. I've spent the whole day reading.'

'Sometimes I envy you not having to go through this.'

At once she knew she'd said the wrong thing. Alex's voice grew sombre.

'Don't be too jealous of me. I've been through plenty. And I'd rather be well enough to support myself than be stuck at home all day.'

'Sorry, love. I didn't mean it to sound like that.'

He gave a deep sigh. 'It's all right. Sorry I snapped. It's been one of those days. And talking about interviews brings back bad memories.'

'Are you saying I shouldn't have told you about it?'

'Of course not. I want to know what's going on your life. I want to be here to support you.'

'Thanks.' She got up from the sofa. 'Maybe I'd better go though, if you're tired. Love you.'

'You too. I'll see you tomorrow.'

After she put the phone down her unease persisted. Alex had sounded glum. He'd been so happy since they got together. What had changed?

As he'd said, it was one of those days. She couldn't expect any partner to be in a good mood all the time, let alone someone with his condition. And she'd made it worse by saying something daft.

When she went to bed she lay awake telling herself the positives that had emerged from the day. Although she hadn't been offered the job, she'd been calmer and had performed better at the interview than ever before. She'd taken the first steps towards believing in herself, and that she was sure was the key to coping.

# 21

To Kerry's surprise, when Sue found out about her relationship with Alex she didn't immediately go around broadcasting the news. But she must have said something to someone in the end because suddenly it was common knowledge.

'I can't *believe* you've been seeing him for two months and you never told me,' Yasmeen said as they sat in the staffroom sorting bric-a-brac.

Kerry looked up from her pile of objects, which included a lavender soap gift set, a snow shaker and a bunch of twigs spray-painted in silver.

'It was nothing personal. We wanted to give it a chance to work first.'

'I'd never have pictured you two as a couple,' Yasmeen said, sticking a label onto a heart-shaped photo frame. 'I can see it though, now I think about it. Is it serious?'

'Oh yes.'

'That's awesome. He's a sweet guy.'

A rush of loving pride swept over Kerry. 'He's the most amazing person I've ever met.'

'Aw bless,' Yasmeen said, smiling as she discarded a threadbare teddy bear into the recycling bag. 'You've really got it badly, haven't you?'

'You could say that,' Kerry said, and she laughed.

She'd been dreading Pete's comments on the subject, and sure enough when he next encountered her alone in the corridor, he stopped to look at her with a leer.

'You and him upstairs, eh? Who'd have thought? You got a thing for old blokes?'

'His age isn't important to me,' she said coolly.

'And it doesn't bother you that he's... you know?'

'That he's what?'

Pete lowered his voice. 'You know. The reason he works here.'

Kerry gave an exasperated sigh. 'Because he has depression? Why should it bother me? It doesn't define who he is.'

'All right petal, calm down. I didn't mean anything by it. I'm heading off out now. Can I squeeze through?'

She felt his hot wheezing breath on her ear as he began to brush past her, but this time she was prepared. As his hands fondled her hips, she spun round.

'Don't do that, please.'

He stepped back in feigned surprise. 'Don't do what?'

'Don't touch me.'

Pete's features contorted into a scowl. 'I wasn't *touching* you. I was trying to shove past you. You're plonked right in the middle of the corridor, blocking the way.'

Her pulse pounded as adrenaline flooded through her. 'You know that's not what happened.'

He stepped backwards and raised both hands in the air. 'Sorry to have displeased you, madam,' he said sarcastically. 'I promise I'll never cross within six feet of you again.'

'I'm asking you not to put your hands on me. Or anyone else.' Her cheeks burned. Pete was red in the face too and breathing heavily.

'Don't flatter yourself, love. You're not my type.'

'Well, that's a relief.'

They glowered at each other, then he turned on his heel and marched out of the shop.

Kerry went into the staffroom where she sank onto a chair, trembling. Her head ached and her nerves jangled from the conflict. She took some slow breaths and congratulated herself for having spoken out, despite what it had cost her.

Not long afterwards Sue came in to fill the kettle.

'Is something up?' Sue asked when she saw Kerry's face.

'Actually there is. One of the men here is behaving inappropriately.'

Sue switched off the tap and sat down. There was a resigned weariness in her manner.

'You're going to complain about Pete, aren't you?'

So this wasn't the first time. If Sue knew, why hadn't she done anything about it?

'No one should have to put up with sexual harassment at work,' Kerry said.

Sue peered over her rimless spectacles. 'Did you ask him to stop it?'

'Yes.'

'Then that'll be the end of it. He only misbehaves with the girls he thinks are too meek to confront him. Once he sees you can stick up for yourself he won't need telling a second time.'

Kerry's eyes widened. Was Sue for real? Did she realise she'd just condoned the abuse of women who were too afraid to raise their voices?

'But it's not *our* responsibility to make him stop. It's *his* responsibility not to do it in the first place. And you're his manager. Shouldn't you be telling him that?'

'Don't you think I had it out with him last time? He denied everything. Acted all hurt and made out he was the one being victimised.'

'And you believed him?'

Sue gave a snort. 'Did I heck. But try to understand. Pete's no angel, but he's not a monster either. He didn't have the easiest childhood. His dad used to beat his mum and left dirty magazines around the house for the kids to see. His manners might seem rough to a lass like you, but that's because he doesn't come from the same sort of world as you do.'

This was getting more ludicrous by the second. It was unheard of for Sue to make excuses for people or be soft on bad behaviour.

'None of that makes it acceptable,' she said, though her voice shook as she spoke. 'You have a duty to create a safe environment for your volunteers. If you don't, well, I'm afraid I'll have to take the matter further.'

Sue was looking at her in surprise now, and Kerry realised that she too was acting out of character. As if they'd experienced a temporary role reversal. At last Sue's shoulders slumped.

'All right. Put down in writing for me what happened and when. I'll have a stern word with him and put him on an official final warning. I'd like to give him one more chance to mend his ways. Is that okay?'

Kerry was beginning to feel shattered from the stress of the morning's confrontations.

'That'll do for now,' she said. 'But I'll be keeping a close eye on how he behaves round the other women.'


As Kerry went out to buy a sandwich for lunch she considered telling Alex what had happened, but then she thought better of it. He'd be furious with Pete, which would make it impossible for them to work together. Besides, she'd already proved she could fight her own battles.

On leaving the shop she bumped into Dan coming in and they stopped on the pavement to chat.

'You look like you've got something on your mind,' he said.

'I just had a disagreement with Sue.'

'What's she got a bee in her bonnet about today?'

She told Dan what had happened and his smile vanished.

'Sorry. That must have been horrible for you. He's done this before, you know. I had a go at him about it myself. You can imagine how well *that* went down. But I don't have any authority to make him leave.'

'I can't *believe* Sue tolerates it,' Kerry said, still outraged. 'I thought she was so tough.'

'She's got a blind spot where Pete's concerned.'

'Because they're friends?'

Dan made a face. 'I hate to say this but it's more because she doesn't want to lose him. She'll struggle to find anyone else who's prepared to lug heavy wardrobes around for nothing when they could get paid to do it. And if the furniture department has to close, it'll hurt our income.'

'And everything's about the shop to her?'

'She doesn't have grandchildren, you see, so it's become her baby. She'll do whatever it takes to make it succeed.'

'And Pete? Why does he keep coming here? To meet new victims?'

He shook his head. 'I'm not sure it's as simple as that. I get the impression he's as devoted to the place as Sue is. As for the groping, he rationalises in his own mind why he's not doing anything wrong.'

'Which is exactly what abusers do.'

'I'm sorry you had to put up with it, Kerry,' Dan said, almost guiltily. 'I hope you're not going to leave. Though I'd totally understand if you did.'

'Don't worry. He won't drive me out. I'm not going anywhere until I get a job.'

'I'm glad about that.' He paused. 'On a different note, I was pleased to hear about you and Alex. You make an adorable couple.'

'Thanks.' She gave him a bashful smile. 'Did you know you helped get us together?'

He stroked his beard, puzzled. 'How did I help?'

'I overheard you and Sue talking about us. You said Alex was wise enough to know his own mind, and he deserved some happiness. It confirmed what I'd been thinking and gave me the courage to ask him out.'

Dan's blue eyes crinkled at the corners. 'Pleased I could be of assistance.' He checked the time. 'I'd better go in and see Sue. I need to head off early this afternoon for a meeting at Libby's school.'

'How is Libby?'

He lowered his head. 'She's being bullied because of her autism. That's what the meeting's about. I'm hoping the school's going to do something about it. She's coming home in tears and begging me not to make her go back.'

Kerry put her hand to her mouth. 'That's awful. I'm so sorry. I can't stand bullies.'

'Me neither. It breaks my heart to see her so upset. She doesn't understand why the other girls don't want to be friends with her.'

'I hope they manage to stop it.'

'Cheers Kerry. Listen, I'd better go. Let me know if you have any more hassle with Pete.'

After lunch Colin came in to help Pete with the furniture. Before Colin left in the van, he and Kerry chatted about their job hunting.

'I was at the job centre today and they said my CV wasn't good enough,' he said. 'I done it on the computer like they told me to, but they still weren't happy. I'm going to be in trouble if I don't get it right next time.'

'What did they say was wrong with it?'

'Spelling mistakes,' Colin said, hitching up his trousers. 'And I done it in the wrong order. Someone told me CV means the story of your life, so I started at the beginning and carried on up till now. But that's not what they want, is it? They said I've got to make it "skills-based", whatever that means.'

'I've had to write one myself. If you want some help formatting it, I'd be happy to take a look.'

That night he emailed her the document, which was rambling and riddled with errors. She made extensive suggestions, and when they were next in the shop together, she asked Sue's permission to spend an hour in the staffroom going through it with him.

'It's much better now, isn't it?' he said, looking admiringly at the draft she'd printed out. 'It's very kind of you to help.'

'You're welcome. It was no trouble at all.'

Colin rearranged his stringy hair, peeped out of the door to make sure no one was approaching the room and cleared his throat.

'I've been meaning to ask you something. I think you're really nice. I've liked you for ages and I know we get on well. I was wondering if you'd like to go on a date with me.'

So he hadn't heard the news. She gave him a rueful smile.

'Sorry, but I'm seeing someone else.'

His face crumpled. 'I didn't know *that*. I thought you was on your own after splitting up with your fella.'

'I was. But I met someone.' She paused. 'In fact it's someone you know. It's Alex.'

Colin looked at her incredulously. 'Alex who works upstairs? Crikey. Well I never.' He tugged at his bottom lip. 'I suppose you'd have said no anyway.'

'I think we're better off being friends.'

'Yeah. That's what they all say.'

He was so crestfallen it made her feel terrible. Had she given him the wrong impression by helping him? It wasn't the first time her kindness had been misinterpreted as sexual interest.

'You won't tell anyone I asked you out, will you?' he said. 'If Pete finds out I'll never hear the end of it.'

'I won't tell a soul.'

'Ta Kerry. Right, I'd best be off.' He shuffled despondently away, clutching his papers.

That afternoon Yasmeen came in to work with Kerry on a new window display. Kerry found herself telling Yasmeen about Pete.

'Ew,' Yasmeen said, screwing up her nose. 'I hope you told him where to stick his rancid hands.'

'Has he ever done it to you?'

'Never, thankfully.'

Of course Pete would have quickly sussed out that Yasmeen wasn't the sort of woman you touched without her consent. But Kerry had decided she wasn't going to feel ashamed of being a victim. It was like she'd said to Sue: the responsibility lay with him alone.

Yasmeen was looking thoughtful. 'It's weird because although he's a creep, he can be as nice as pie when it suits him. Last term, when I was stressed about moving house, he offered to bring his van and help. I wasn't keen at first, but I got desperate and took him up on the offer.'

'And he behaved himself?'

'Totally. He worked flat out all day and was careful not to damage my stuff. Then I made him a cup of tea and he went home. He refused to accept any payment, which saved me a ton on hiring a removal man. It's strange isn't it? As if he's trying to make up for his other faults.'

'I don't know. I'm not convinced he thinks he has any,' Kerry said.

They sorted through the boxes of bric-a-brac for objects to use in the display.

'This tea set is cute.' Yasmeen picked out a miniature mother-of-pearl teapot, four little cups with saucers and a matching milk jug.

'There's a cake stand to go with it,' Kerry said, lifting up the three-tiered white stand.

'How about we bring down that trestle table from upstairs, lay a cloth over it and set out the china like a tea party?'

'Like in Alice in Wonderland?'

'Awesome. The Alice theme is so on trend. We could Instagram it when we're done.' Yasmeen's dark eyes sparkled. 'Let's see what else we've got that would fit.'

Together they hauled the table into the window area and covered it with a delicate lace-edged cloth. In the staffroom Yasmeen clambered up the step ladder to the highest shelf where to her delight she discovered an old top hat, dusty and bent out of shape. They cleaned it up and tied a red satin ribbon around its brim.

Among the clothing they found a plain blue linen dress. Yasmeen cut an apron shape from a square of white cotton and they dressed the mannequin as Alice. Also in the bric-a-brac were two brown glass bottles, on which they stuck handwritten labels, 'Eat Me' and 'Drink Me.'

'What else? I'm sure I've seen a pack of cards somewhere,' Yasmeen said. 'I think it was upstairs with the board games.'

Kerry offered to go up and fetch the cards.

'Can I borrow these?' she asked Alex, who was covering the till while Ruth was out. 'I promise I'll put them back.'

'Course you can,' he said with a smile. 'What are you doing down there, playing poker?'

'We're making an Alice in Wonderland display.'

'Fantastic. I'll come down and look at it later.'

He blew her a kiss as she left. A customer noticed and gave him a curious stare.

'It's a shame we haven't got a white rabbit,' Yasmeen said as they stood in the window arranging objects on the table. They'd placed the top hat on the other mannequin next to Alice.

'Or a dormouse,' Kerry said, laughing. Dressing the window with Yasmeen was one of the highlights of her week. They were both in their element seeing what they could create by raiding the stock.

Outside the window a middle-aged woman with short wiry hair was taking photographs with her phone. From her grim expression it didn't seem she was admiring their creativity. The woman entered the shop and approached them.

'Excuse me,' she said, bristling with indignation, 'is this some kind of sick joke?'

Yasmeen stared at her, puzzled. 'I'm sorry?'

'Have you forgotten you're meant to be a mental health charity?'

Yasmeen remained bewildered but with a surge of alarm, Kerry realised what they'd done.

'Is this about the Mad Hatter?'

'I'm shocked you could think it was appropriate.'

'I'm very sorry if we've been insensitive.' Instinctively, Kerry adopted the soothing voice she'd used throughout her career to placate angry clients. 'We had no intention of upsetting anybody.'

'I'm disgusted. I'll be reporting this as widely as I can.'

Fear squirmed in Kerry's stomach. If they got negative publicity it could be a disaster for the charity. 'We're more than happy to take the display down now. As I said, I'm sorry if it caused you any distress.'

The woman sniffed. 'It's not *me* who's distressed, is it? It's people with mental health issues. You know; the ones you claim to care so much about?'

Kerry was beginning to resent the woman's snarky tone.

'To be fair,' she said, 'the Mad Hatter's tea party is a classic scene from literature, and very popular. Perhaps we should have thought more carefully about it. But I do think you may be seeing offence where none was meant.' She trembled as she spoke but was determined to hold her ground.

'You must be the worst kind of hypocrite if you think it's funny to laugh at madness,' the woman said. 'It's *extremely* offensive to people with mental health issues.'

'How do you know? Have you asked any?' said a familiar voice. Alex had wandered downstairs to see the display and had overheard the conversation.

'Why would I need to? It's obvious,' the woman said in the same aggressive voice.

'Not to me, and I've spent many weeks on psychiatric wards,' he said. 'Personally I see the Mad Hatter as a harmless fictional character. However, the difference between you and me is that I don't presume to speak on behalf of everyone with a mental illness.'

'I have a mental health condition too,' Kerry said, making Yasmeen glance sideways at her in surprise. 'Don't *we* get a say in whether we find something upsetting or not?'

The woman seemed unmoved by their confessions. She stuck out her jaw.

'Let's see what other people have to say about it,' she said triumphantly, brandishing the photograph on her phone. It was a close-up of the hat. Yasmeen had to smother a laugh.

'That's an interesting insight into your priorities.' Alex was getting rattled now. A muscle in his cheek twitched and he clasped his hands together until the thick blue veins stood out.

The woman glared at him. 'What do you mean by that?'

'That you feel the need to express your outrage in public at any cost. Even if it harms an organisation raising money to help people in desperate need.'

'You should have thought about your reputation before you did *this*,' she said, pointing at the window.

'But we've already apologised and offered to remove it. I assume you'll mention that too?' Kerry said. Yasmeen flashed her a discreet thumbs-up.

Then they all turned, because Sue had returned from a trip to the bank and was standing with her hands on her hips.

'What the heck's going on?' she said.

Kerry explained. Sue pursed her lips, then she rounded on the woman.

'I never heard anything so bloody daft in my life. It's a children's story. If you're really offended by that, you need to grow up. Now be off with you.' Sue flapped her hands, as if shooing away a pigeon.

The woman opened and closed her mouth. Speechless with surprise, she turned and left.

'Well, that was one way of dealing with it,' Alex said with a grimace.

'I've no time for her sort,' Sue said briskly. 'They've got no real problems so they go around looking for things to get the hump about.'

'She'll be super pissed off now,' Yasmeen said.

'I don't give a damn if she is,' Sue said. 'Nobody bullies me or my staff in my own shop.'

'We should take the display down all the same,' Kerry said. 'We don't want to upset anyone else.'

'I'm not having you two changing the window every five minutes. It's fine as it is,' Sue said.

'Maybe if we removed the hat the rest would be okay,' Yasmeen suggested. She went into the window and retrieved the top hat. Sue bustled off into the corridor, muttering under her breath.

Later at home Kerry reflected on the changes taking place in her. It wasn't that her fear of conflict had gone, but she was learning she could still speak the truth even when her insides were knotted and her voice wavered. She would remember to tell Magda in their next session how much progress she'd made.

# 22

Early April sunlight poured in through the sloping window of Kerry's attic room, where she was packing for her flight to Rome that evening. She'd treated herself to two new dresses from the shop, which fitted well and made her feel confident and attractive.

It helped that she'd lost a few pounds since she'd started seeing Alex: love had diminished her appetite. He'd said nothing about it, although no detail of her appearance ever escaped his notice. Instead, he constantly told her how beautiful she was. She sensed he had the insight to know that if he complimented her on her weight loss, she'd interpret it as a criticism of how she'd looked before, so instead he sought to reassure her she was intrinsically desirable.

It was a miracle how her life had improved since that gloomy November day when she'd first stepped into the shop, unemployed, lonely and struggling with crippling anxiety and self-doubt. Although she was still out of work and still in financial difficulty, she'd travelled a million miles from the place she'd been in then. She could only attribute her recovery to a combination of the medication, the therapy, Alex's support and her own determined efforts.

And now she was preparing to go on a wonderful holiday with the man of her dreams. By tomorrow she'd be walking through the Eternal City with him, looking at sublime works of art, watching him as he took endless photographs, eating delicious food on a restaurant terrace under the stars, returning to their hotel room at night…

Her phone beeped with a text from him. 'Are you busy? If not, can I come round?'

When the downstairs doorbell rang she buzzed him in. He took a long time to come up the stairs and when she let him into her flat she knew at once something was wrong. He was struggling to catch his breath, his face was ashen and his skin clammy. Without a word he sank onto her sofa.

'What's happened to you?' she said, coming over and slipping her arm around his shoulders.

'I walked upstairs too fast.'

'Alex, I've seen you run all the way up those stairs without getting out of breath. What's wrong?'

'I don't want you to get too worried about this,' he began. 'But last night I had some pretty severe chest pain. Worse than I've had in years.'

Her hand crept to her mouth. 'Jesus. You poor thing. Were you okay? Did you call an ambulance?'

'I didn't need one. I have a spray I use under my tongue that makes the angina go away. It was my own fault. I raised the resistance too high on my exercise bike. I'm not as fit as I thought I was and my heart decided to protest.'

She swallowed hard, hating to imagine him alone and in pain. 'What does that mean? Do you need to go to hospital?'

'Not urgently. The pain's gone now and I know what caused it. But I'm afraid it's had quite an impact. The thought of going abroad is making me really anxious.'

'In case you have another attack while we're away?'

'If anything happened to me in Rome I'd hate you to have to deal with it.'

Images flashed through her mind: strange hotel rooms and telephones and confusion and having to communicate his medical needs to doctors who spoke a foreign language. Alex in agony or unconscious or dying. The panic that would engulf her as she struggled to save him.

This wasn't the time for her to be freaking out. He was the one who was sick. She put on her brightest voice.

'Why don't you phone the surgery so they can advise you whether it's safe for you to travel? I'm sure it'll be okay. You'll have your medication and we can take it easy once we get there.'

'I suppose so.' He laid his head against the back of the sofa. He was looking less clammy now he'd rested but his eyelids were puffy with a bluish-purple tinge.

'You're exhausted, aren't you?' she said.

'I hardly slept last night. When I did, I had nightmares about having a heart attack on the plane. I'm shattered.'

'Would a coffee help?'

Kerry went over to the kitchen area to put the kettle on, partly to give herself a minute alone to process the news. When she glanced up from the coffee pot he was sitting with his head buried in his hands. Everything in his body language told her how much he didn't want to go.

She came back, placed the two mugs on the table and sat next to him.

'You know we can cancel it if you don't feel up to it?'

He looked up at her, his eyes full of painful indecision.

'I couldn't bear to let you down. I know how much you were looking forward to it. I was too.'

'We can see Rome another time. Your health is more important than any holiday.'

It was dreadfully disappointing not to be going but she'd get over that. She couldn't watch him suffer like this on her account.

His face sagged with relief, and she realised how afraid he'd been of asking her. He reached for her hand. 'That's so kind of you. I'm so glad you're not annoyed with me.'

'Why would I be? You can't help being ill.' She squeezed his fingers. 'Since we've booked the time off, we can have a relaxing week at home instead.'

Worry came over his face again. 'I'd better check the cancellation policies for the flights and hotel. I might have to kiss goodbye to most of the money, but that can't be helped.'

'That reminds me. You never did tell me how you paid for this trip.'

'Does it matter now?' he said wearily.

'No. It's your business. I'm just curious.'

'All right, I'll tell you. I sold some jewellery my mother gave me. I won't inherit much when she dies because the nursing home's eating up her savings. She wanted me to have her last valuable possessions to keep in case of an emergency.'

She winced. 'Oh love. And you used it to pay for a holiday.'

'You don't need to tell me it was stupid, Kerry,' he said bitterly. 'I've always been an idiot when it comes to money. I wanted to take you somewhere special and for you not to worry about the cost. Now I doubt I'll ever be able to do that again.'

He put his head in his hands again. When he looked up, the whites of his eyes were bloodshot. 'You must be wondering what the hell you've got yourself into.'

'Don't be daft.'

'Maybe you'd be better off with a man who had anything whatsoever to offer you.'

'Just stop it, okay?'

221

'Sorry.' He clutched her hands tight, as if trying to steady himself from plunging into an abyss. 'That's my other problem creeping in, I'm afraid.'

'Are you feeling depressed?'

'A little dark around the edges. Knowing I could collapse and die at any minute tends to have that effect.' He thumped the arm of the sofa with his clenched fist. 'God. I wish I hadn't fucked up my whole life.'

Kerry had never known him act like this before. She gave him a hug. 'You haven't. None of this is your fault.'

'Isn't it?'

'Not at all.' She kissed him on the cheek. 'Don't worry about the money. I'll get a job eventually and then we can go away.'

'And how do you think that makes me feel?'

'Surely it's not important which one of us pays?'

'Maybe that's our age difference showing. I was brought up the old-fashioned way. To believe I should provide for you.'

'Oh Alex,' she said, laughing. 'Come on, you're more enlightened than that. I know you are.'

At last she saw him smile. 'Sorry about all the self-pity.'

'It's okay.' She stroked his hair. 'I understand you must be feeling wretched right now.'

By the time he left he seemed more cheerful, and she was relieved she'd been able to comfort him. The next evening, however, she learned she was also capable of doing the complete opposite.

They were lying in bed in her flat, the room lit by a single lamp. He'd been craving affection from her all evening, and now he was on top of her, kissing her neck and her face with passion over and over again.

'I love you so much,' he whispered in her ear.

'I love you too,' she said, but a tiny worry was building inside her. She tried to ignore it but as he continued to kiss her urgently and his breathing grew heavier and more strained, the fear expanded in her chest until she couldn't contain it any longer.

'Alex,' she said, 'are you all right? Maybe you should be careful.'

He brushed her hair from her face and kissed her lips. 'Careful about what, darling?'

'You know. Not to tire yourself out.'

He froze. 'Why? In case I drop dead during sex?'

'I didn't mean that exactly…'

'Yes, you did.'

He rolled off her and onto his back, where he lay staring up at the ceiling.

'So that rather killed the mood, didn't it?' he said.

*Jesus.* What the *hell* had she been thinking? She could have bitten off her own tongue. She attempted to look into his eyes but he turned his face towards the wall.

'Alex, I only said it because I care about you.'

'Well, your timing could hardly have been worse.'

'I know. I'm sorry. I'm stupid. I hate myself. What else can I say?' She wrapped her arms around him, but he pushed her away and sat up. 'Please don't be angry with me.'

Alex threw off the embroidered patchwork bedspread and fumbled around for the clothes he'd cast all over the floor in his haste to undress.

'It was absolutely the last fucking thing I wanted to hear from you tonight,' he said in a low voice as he pulled on his shirt. 'I can't stay here now. I need to be on my own.'

The intensity of his anger was beginning to alarm her. He'd always been so gentle.

'Try to understand,' she said as he laced his shoes. 'I've been worried about you. I appreciate it was tactless, but can't you forgive me for that?'

'Not right now. I'll call you tomorrow.' He finished dressing and left her apartment. His footsteps pounded down the stairs. The door slammed behind him.

Retrieving her phone, Kerry sent him another heartfelt apology. Half an hour later she'd received no reply. She'd have to let him calm down in his own time. She switched out the lamp and tried to sleep but, after several hours of restlessness, she took some diazepam for the first time in months, and finally she passed out.

On waking up to nausea and a pounding headache she sent him another text. An hour later he still hadn't answered. How long was he going to punish her?

Then again he was often slow to respond to messages, having never acquired the younger generation's habit of constantly checking his phone. Nevertheless a paralysing fear gripped her as his silence continued. She composed a third message.

'Alex, even if you don't want to talk, can you let me know you're all right? My anxiety is really bad this morning. I feel so panicky and worried. I just need to know you're okay.'

To her immense relief, he replied.

'Sorry I ignored you before. I've been writing you an email. Let me know when you've read it and we'll talk. Sorry to hear about the anxiety. I love you.'

Kerry got up, slipped on her dressing gown and made herself a coffee. She sat at her computer refreshing the browser for the next ten minutes until his email arrived.

My darling Kerry,

I am so very sorry about last night. I should never have taken my temper out on you. There are no excuses for what I did, but the truth is I was feeling very low, and I needed you to soothe me. And that thing you said, it just wounded my stupid male pride. I suddenly felt so afraid of being old and useless. But it wasn't your fault. You were only expressing legitimate concerns about my health, and I was the one who over-reacted. So please don't blame yourself any more.

The other thing I need to tell you is this. I'm afraid the depression is really taking hold again and I may be in it for the long haul. I thought I was just pissed off about the angina and the holiday, but it's starting to feel more significant than that. I'm seeing my psychiatrist tomorrow and he may adjust my medication, but I'm not expecting a miracle.

I've ridden these storms out many times before, but this time I've got you with me and I'm terrified of driving you away. You caught a glimpse last night of what I'm like when I'm low. There are going to be days when nothing you can do will cheer me up. I'll say negative things that will be unpleasant for you to hear. I may not be up to washing or dressing or leaving the house. I may get impatient with you, even though you're being an angel.

I wish to God I didn't have to put you through this, but try to understand it's my silly sick brain that's at fault, and that I love you madly, even when I'm being a pain in the arse. And if it gets too much for you, Kerry, don't torture yourself by staying with me. You have your own health to take care of, and it would crucify me to think I was taking you down with me.

You know, all my life people have told me I'm too sensitive. That I'm too thin-skinned. And they're probably right. That I lack some essential barrier to separate me from the rest of the world, and so everything gets in. All of the light and the noise and the beauty and chaos and pain. It flows in and out and I have to experience it all, whether I want to or not.

I sometimes wonder if that's why I became a photographer. To distance myself by viewing life through a lens, instead of being fully immersed in it. Like watching a solar eclipse through a pin-hole camera to protect your eyes from the sun. That could be utter bullshit of course, but I'm feeling the truth of it as I write, so I'll let it stand.

Kerry, I've never been keen on regarding myself as special or some kind of tortured artist. At the same time, I honestly can't believe most people feel the way I do. You're the only woman I've met who I sense may be similar, and it's one of so many reasons I'm hopelessly drawn to you.

I hope you can forgive me for my many faults. I can hardly wait to see you and be in your arms again.

All my love forever,

Alex.

When she'd finished reading, Kerry wiped the tears running down her cheeks and drew in a shaky breath. She picked up her phone and dialled his number.

'How soon can I come over?'

# 23

The next day, following a reconciliation with Alex so passionate it left her lips bruised, Kerry went to visit her parents. She took the train to Buxton and as usual her mum fetched her from the station.

'Any news on the job front?' her mum said before Kerry had even fastened her seatbelt. Although she understood her mum's concern, it was frustrating that it was all anyone asked her about her nowadays. It was one of the reasons she avoided meeting up with old friends. It gave her an insight into what it was like to be long-term unemployed like Alex. How your worklessness could become your identity.

'Nothing yet. But I'm enjoying working in the shop,' she said in a cheery voice.

'It's shame they can't pay you a wage,' Mum said. 'Sometimes I wonder if these charities are exploiting unemployed folk like you, using your skills for nothing.'

'I'm free to leave if I want. Besides, if I hadn't chosen to volunteer there I'd be on some awful government training scheme by now.'

Her mum tutted as she navigated her way out of the station car park.

'I don't know what the world's coming too these days, I really don't. Neither does your father. He's talking about getting involved in politics, God help us.'

'Good for him,' Kerry said, admiring his nerve.

They arrived home and she curled up on the sofa with the golden retriever. Dad was in his usual seat, absorbed in the newspaper.

'By the way,' Mum said with a gleam in her eye as she handed Kerry a cup of tea, 'I was on the phone to Fran last night and she let slip there was a new man in your life.'

Kerry had suspected that would happen. Her sister was never able to keep a secret for long; she had too much instinct for a good story. 'Yep. But it's still early days.'

'Fran said you met him in this charity shop.'

'That's right.'

An expectant pause followed.

'Come on love. I'm dying to hear about him,' Mum said. 'What does he do?'

So Fran hadn't told them everything. 'He's a photographer.'

'Oh right. Is that for the magazines or something?' Mum said.

'Alex is more of an artist. He takes amazing photographs of people and places all around the city.'

'And he makes his living from that?' Dad asked.

'That's right.'

Kerry petted the dog, feeling uncomfortable. Why was she lying to her parents? She wasn't ashamed of his situation. Only afraid of how they'd react.

'Fran said there was quite an age difference between you,' Mum said.

'Yep. He's sixty next month.'

Dad peered over the edge of his paper. Mum composed her features into a smile. 'I suppose sixty isn't that old nowadays. I take it he's in good health?'

Kerry twiddled one of her earrings and declined to answer.

'What is it?' Mum said. 'Come on, you can tell us.'

Kerry fondled the retriever's warm ears, drawing comfort from his innocent presence.

'Okay. This is the truth. Alex doesn't make any money as a photographer, even though he's brilliant. He has a mental health problem and heart disease, which stops him from working. Because of that he's on benefits and lives in a council house. I'm sorry if that isn't what you wanted to hear. But it doesn't bother me. He makes me happy and I love him and that's all that matters.'

A tense silence ensued as her parents digested what they'd been told. Mum shifted in her seat and crossed her legs.

'When you say mental illness, what do you mean? He's not…? I mean, he's not likely to…?'

'He's not insane and he's not a danger to me, if that's what you were thinking. He has severe depression. It means he can't work a regular job.'

Another prolonged pause. The dog thumped his tail lazily on Kerry's knee.

'Of course, it's up to you who you go out with,' Mum said. 'But just because you're forty-three doesn't stop me worrying about you. Any mother would be concerned about her unemployed daughter caring for an older man who's unwell and financially insecure.'

'The money isn't an issue,' Kerry insisted. 'I'll get a job soon enough.'

'What about when he gets to retirement age? I don't suppose he's got a pension lined up, has he?' Dad said.

Kerry drew in a frustrated breath. 'Is that seriously the most important thing to you?'

'No need to be like that, love. I'm only trying to ascertain the facts.' It was one of Dad's favourite phrases that had used to drive her and Fran mad.

She needed to be patient and see it from their perspective. Perhaps she'd been unwise to bash them over the head with all the details at once. But she couldn't have maintained her dishonesty either.

'I'd like you to meet him,' she said, 'so you can form your own opinion.' Surely they'd appreciate Alex's intelligence and charm once they got to know him.

'We'd be happy to meet him,' Mum said. 'Wouldn't we, Fred?'

Dad mumbled something non-committal and retreated behind the paper.

Kerry recalled how she'd won Fran over. 'Before he was ill, Alex was one of the best photographers in the country. Fran said her fashion journalist friends speak of him as a legend.'

She told them about his career, and despite themselves they grew interested. On her phone she showed them the photo of herself under the cherry tree.

'That's how talented he is,' she said.

Mum removed her distance glasses and screwed up her eyes to see close. Dad stood up and peeked over her shoulder.

'That doesn't look like you, love,' Dad said.

'That's what I said at first, but it does. It's what I look like in his eyes.'

'It's very flattering,' Mum said. 'You look quite slim there.'

'He can make anyone look amazing,' Kerry said. 'And it's not because he alters the images afterwards. He sees the beauty that's already there.'

She stopped, because her voice sounded shaky with emotion.

'It's a pity he had to give it up,' Mum said. 'Is he sure he couldn't go back to it again?'

'I asked him that myself. But he finds it too hard to be reliable. And he'd never forgive himself if he let someone down. He's very conscientious.'

'It's all in the mind though, depression, isn't it?' Dad said when he'd resettled into his armchair.

'Everything's all in the mind. How else do you think we experience things?' Kerry said.

'I'm not saying it doesn't exist. But it's not the same as a physical thing that can't be fixed, is it? Like having cancer or losing your legs, which you can't do anything about.'

'What Alex has can't be fixed,' Kerry said. 'It's not a temporary bad patch he's going through. It's a condition he has to manage for the rest of his life.'

'I do find it odd that he was so unhappy when he had so much going for him,' Mum said.

'That's the thing. It can happen to anyone, however lucky you think they are.'

Would she ever be able to confide in them about her own state of health? It didn't feel like the right decision today.

During lunch her phone vibrated in her pocket with a message she suspected was from Alex. She couldn't resist a glance, despite knowing her parents considered it bad manners during mealtimes.

'Do you know what time you're getting back tonight?' it read.

'Probably not until late,' she replied. 'Are you okay?'

He didn't answer for a few minutes. 'Not really. Feeling pretty low. Don't worry though. It'll pass.'

Anxiety seized her. Under the table she typed a quick message. 'I can come back now if you like?'

'No, don't ruin your day with your family. I'll be fine. See you soon.'

Both her parents had stopped eating in order to watch her.

'Sorry,' she said, putting the phone away. 'I didn't mean to be rude. I just had to check if it was anything urgent.'

On closer observation their expressions suggested they weren't so much annoyed with her as concerned by seeing her reaction to the texts.

'Are you sure you're all right?' Mum said.

She put on her brightest voice. 'Oh yes. Everything's fine.'

# 24

Soon Alex's condition took a sharp turn for the worse and he became confined to his house. Kerry found it impossible to concentrate on her duties in the shop while she knew he was suffering at home. One afternoon she went upstairs, where Sue was restocking the bookshelves.

'Sorry to ask, Sue, but would you mind if I took the rest of the day off?'

Squatting on the small metal stool, Sue pulled a face. 'I could do with having you here, if I'm honest. We're short-staffed again today. But you're a volunteer. If you want to go, it's up to you.'

'I wouldn't ask normally. It's just…'

Sue cut her off. 'It's all right. I know where you're going.'

'I want to see if I can help him feel any better.'

'Good luck with that,' Sue said as she opened a hardback to find the price. 'I know what he's like in that state. You can't say anything right, no matter how hard you try.'

'But at least I'll have tried, won't I?'

'All right love. I'm just warning you it won't be easy.'

Kerry sighed inwardly. Sue still doubted her ability to cope. The truth was she doubted herself too. She'd already proved her capacity for saying the worst possible things. She turned to leave, then something occurred to her. 'I forgot to ask; how did you get on this morning?'

Sue had arranged to visit Shaun, who after being charged with burgling the shop had been denied bail on account of his previous record. He was now on remand in Strangeways Prison.

'I wasn't expecting him to welcome me with open arms,' Sue said. 'I went in and said my piece: that I was sorry about accusing him over the money and so on. He didn't say much, just sat there looking sullen. But right at the end when I got up to go, he thanked me for coming. So who knows; maybe it was worth it.'

'It was a brave thing to do,' Kerry said.

'I felt I owed him that, even after what he did to us. And you know, when I saw him inside, I felt sorry for the lad. That place gives me the creeps with those high walls and that grim tower overlooking it.' She shuddered. 'I'd sooner kill myself than be stuck in there.'

A silence fell as Kerry thought about Alex.

'I'd better go,' she said.

'Send Alex my best wishes, won't you?' Sue said, her face softening into a smile.


Kerry rang Alex's bell and waited. No reply. Her insides tensed. She rang again. At last he padded down the stairs and opened the door in his dressing gown. His eyes were thick-lidded and he was unshaven. He gestured for her to come in. They sat together on the scuffed leather sofa in his living room.

'You don't need to tell me I look like shit,' he said. 'I haven't slept in days.'

She put her hand on his bare knee. 'Can I make you a cup of tea?'

'Would you mind? I should offer to make one for you but I haven't got the energy.'

The kitchen looked much as usual. The recycling boxes were overflowing, but they always were. What had she expected? Some kind of unimaginable chaos that reflected the disorder of his mind? The milk in the fridge had gone off so she threw it away and made black coffee.

She returned to the living room. He'd switched on the television and was watching the news with the sound on low and a vacant look in his eyes.

'I'll go out and do some shopping for you,' she offered.

'You don't have to bother.' His gaze was fixed on the flickering screen. 'I'm sure you've got better things to do.'

Was that cigarette smoke she could smell? Her glance fell on a packet of Marlboro and a lighter on the shelf below the coffee table.

'I thought you quit smoking years ago, Alex.'

'I did.'

She looked questioningly at the packet, prompting an irritable groan from him.

'I still have one occasionally when I'm stressed. It's not like I'm injecting heroin, is it?'

Kerry gave his knee a squeeze. 'I didn't mean to sound critical. I'm just worried about your poor heart.'

'My heart can go to hell.'

'You don't mean that.'

'Actually, I do.' He stared fiercely at the television and then he turned to her. 'Sorry. I'm being vile, aren't I? Maybe you should go home.'

'Do you *want* me to go?'

Alex screwed up his eyes and frowned, as if it was difficult for him to decide either way.

'I'd rather you stayed. If you can bear it.'

'I'll be here as long as you need me. How are you feeling?'

'How am I feeling?' He spread out his hands. 'Christ, I don't know. Numb. Empty. Desolate. As if there's a black hole inside me consuming all the light. Do we have to talk about this?'

'Are the new pills not helping?'

'It's hard to tell. It's possible they're taking the edge off it.'

He grasped the mug of coffee as if to drink it but then replaced it untouched on the table. Kerry didn't know what else to say. For a while she watched the news, the discomfort in her insides growing, until he edged closer to her and put his arm around her shoulders.

'Thank you for coming here. It means a lot to me.'

She settled into him, her hands on his chest and her head resting on his shoulder. His hair was matted and he stank of stale smoke but she couldn't have cared less. It was comforting to be close to him once more.

'I suppose I should get washed now you're here,' he said without enthusiasm.

'What about a hot bath? It might be soothing for you.'

She went upstairs and ran the bath, sprinkled it with lavender oil, then encouraged him off the sofa and up to the bathroom, where he took off his dressing gown. To her alarm he was losing weight rapidly: his stomach had hollowed out and when he stretched his arms upwards, his ribs showed beneath his skin.

'You're looking very thin, love,' she said. 'When did you last eat?'

'I don't know. Yesterday lunchtime maybe. I haven't been hungry.'

Kerry turned her face so he couldn't see how distressed she was to see him in this state.

'Shall I leave you here to relax while I get you some food? I won't be long.'

Taking his keys, she headed through the estate where clusters of daffodils twinkled on the verges, out along the main road and into the supermarket attached to the petrol station. What might tempt him to eat? Treats maybe, but he should have something healthy too, a salad perhaps, or fruit. She filled her basket with more than she'd intended. It was going to add to her debts, but it was worth it.

She was approaching the counter when she stopped dead in the aisle next to the newspapers as something occurred to her. Spiders of panic crawled in her stomach. She breathed out hard through her nose. It was a silly irrational thought. A product of her stressed-out imagination. All the same she needed to get home at once to be sure.

Kerry waited in line in an agony of impatience. As soon as she'd paid she shoved the food into plastic bags and dashed out of the shop, almost bumping into the person in front, and then she was outside on the street, inhaling the fresh air and trying to calm her hammering heart. She set off down the road, hampered by the weight of the bags. At last she reached his house and unlocked the door.

'Alex?' she called out in the hallway. 'Are you okay?'

No answer. An eerie silence enveloped the house. The pungent scent of lavender drifted down the stairs. Fear swooped through her. She dumped the shopping on the floor, tore upstairs and charged into the bathroom.

He lay motionless in the bath. His chin had dropped onto his chest and his eyes were closed. She bent over him and touched his face.

'Jesus, Alex. Wake up.'

His eyelids parted. He looked up at her, confused, until he moved his legs in the water and realised where he was.

'Hello,' he said. 'Are you back already? I must have drifted off to sleep.'

Kerry sank down on the wet lino floor next to him, her knees weak, as relief washed over her in waves. He peered over the edge of the bath at her

'What's wrong?'

'Nothing. It doesn't matter,' she said in a shaky voice.

'Yes, it does. You look like you've seen a ghost.'

'Really, it's nothing. Just when I saw you lying there not moving, I thought for a second…'

'That I'd drowned myself?'

She squeezed her eyes shut. How absurd it sounded, now he'd said it out loud. As if he'd have chosen to do it just before she was due to return and find him, when he could have taken an overdose any night he was alone in the house.

'I know it was stupid. But I read in the paper yesterday about a woman who drowned herself in the bath at home. When I remembered it in the shop I got myself in such a panicky state I couldn't think rationally. And the anxious feelings built up and built up, and spiralled out of control, and then when I came back, and you were so quiet and still…'

Alex closed his eyes and gave a long sigh. 'Oh darling. This is hard for you, isn't it? I'm sorry.'

She bit at her thumbnail, bitterly ashamed. Sue's sceptical voice spoke in her head.

*Do you think you can be a rock, Kerry?*

'This isn't about me. I'm fine,' she said as bravely as she could. She stood up and fetched a towel from the rail. 'Maybe you should get out. The water must have gone cold by now.'

He climbed out of the bath and she wrapped the towel around him. She held him close to her until her clothes were soaked.

'You don't need to worry,' he said. 'I feel horrible, but I'm not suicidal.'

'Would you tell me if you were?'

His eyelids flickered, and she feared that from now on he'd conceal the truth in order to protect her.

'I know where to get help if I need it,' was all he said.

'I'll leave you to get dressed,' she said, kissing him as she let him go. 'Then I'm going to make you something to eat.'

Downstairs she fished a packet of diazepam out of her bag and swallowed a pill. Would it always be like this? Could she ever feel safe, knowing he'd attempted to end his life before and was capable of doing so again?

On impulse she took one of his cigarettes and went into the garden to smoke it. The first one she'd had since leaving university. Halfway through she wished she hadn't, as it made her dizzy and nauseous.

She stubbed it out and returned inside, where she began preparing dinner. Alex came downstairs, still in his dressing gown, and switched on the television. When she asked him if he wanted a drink he seemed lost in thought and she had to repeat herself several times to get a reply. She wondered if the new medication was making him drowsy. Soon her own pill took effect, and she chopped tomatoes in a semi-daze.

Was this to be their future, both spaced out on drugs?

Disorientated, and unfamiliar with the kitchen appliances, she burned the inside of her wrist on the hot interior of the grill.

'*Shit.*' She winced and put her hand between her knees as the blistering heat stung her skin. She ran the cold tap and held her wrist under it. Already it had turned an angry scarlet. She held it there until the pain subsided, then went into the living room.

'Alex love, I don't suppose you've got any cream for burns? I caught my hand on the oven.'

He got up, suddenly alert.

'Let me have a look.' He examined her hand, frowning. 'I'd keep that under the tap a bit longer.'

When her burn had cooled he rubbed on a pink ointment that smelled of disinfectant.

'It's my fault,' he said in an agitated manner. 'I should have been helping you, not leaving you to struggle on your own.'

'It was an accident. I wasn't concentrating on what I was doing. It was nothing to do with you.'

'I hope it doesn't leave a scar.'

'It won't be the end of the world if it does, will it?' she said. 'Why don't you sit down? You're supposed to be resting.'

She persuaded him to return to his seat. When she came in to put cutlery on the table, he looked up at her.

'Did you take one of these?' he said, indicating the open packet of cigarettes.

'I didn't think you'd mind.'

'I don't. But I know you're not a smoker. I don't want to encourage you into bad habits. I can't have that on my conscience as well.'

'As well as what?'

'You know. Everything,' he said with a vague wave of his hand.

'It's all right. I didn't even enjoy it. I remember now why I never developed a taste for smoking.'

'I wish I'd been so lucky,' he said gloomily.

She served him a bowl of pasta with grilled vegetables and an olive and tomato sauce, parmesan sprinkled on top.

Although he complimented her on the dish she could see it was a struggle for him to eat it.

'Don't feel like you have to finish it,' she said. 'As long as you've eaten something today.'

'It's kind of you to make so much effort.'

He seemed surprised she was doing the things she took for granted she'd do for someone she loved. Had no one ever cared for him until now?

After dinner he retreated deep into his mind and she couldn't get any conversation out of him, so she sat next to him and held his hand. They watched a film, although he didn't pay it much attention. When it had finished he turned to her.

'I love you, Kerry,' he said for the first time that day. Normally he'd have declared it within minutes of her walking through the door.

'I love you too. Do you want me to stay the night?'

'If you'd like to.' He regarded her gravely. 'So I haven't fucked this relationship up yet?'

She smiled. 'Not even close.'

They went upstairs to bed, where for once they had no desire for each other, only tenderness. She got undressed and climbed into bed beside him, as if they were a long-married couple. He kissed her shoulder and switched out the bedside light.

In the middle of the night she woke, because the bed was shaking. He was awake and weeping.

She rolled towards him. 'What is it, love? What's wrong?'

He turned and hugged her with a fierce grip, burying his head in her hair. His warm tears trickled onto her ear.

'Please don't get sick of me,' he whispered. 'I can't cope with the thought of you leaving.'

'Alex, I'm not going to abandon you because you're ill.'

'Why not?' he said savagely. 'Everyone else has.'

'I won't. I love you. I promise I'll be here for you. You can trust me.'

His body convulsed with stifled sobs but as she rubbed his back soothingly, he grew calmer, and eventually he fell asleep in her arms. She continued to hold him as he slept, and never had she felt so loving and so sad. In the morning he said he had no recollection of the incident.

# 25

Alex's depression lasted for several weeks, during which time Kerry visited him every day. She cooked him fresh healthy food, cleaned and tidied his house, talked to him if he felt like it and watched television with him if he didn't. When she sensed he needed time alone she'd cut short her visit and leave him to sleep in peace.

As his condition remained stable, her fear of discovering him dead in the house lessened. She became accustomed to the fact that she didn't always say the most tactful things, and he didn't always respond well even when she did. Their once-passionate sex life had dwindled almost to nothing, and they adored each other regardless.

Towards the beginning of May she noticed a change in him. Although his mood was still low, and he was often irritable, he was getting dressed in the mornings and walking to the supermarket to buy milk. He seemed more engaged when she told him what was going on in the shop.

'I should get back to work soon,' he said when she remarked that Sue was struggling to fill the rota. 'I feel guilty for letting everyone down.'

'Sue misses you but she can manage.'

The next day she arrived to find him drenched in sweat and exhausted after an hour on the exercise bike. He hadn't had the energy to use it since his illness had started.

'Be careful, won't you?' she said, pushing his damp hair out of his eyes. 'You don't want to give yourself chest pain again.'

'I need to get fit. I'm sick of being so tired and weak.'

'Wouldn't it be safer to ease into it gently?'

'I need to go fast. It releases endorphins.' Alex gave her a smile. 'Don't worry. I won't push myself past my limits. I've learned my lesson about that.'


Then one morning he turned up in the shop. Kerry was starting her shift on the till when to her astonishment, he wandered in.

'Morning,' he said, as if he'd never been away.

'What are you doing here?'

'I work here, remember?'

'Are you sure you're well enough for this?'

'I feel fine. I think all the exercise must have paid off.'

On her break Kerry went upstairs to see him. She found him crouched in the stockroom, wearing his reading glasses and surrounded by books.

'Everything was in a mess,' he said. 'There were bags piled halfway up the walls.'

She'd been intending to sort through them before he got back but hadn't expected him to return so soon.

'Sue tried to keep on top of it, but we've been so busy, and most of the volunteers don't know how to price them.'

'Oh, I don't mind.' He smiled up at her. 'If anything, it makes me feel useful.'

'Alex, why didn't you tell me you were coming back?'

'I only decided this morning. I woke up in a good mood at last and realised there was no reason for me not to be here.

By the way, have you seen the latest arrival in the furniture department? You're going to love it.'

Alex led her to an Art Deco table and six chairs made from gleaming walnut, upholstered in white leather and finished with chrome studs.

'They're beautiful,' she said.

'Yes, aren't they? They're authentic 1920s. I'm no expert but I think they could be worth a couple of grand. I'm going to ask an antiques dealer I know if he'll value them for us.'

'It's amazing someone gave us these instead of selling them.'

'They were from a house clearance in Didsbury. An old lady died and left all her things to charity. Pete brought them back in the van this morning.' Alex ran his fingers lovingly along the top of the shining wood. 'They were covered in dust, but Pete and I cleaned and polished them, and they're gorgeous.'

As always, his love of exquisite objects enthralled her. 'I'm glad you're feeling better.'

'Oh, I am. So much better.' He put his hand on her arm. 'Shall I come to your flat later? It's the least I can do after all the days you've had to travel to mine.'

That night he came round and she made dinner. For once he finished it, and he even asked if there was more.

'I see you've got your appetite back,' she remarked as she returned from the kitchen with a pan of risotto.

'What have you been up to?' he asked her when she'd sat down, enveloping her hand with his. 'I feel terrible that I've neglected you recently.'

'Nothing special. Working in the shop. Signing on. I had another interview but I didn't get the job.'

'You never told me about that.'

'It wasn't a big deal. I knew I wouldn't get it. They were looking for someone with events management experience, which I don't have. I only went along to keep the job centre happy.'

'Are they putting a lot of pressure on you now?' he asked, concerned.

'Kind of. But I guess they have to. Oh, and there's this party of Fran's I'm dreading.'

'What party?'

She'd definitely mentioned it to him before. He must have been too preoccupied to take it in.

'I'm going to London for her fortieth birthday a week on Friday. I know I should be looking forward to celebrating with her. I'm just anxious at the thought of staying in a hotel on my own and talking to strangers for a whole weekend.'

'I can imagine that would be daunting.'

'Fran's friends are all so successful. They're journalists or musicians or people managing their own businesses. The thought of making small talk with them terrifies me. Plus I've no idea what to wear.'

'I'm sure you'll look gorgeous as usual.' Alex leaned forward to kiss her. 'And you've no reason to feel inferior to anyone.'

'I hope I can get through it without being too awkward. I can't expect Fran to look after me when she's supposed to be the centre of attention. She's invited over a hundred guests.'

'Do you think she'd like to have a photographer for the night? Or has she already got someone in mind?'

Kerry stared at him. 'Are you offering to do it?'

'If she'd like me to. If not, I'll come with you anyway. If I'm allowed?'

'Of course you're allowed. And I know Fran would be thrilled. But are you sure? I assumed you wouldn't be well enough to go, let alone to photograph an event.'

'Last week I wasn't. But now I am. So let's do it, shall we?' He gave her a broad smile. 'I'll sort out a train ticket tomorrow. The money I got back from the Rome trip should cover it. Have you booked a room? I can't afford that as well, I'm afraid.'

'My room was paid for ages ago, so that's not a problem. And you don't mind meeting my sister and her friends?'

'Not at all. You may not have seen that side of me yet, but I'm quite capable of dressing up and being passably charming for a few hours.'

She got up and gave him a hug. 'All the other women will be so envious of me when they see how gorgeous and talented you are.'

'I doubt that very much,' Alex said, but he was smiling.

For the rest of the evening he showered her with affection and compliments. Although flattered, she couldn't help feeling he was over-compensating.

'You don't have to keep thanking me,' she said as he told her for the umpteenth time how grateful he was for everything she'd done while he was ill.

'Sorry. Is it annoying?'

'I'd rather you took it for granted that I'll be there for you when you need me.'

'I could never take anything about you for granted,' he said, and kissed her lips. 'I can't wait to go away with you. Will your parents be there too?'

'No. It's not their scene. Half Fran's friends will be off their heads on coke by the end of the night.' Kerry paused. 'That's not going to be difficult for you, is it? Being around people on drugs?'

He seemed surprised she'd asked. 'I haven't touched the stuff in twenty years. Nothing could tempt me back to that lifestyle now.'

'Just checking. As for my parents, I suppose I should introduce you to them soon.'

Alex noticed the reluctance in her voice. 'I take it they wildly disapprove of you going out with an older man?'

'Kind of. But I'm winning them over.'

'Good. Because if we're going to be together, it's important to me that I have a positive relationship with your family.'

It was incredible to witness the difference in him. And when they went to bed that night, she was transported back to the early days of their relationship, as if nothing had taken place in the meantime.

# 26

Kerry had expected to be relieved once Alex was better and she no longer had to worry about him so much. To her surprise she found her stress levels rising. She'd been so focused on his recovery that her own problems had receded into the background. Now they were agitating to get back in the driving seat.

A review of her finances revealed that her situation had reached crisis point. The repayments on her card had gone up again and her benefits were no longer covering her basic costs. Although she avoided frittering money away, she'd spent a lot on shopping for Alex. She'd done it out of love and would never resent him for having no means to pay her back; nevertheless, it hadn't helped. Now there was this party to get through. Fran had paid for her train ticket and hotel room, but she couldn't arrive without a present or expect other people to buy her drinks all night.

With gritted teeth she trawled through her monthly bills to see where she could cut down. Heating was less of an issue in the summer but her electricity had gone up since last year. As a jobseeker she couldn't afford to be without her phone and internet. She had no car, didn't smoke and only drank occasionally. Aside from the second hand dresses for their abortive holiday, she hadn't bought anything for herself in ages. It was hard to see how she could make any significant changes.

She could try putting pressure on Stuart to sell their house, but he'd been paying their mortgage on his own for so long now she wasn't sure he'd owe her much from the proceeds of the sale. In fact, it was possible she would owe him. So that was a can of worms she couldn't risk opening yet.

A few days before the party she got home to discover an answer phone message. It was from a telemarketing company she'd emailed her CV to, informing her she had an interview on the morning she was due to go to London.

There was no way she could not attend. The job centre had suggested she apply for the role. They could easily find out if she declined the interview. In retrospect she shouldn't have planned to be away on a Friday, but the weekend had been arranged long before she lost her job.

With a sick stomach she switched on her computer and located the company. Assuming the interview only lasted an hour as stated, she could just about make it in a taxi to the station in time to meet up with Alex and catch her booked train. The cab was another cost she couldn't afford, but she didn't have much choice. She'd have to take her luggage with her to the interview.

There were ironed clothes and polished shoes ready in her wardrobe. All she had to do was to find out about the company and prepare herself for questions. As she researched, her spirits fell further. They specialised in making outbound calls to business customers about photocopier and printer contracts. The sort of calls everyone in offices hated receiving. The salary wasn't much above minimum wage, though they promised the chance to earn more in commission.

It sounded like hell on earth.

They wouldn't actually offer it to her. Would they?

She wouldn't allow herself to perform badly in the interview on purpose, but they were bound to have other more suitable candidates. Surely when they met her they'd realise she wasn't destined to be making over a hundred sales calls a day?

The next day in the shop she told Sue about the interview.

'That's good news, isn't it? I hope they have the sense to take you on this time.' Sue had been furious on Kerry's behalf over the charity interview.

'The thing is, it's in telesales. And I'm not very good on the phone.'

'That's your insecurity talking, Kerry. You'll be perfectly okay, especially with your sweet manners. Just go in there and show them what you can do.'

Kerry looked at the floor.

'Come on love,' Sue said, nudging her elbow. 'You need a job. You can't volunteer forever, much as I'd love you to.'

Perhaps Sue was right. She should look on the bright side. She was lucky to be in the running for anything. It wasn't as if she'd be working in a coal mine or a sweatshop. And she wouldn't have to stay there for the rest of her life. Only until something better came up. Whenever that might be.

The night before the interview Kerry lay awake for hours and got up feeling sick and tired. She'd been nervous before the charity interview but at least there'd been a positive energy to her nerves. Today there'd be the added stress of having to rush to catch her train. What if the interview overran or her taxi didn't turn up? There was no room in her schedule for delays.

She left the house, dragging her case on noisy wheels. On arriving at the big glass office building she asked the man on reception if she could leave her luggage at the desk.

'This ain't a hotel, you know,' he said.

'Sorry. I had to bring it because I've got to go somewhere straight afterwards.'

'Give us it here then,' he said with a smile. In her preoccupied state of mind, she'd failed to recognise he was only teasing her. He pushed back his chair to create space below the desk. 'I'll call Dave and let him know you've arrived.'

She sat in the waiting area, twisting the strap of her handbag while people strode towards the lifts clutching take-out coffees. As the clock on the wall ticked she grew anxious in case they were running late. At last a shiny-faced bald man came out of the lift and headed over to her. His tie featured a Homer Simpson design. So people *did* wear cartoon ties, instead of giving them straight to charity.

'You must be Kerry,' he said, shaking her hand. 'Did you sign in? Just making sure. You know. Elf and Safety.' He winked, then led her down the corridor into a bare anonymous office. He didn't offer her a drink. After explaining at length about the company he turned his attention to her CV on the table.

'It says here you've negotiated with suppliers and customers over the phone,' he said, twiddling a biro in his fingers. 'And I see you've worked in marketing. My wife works in marketing. Or at least she *was* my wife, until she walked out on me last month.' He looked Kerry up and down. 'You married?'

'I'm separated.' Wasn't it against the law to ask about marital status in an interview?

Dave grinned and ran his tongue over his flaking lips. 'Righty-ho. Back to the official questions. Can you tell me how you've dealt with difficult people in the past?'

'I suppose I've listened to them and tried to understand their point of view.' She gave a few examples.

'And what does customer service mean to you?'

'Making sure customers are satisfied by finding a solution to their needs as quickly and efficiently as possible.'

'Excellent,' he said, scribbling a note on her CV. 'Those are the best answers I've heard so far. You have a lovely speaking voice too, if you don't mind me saying. I could happily listen to you all day.'

Somehow she forced herself to smile at him.

'And how do you see yourself coping in a high-pressured sales environment?'

'I've worked in PR. That can get pretty stressful. I guess I dealt with it by prioritising my time.'

For once her responses were coming too easily. She was practically talking herself into the role. He asked her more questions about her experience, nodding and sucking the end of his biro as she answered.

'And why did you leave your last position?'

'I was made redundant. But I've been volunteering in a charity shop since then.'

'Really?' He gave her a smirk, as if he found it odd or quaint. 'You must be a better person than me to work for nothing.'

'I enjoy it.'

'Bet you'll be glad to get your first pay cheque though. You'll have seen from the ad that we offer a very competitive salary.' That was an outright lie but she let it pass. He took the pen out of his mouth. 'Are you available to start straight away?'

Everything in Dave's manner suggested he was considering offering her the job. With resigned horror, she confirmed her availability.

'Righty-ho. Well, it's been an honour to meet you, Kerry.' He checked his watch. 'Fancy a quick snoop around the office before you dash off?'

He showed her into a stuffy overcrowded room in which employees wearing headphones with mouthpieces sat at tiny desks partitioned by screens. Harsh strip-lighting glared overhead. The hum of chatter filled the air.

'Okay, Mrs Steinberg,' said a spiky-haired young man nearby, 'you'll get your confirmation letter in the post in the next fourteen days. Is there anything else you want to ask me? Are you sure? Then it's been a pleasure talking to you today, Mrs Steinberg.' He ended the call and fist-pumped the air in triumph before typing something into a database on the screen.

A supervisor was stalking around the floor. He leaned over a small elderly Asian woman and said something Kerry couldn't hear that caused the woman to shrink into herself and nod repeatedly in a vigorous, flustered manner.

'There you go,' Dave said. 'Plenty of opportunities here for team players who work hard. What do you think? Have you got any questions for me?'

'When can you let me know?' was all she could think of.

'I've got a few more people to see today. Then I need to have a chinwag with HR. But I'll let you know on Monday either way. I believe in putting people out of their misery.'

Except her idea of misery was probably the opposite of what he imagined. The clock on the wall informed her it was gone eleven.

'I ought to get going, if that's okay,' she said awkwardly. 'I've booked a taxi. I'm getting the train to London for a party.'

'I see you live life in the fast lane,' he said with a wink. 'I like that. I'll be in touch, Kerry.'

She retrieved her luggage and ran out to the waiting taxi. The car crawled at a sickeningly slow pace through the busy streets. She glued her gaze to the time displayed in red on the meter as her mind whirled with frantic thoughts.

If she were offered the job she'd have to accept it. She desperately needed the money, and as a welfare recipient she had no right to turn her nose up at an offer of work she was capable of doing. But the thought of sitting in that hot, noisy call centre with no space or privacy for eight hours a day made her stomach clench like a fist.

The only alternative was to stop claiming benefits. Clearly Alex couldn't support her until she found work, so she'd have to give up her flat and move in with her parents. Aside from the obvious humiliation, she'd be marooned in the countryside, reliant on them for transport to the city, and without any means to pay off the debts they didn't know about.

How the hell had she ended up so powerless?

At least she'd see Alex in a few minutes. She'd talk through the situation with him and draw comfort from his presence.

Only ten minutes until the train left. She closed her eyes and prayed for the taxi to hurry up. At last the driver pulled up close to Piccadilly Station. She grabbed her case from the boot and set off, almost tripping on the kerb in her heels.

Inside, the station was a claustrophobic hell as people milled around in all directions and announcements blared over the buzz of voices. She located the platform for the

London train and hurried towards it, where she was due to meet Alex outside the ticket barrier. There was no sign of him.

He must be delayed in traffic too. Now *he* was going to miss the train. She snatched her phone out of her handbag, realising she'd put it on silent before the interview and forgotten to turn the sound back on. Sure enough, there were numerous missed calls from him. With stiff clumsy fingers, she called him back. He answered at once.

'Kerry. Thank God. I've been trying to reach you for ages.'

'What's wrong? Are you stuck on the bus?'

'I'm at home.'

Her face flushed and her breathing grew rapid as her anxiety spiralled out of control. 'What the bloody hell are you doing there? We're supposed to be getting the 11.35 train. It's leaving any minute now.'

'Hang on. Let me explain.' His voice sounded flat and heavy. 'I'm afraid I may have been over-optimistic about my recovery.'

The announcer's echoing voice informed them the train was about to depart.

'If you need to run for your train, don't let me stop you,' Alex said.

She stood clutching the phone to her ear. Passengers laden with luggage were pushing past her, tutting. Moving aside from the ticket barrier she struggled to collect her thoughts.

'Are you saying you're not coming?'

'I didn't get any sleep last night, and this morning I was so exhausted I literally couldn't get out of bed. I don't feel well enough to leave the house, let alone go to a party and take photographs.'

'And you're telling me this *now*?'

'I tried to call you earlier, but you must have been in your interview. I hope it went well, by the way.'

A shrill whistle blew. Her train pulled away from the platform. There was no way she could pay for another ticket, which could cost hundreds now. She'd have to ask her younger sister, on her birthday, to lend her the money for the second time. The last shreds of her composure vanished.

'The interview went fine,' she snapped. 'In fact, I think they're going to offer me the job. So now I get to show up to a swanky party on my own and talk to posh couples about how I'm forty-three and penniless and soon to be working in a sodding call centre. Oh, and I missed my train. So thanks for that.'

As she yelled into her phone, people turned to stare, but for once she couldn't have cared less.

'Darling, I feel as guilty as hell,' Alex said in a low voice. 'I've been trying all morning to summon up the energy for it, but I can't.'

'I never *asked* you to come in the first place. *You* were the one who offered.'

'I know. And I shouldn't have made that promise in the circumstances.'

'No, you shouldn't have.' She shuffled over to a latticed metal bench near the platform and sank onto it. 'I've been feeling dreadful all morning. Knowing I'd be with you was the only thing keeping me sane.'

'Why don't you ring Fran and cancel? She won't want you to suffer needlessly over a party.'

Kerry sucked in an impatient breath. Did he not understand that family loyalty demanded her presence on special occasions?

'How can I do that? She doesn't know I have anxiety. She'll think I'm being pathetic.'

Hot dizziness swept over her. On the departure board the train times flashing in orange swam before her eyes. The announcements merged with the hum of voices into a torrent of sound. Nausea punched her in the guts. She bent over and retched, but nothing came up. She hadn't eaten since last night.

Breathless, she replaced the phone to her ear. 'I can't handle this. I'm terrified I'm going to be sick or have a panic attack on the train.'

'Kerry,' he said firmly, 'you're in no fit state to be travelling either. Go home, calm down, have a rest and then talk to her. You've *got* to learn to say no, even if it inconveniences someone. If you don't take care of your health, no one else can do it for you.'

Fury seized her that he had the nerve to lecture her. 'And *you* need to learn that sometimes you have to make an effort, whether you feel like it or not.'

A silence ensued as she reflected on what she'd said.

'Are you calling me selfish?' Alex asked incredulously.

She winced inside. 'No.'

'It sounded damned like it to me.' He raised his voice. 'I suppose you think I should be a man and pull myself together?'

She cradled her head in her hands, stung with remorse. Despite all her talk about fighting mental health stigma, for a second she *had* wanted him to pull himself together, for her sake. Because she felt so vulnerable herself, and she needed his arms around her.

'Alex,' she began, but he interrupted her.

'Like an idiot, I assumed you meant it when you said I could take your support for granted. I bet if I'd fallen over and broken my ankle, you wouldn't be having a go at me like this.'

'Alex, please…'

'Do you want to know why I didn't get any sleep last night? Because I was on the phone to the Samaritans for hours, telling them I felt like killing myself so I didn't have to live with the depression any more. I wasn't going to tell you because I didn't want to burden you with it. But I see now I've got to fucking *prove* to you that I'm not making excuses.'

A pigeon limped past, stopping to inspect Kerry's suitcase for any sign of food. One of its little red feet was mangled into a stump from an accident or disease.

'Oh love,' she said in a choked voice. 'I hate to think you were suffering like that, and I was so awful to you.'

He didn't reply, and she sensed he too was trying to control his emotions.

'I think I'd better go,' he said.

'No.' She gripped onto the phone as if it were a lifeline. 'Don't go. We need to talk.'

'I can't talk about this now.' He didn't sound angry any more, only shattered. 'My brain feels like it's closing down.'

Abruptly he ended the call.

Kerry remained on the bench, brooding on everything he'd said. Then she got up and slowly walked out of the station.

# 27

Back in her flat Kerry made a cup of tea, took some diazepam and phoned Fran.

'Hey Kez. Are you on the train yet?' her sister asked.

'No.' She was stretched out on her sofa, her aching head resting on a cushion. 'I'm afraid Alex isn't well. He asked me to apologise to you about the photography.'

Fran gave a disappointed sigh. 'That's such a shame. I've already told everyone all about him. I was so excited about him being there.'

'I know you were. But he's not up to it tonight.'

'Is it his heart?'

'No. It's the depression.'

'Can't he take pills for that? Most of my friends seem to be on something or other these days.'

'He's already on a high dose of anti-depressants. But even so, it's often impossible for him to go out.'

'You're still coming though, right?'

Kerry raised her head from the cushion and braced herself. 'I'm so sorry, love, but I can't make it either.'

Fran gasped. 'You're *kidding* me. Why?'

'It's a long story.' She hesitated. 'You know you just said half your friends are on medication? Well, so am I.'

A pause. 'Jesus, Kez. What for?'

She explained about her panic attacks and social anxiety. To her surprise Fran listened without interrupting.

'Sounds like you've been having a tough time,' she said when Kerry had finished. 'Why didn't you tell me?'

Kerry picked up her mug of tea. 'I wasn't sure you'd understand. You're so confident and together.'

'Just because I'm assertive doesn't mean I'm insensitive,' Fran said. 'Besides, it's understandable you'd have a reaction to splitting up with Stuart and losing your job at the same time.'

'It started before I met Stuart.' Kerry related some of the feelings she'd been struggling with since her childhood.

'I'd no idea things were so bad,' Fran said. 'Tell you what; I'll drive up to visit you soon and we can have a proper chat over a bottle of wine.'

'That'd be cool. And you can meet Alex. Though we've just had a huge argument.'

She told her sister what had happened.

'Kez, love,' Fran said slowly, 'I'm not trying to interfere in your life, but are you sure he's right for you? I know he's smart and talented, and I see the appeal of that. But he seems troubled too. It sounds like hard work. Especially with everything else you've got going on.'

'Alex makes me happy. And I love him.'

'Okay. I guess you know best. I'd better be off anyway. I need to phone the caterers to check what time they're arriving.'

'I hope the party goes well. I'm sorry we couldn't be there. Happy birthday. And… thanks for listening.'

Kerry hung up to let Fran get ready. She couldn't imagine hosting such a big event. On her fortieth birthday she'd gone out for a quiet dinner with her parents and Stuart.

Stuart had always been so dependable. Throughout their marriage he'd never once failed to turn up to a family occasion. She gave herself a mental shake. Why was she even thinking about him? Their relationship had stifled her in ways she was only beginning to understand.

It was just a rocky patch she was going through with Alex. The end of the honeymoon period when they came face to face with each other's flaws. Though she had to admit the honeymoon had been somewhat shorter than she'd anticipated.

Sue's critical voice spoke in her head.

*You've both got too many needs. You'll burn each other out.*

And that was what had happened today. Their needs had flared up at the exact same moment and they'd both got hurt.

She lay on the sofa mulling it over, then sent him a text.

'Are you feeling any better? I told Fran everything and she was fine. More understanding than I expected. Can I come over later?'

As usual he kept her waiting. When he did answer his tone was cool enough to plunge her back into dismay.

'Glad it went well with Fran. I'm okay, but I'm afraid I can't see you tonight. My friend Vanessa is in town unexpectedly and she's coming to visit, and we need to catch up. I'll be in touch tomorrow.'

Kerry got up and switched the television on, searching for anything to distract her from the jealousy gnawing at her. What did Vanessa the artist look like? She pictured a sophisticated mature woman with flowing hair and floaty skirts.

Alex had known Vanessa for years, and Kerry trusted him not to be unfaithful, but she was sure he'd confide in his closest friend, just as she'd confided in her sister. Would Vanessa express her disapproval of his neurotic new girlfriend?

Unable to focus on the television she went to lie down on her bed. How exhausting love was, like some horrible debilitating illness. Was it worth enduring all this for a few elusive moments of ecstasy?

Of course it was worth it. Of that she'd never been more certain.


The next morning she received a much-awaited message. 'Kerry, I need to talk to you as soon as possible. Are you free now?'

She replied. 'I'll be straight over.'

When she arrived and Alex let her in he didn't kiss her, or even smile. When she sat down, instead of taking his usual place at her side, he perched on the sofa opposite her. He must still be very angry with her.

'How was Vanessa?' she asked.

'She was well.'

An awkward pause. She crossed over and sat next to him, slid her arms around him and caressed the back of his neck. 'Let's not be cold towards each other. I'm sorry about what happened yesterday.'

'You don't need to apologise. You were only standing up for yourself.'

He disengaged her hands, got up and stood in the centre of the room with his arms folded.

'Kerry, I let you down badly yesterday, and I can't forgive myself for that.'

She looked up at him. 'You were ill. I should have been more sympathetic.'

'You were anxious and distressed, and I should have been there for you as I'd promised. Instead I lost my temper. Then I left you stranded in a public place with no one to look after you. Any decent partner would have come to pick you up and take you home. No, don't make excuses for me,' he said as she was about to speak. 'I'd rather take responsibility for who I am.'

'But nothing terrible happened, did it? In fact, it worked out for the best, because I admitted to Fran that I had a problem. I learned that I'm capable of asking other people for support.'

She wasn't sure he was listening to her. His gaze was fixed on the photograph of the cathedral shrouded in violet mist. The one she'd admired the first time she visited.

'I should never have asked you to get involved with me, knowing how I'd treat you,' he said. 'It was unfair of me and I'm sorry.'

'I told you; it's all right. Let's put it behind us now, shall we?'

'I can't. I'm not the man you need me to be. And I can't spend the rest of my life with you, knowing that.'

Her heart began to thump. Sweat broke out on her neck and chest. 'Alex, you're not yourself. This is the depression talking.'

'The depression is part of me. And sometimes it speaks the truth, however difficult that may be to hear.'

'Are you saying you don't want to see me any more?'

He said nothing, but turned to stare out of the window.

Could this be happening? Was she going to wake up in a second and realise it had been some awful dream? She bit the inside of her lip and tasted blood.

'Can't we give it another try?' she said. 'Once you're feeling better, things might look very different...'

Alex turned to her, his eyes tawny in the light coming in through the window behind him. 'I'd rather make it a clean break. No second thoughts or reconciliations. I won't survive this more than once.'

A wild thought gripped her. 'Did Vanessa tell you to do this?'

'What?' Alex's shoulders stiffened. His voice became sharp. 'Of course Vanessa didn't tell me to do it. Do you think I'm the sort of person to take orders from my friends? Maybe you think I am.'

In a daze of panic she stood up and approached him. She cupped his beloved face in her hands. 'Sweetheart, please don't do this, we love each other so much, we can work through it…'

He backed away and held up his hand to stop her. 'Don't touch me, please.'

Then to her astonishment, he turned his back on her and walked to the other side of the room. She waited for him to say something else but he remained facing the wall in silence, his hands pressed over his eyes.

'So that's it?' she said. 'I'm just supposed to leave?'

'I think that would be a good idea. And I'd prefer you didn't call or text me again. And for Christ's sake, don't ask me if we can be friends.'

She stared at his rigid spine and shoulders. How could he be acting like this? As if he was oblivious to the agony he was causing her. Where the hell was the sensitive man who adored her?

Sudden anger gripped her. She grabbed her handbag from the sofa.

'Okay. Fine. Have it your way then, Alex.'

'I know this is beyond brutal,' he said quietly, still not looking round. 'But one day you'll thank me for it.'

'Believe that if it makes you feel better,' she said, and she marched towards his front door and slammed it shut behind her so hard that the house shook.

# 28

Kerry was sitting on her embroidered bedspread, tears stinging the swollen skin around her eyes. The curtains were drawn. Her head throbbed and her ribs ached from frenzied weeping.

She'd loved him so much. So much that what he'd done to her had left her raw inside. He might as well have slit her open and gutted her like a fish and left her dying on a slab.

How could she bear to be without him? How could she live knowing she'd never feel the warmth of his arms around her? How *dare* he give her such immeasurable happiness and then take it away from her?

'You selfish, self-pitying bastard, how could you do this to us?' she said out loud.

It was her own fault. If only she'd been strong and patient enough to care for him as he needed her to. If only she hadn't allowed her moment of weakness to wreck their love for each other.

No, it was nothing to do with the argument. That was just his crappy excuse. The truth was he didn't want her any more. All of his passionate declarations had been a lie. If he'd loved her a tenth as much as he'd claimed he could never have given her up so easily.

Outside, the last glimmer of light was fading. She dragged herself into the kitchen and ran a glass of water from the tap. Eating was out of the question. Should she call someone? Fran or her mum would be sympathetic, but also relieved, and that was the last thing she wanted to hear. There was no one else she could tell except Magda, and her next appointment wasn't until the end of the week.

She went the bathroom to clean her teeth. Her makeup was smudged and her burgundy hair was a tangled mess. The skin around her eyes and mouth drooped and sagged. She was old and broken, and unrecognisable as the radiant woman Alex had photographed. Her glance fell on the toothbrush he kept on her bathroom shelf. She cast it into the bin, then went back to bed, took a pill and passed out.

When her alarm went off she awoke with a jolt. Sunlight stole through the curtains. After a few seconds of blissful ignorance, memory struck. She rolled over and buried her face in the pillow, wishing she never had to face the world again.

But she did have to face it, and the next thing on her schedule was a shift in the shop on Monday morning. In the turmoil of their break-up she and Alex hadn't discussed what to do about encountering each other there. The obvious solution was for her to switch her days, since she was more adaptable to changes in her routine than he was. She was certain he'd phone in sick that day. If he didn't, he'd just have to deal with her presence when she arrived.

As she reached the shop, its associations with him made her catch her breath. She squared her shoulders and pushed open the door.

'Morning,' she said to Sue in her best attempt at a breezy voice as she came into the corridor.

'Morning love.' Sue removed a price tag from her mouth. 'How did the interview go on Friday?'

She'd hardly given it a thought in the aftermath of losing Alex, but now the threat of the call centre job returned to haunt her. Maybe she could turn it down and move to her parents' house, now she wasn't tied to being near him.

'I'm hoping they'll let me know today.'

Kerry hung up her bag and coat and set to work on a pile of clothes Sue had laid out.

'Have all the volunteers turned up?' she asked Sue, who was heaving bin bags onto the bench.

'Have they heck,' Sue said with a grunt. 'Alex and Joe are both off sick. And the new lady I was counting on to cover downstairs phoned to say she's changed her mind. She doesn't think working in a shop is for her after all. I don't know why she couldn't have figured that out in the first place.'

'That reminds me,' Kerry said, 'if it's all right, I'd like to change my days. I'm finding job adverts often come out on Mondays, so it's best if I get my applications done early in the week. So maybe Thursday, Friday and Saturday would be best.'

Sue stopped in her tracks. 'Now, that *is* interesting. Because before you got here, Alex called to ask me exactly the same thing.'

'In that case, if he's changing his hours, I'll keep mine as they are, so the number of volunteers is spread across the week more evenly.'

Sue gave a snort. 'Come off it, Kerry. How daft do you think I am?'

Kerry fiddled with her nose ring and stared at the floor. 'I suppose it is pretty obvious.' Tears sprang to her eyes. She took a deep breath and blinked them away. 'I'm sorry.'

Sue's voice softened. 'It's all right, love. Let's sit down for a sec, shall we?'

They retreated into the staffroom.

'Please don't say I told you so,' Kerry said in a dull voice as she pulled up a chair.

'I'm not saying anything,' Sue said. 'I'm just going to make you a brew.'

They sat in silence for a while as Kerry drank the hot tea.

'You were right,' she said at last. 'It was too hard.'

'You know, despite everything I said, I honestly hoped it would work out for you.' Sue sat back in her chair and ran a hand through her blonde bob. 'What was the straw that broke the camel's back? I mean, what did he do that made you call it a day?'

Kerry glanced up from her mug in surprise. 'It wasn't me who finished it.'

Sue peered over her spectacles. 'That's unusual. In the past, Alex has always been the one who refused to let go.'

'Well, this time he wasn't,' Kerry said. It confirmed what she'd feared. That he hadn't loved her as much as he'd implied.

Sue clicked her tongue against the roof of her mouth in sympathy. Kerry took another sip of tea.

'How was he when you spoke to him?' she asked Sue.

'He didn't say much. Just that he wasn't coming in today and he wanted to change his hours. I'll give him a ring later to check he's all right.'

'Thanks. I'd do it myself, but he asked me not to.'

Sue puffed out her cheeks and exhaled. 'It's for the best, love. I'm sure you must feel pretty sore right now. But in a few weeks you'll be right as rain. You'll see.'

Perhaps Sue didn't know what it was like to feel this way about someone. After all, if Kerry had never met Alex, she might not have known either.

When she got home she found an email from the call centre lurking in her inbox. Her pulse beat in her throat as she opened it.

'Kerry. Thanks for coming in on Friday. I enjoyed meeting you, and you did a great interview, but I'm afraid we offered the job to someone with more telesales experience. We have new vacancies coming up all the time though, so do keep in touch. You can call me any time on the number below. Best, Dave.'

Relief flooded through her. As always, it was tainted by the fear of what lay ahead, but at least she'd escaped the hell of working in that place. She couldn't have endured it on top of everything else.


Somehow she survived her first week without him. The pain gradually dulled, though she ached for his touch, and little things affected her without warning. One day in the shop she went upstairs to discover he'd left his reading glasses on a bookshelf. She imagined him at home trying to watch television or read without them and cursing his absent-mindedness, and the thought made her breathless with sorrow.

On Saturday she went for her counselling appointment with Magda. She sat in the grimy church room in the old armchair, which was now shedding its stuffing everywhere, and crumpled up a tissue. Magda sat opposite, her herbal tea cupped in her hands. The window was open and the curtains fluttered in the breeze.

There was a new poster on the wall. It depicted a sea of glum blue faces with one smiley yellow face shining out in their midst. The caption read Happiness is a Choice. There was something about all of the faces that Kerry found unutterably bleak.

'It sounds like things are very hard for you at the moment,' Magda said when Kerry had finished telling her what had occurred.

Kerry picked at the remnants of the stuffing. 'It's not been the best week of my life.'

'It's never easy breaking up with someone, is it?'

'I was happier with him than I thought was possible. We were so connected. Then it all went wrong.' She sighed. 'I should have known he was too good to be true. People warned me, but I ignored them.'

'Are you talking about the shop manager, Sue?' Magda asked.

Magda never seemed to forget anything. How the hell did she recall all the names of the people her clients told her about?

'Sue, my sister, my parents. They could see the difficulties a mile off.'

'And you think Alex ended your relationship because of those difficulties?'

'Why, do you think there was some other reason?'

Magda said nothing, which meant she was waiting for Kerry to dig deeper into her feelings.

'What's been tormenting me is the thought that he never loved me at all,' she admitted. 'He was so cold towards me at the end. As if he didn't care. I'm still furious when I think how he treated me.'

Magda looked thoughtful. 'When you recall that conversation with him, are you sure there was nothing in his behaviour to indicate he was upset?'

She screwed up her eyes to revisit the scene. How he'd stood facing away from her, his hands pressed over his eyes.

The way he'd backed off when she'd tried to show him affection.

*Don't touch me, please.*

'You're right. He was upset. Actually, he was devastated. He was switching off his feelings to protect himself. Despite all his issues, he has a strong instinct for self-preservation.'

'And when you look back over your relationship, how do you think he felt about you?'

Kerry closed her eyes. Alex was behind the camera, taking photos of her under the cherry blossom. He looked up at her, his eyes amber-brown in the evening light.

*Have you any idea how much I love you? More than you can conceive of.*

He'd meant every word. She knew. It was intuition.

'It must have been difficult for him to end it,' she said, acknowledging it for the first time. 'But he did it because he believed it was the right thing to do.'

'Do *you* believe it was the right thing to do?'

Kerry regarded the glum blue faces on the poster. 'Maybe. But that doesn't help much.' She looked back at Magda. 'I mean, how do I stop loving him and feeling so hurt?'

'It's understandable you feel hurt. You were very close. It's going to take time for those wounds to heal. In the meantime, I think you need to practise some intensive self-care.'

Self-care was one of Magda's favourite phrases. It had taken Kerry a while to realise it meant more than having a hot bath or painting your nails. It required treating yourself with compassion and forgiving yourself for your mistakes.

'I suppose I should stop blaming myself for ending up with the wrong man again.'

'Exactly,' Magda said. 'You're only human, as we all are.'

'Do you have a partner?' She'd never dared ask Magda anything about herself before, having the impression it was frowned upon in a therapeutic setting. But Magda smiled.

'I've been single a long time now. Twelve years ago I thought I'd met the love of my life while on holiday. I moved from Holland to be with him here. It turned out he'd been sleeping with other women all along. I was horrified someone could do that to me.'

Kerry put her hand to her mouth. 'What a bastard. Expecting you to change your whole life, when he wasn't even faithful to you.'

'At the time it was dreadful. But now I'm grateful for the experience. I learned so much about myself from it.'

'What did you learn?'

'I realised I'd excused his bad behaviour and prioritised his needs over my own because I had an unhealthy need for his approval. It's called co-dependence. You may have heard the word before.'

'Sure,' Kerry said. She hadn't been co-dependent with Alex though. Had she?

'What happened after that?' she asked.

'I went into therapy, where I learned about boundaries and self-respect. I realised that no one else can give you happiness. And that you can't truly love another person until you love yourself.'

She frowned. 'You really believe that?'

'It's true in my experience,' Magda insisted, crossing her legs. 'It was such a revelation it inspired me to train as a psychotherapist.'

'And are you happy now?'

Magda tucked a ribbon of her treacle-coloured hair behind her ear. 'No one's life is perfect, but I'm basically content. I enjoy my work, I have lots of friends and hobbies and I like who I am.' She glanced at the clock on the table. 'You know Kerry, the most important relationship you'll ever have in your life is your relationship with yourself.'

# 29

On Friday Kerry discovered that Alex hadn't been into the shop at all in the past fortnight and that Sue had heard nothing from him.

'I've rung him loads of times but he doesn't pick up,' Sue said.

'Did you leave him a message?'

'I left several, but he never called back. I wouldn't fret about it too much, love,' Sue said in an unconvincingly reassuring voice. 'You know what he's like.'

Dread lurked in the pit of Kerry's stomach. Although Alex could be slow to respond, it was very unlike him to ignore someone completely.

'Shouldn't someone go to his house and make sure he's okay?'

'I went yesterday afternoon. He was out. His neighbour said he'd seen him go off somewhere with his camera.'

So he was alive and well enough to be out taking photos. But it was worrying he was cutting off contact with the shop when it had been his sanctuary for so many years.

'Can you go upstairs and have a tidy up?' Sue said. 'Ruth's stuck on the till and the books have gotten out of order again. When you've finished, you can take over from her while she has her break.'

Upstairs Kerry said hello to Ruth, who was wearing another of her subdued linen dresses that hung baggily on her petite figure.

'How's it been today?'

'Quiet this morning,' Ruth said, 'but it's getting busier now.'

The books, records and CDs were in disarray as customers had browsed through and stuck them back at random. The promotional display hadn't been updated in ages and most of the books on it had been sold, leaving the shelf bare.

Alex would hate to see it in this state. She'd sort it out for his return. If he ever came back. She entered the stockroom, switched on the light and scanned the boxes he'd sorted and labelled by genre in his looping handwriting. A box entitled Psychology and Self-Help was overflowing but she couldn't face going through that today.

Instead she heaved down two boxes marked Cookery, deciding the recipe books would make a colourful display. The interior of the stockroom was bringing back painful memories of kissing him, so she took the boxes outside and sat on the small metal stool. She opened the boxes and searched through the contents. Which books would he choose to put on display? The ones that were unusual or beautiful in some way.

A book on Italian cookery caught her eye. She flicked through photos of scarlet tomatoes, green basil and milk-white mozzarella. A recipe for Roman spaghetti made her pause. If only Alex hadn't had that chest pain the night before their holiday, they'd have gone to Rome. Perhaps he wouldn't have got so depressed and things might have worked out differently.

This speculation wasn't helpful. His illness would have been triggered by something else eventually. There was no point in wondering what might have been. She cast the book aside and picked up one on Moroccan street food. As she turned the pages a shadow fell over her.

Ruth bent down and retrieved the Italian cookery book Kerry had discarded on the floor beside her.

'Have you been to Italy, Kerry?' she asked in her soft voice.

'No. I was planning to, but the trip was cancelled. Have you?'

Ruth nodded. 'I went to Florence last year. On one of those coach trips for single people.'

Kerry looked at her in surprise. It was unheard of for Ruth to initiate a conversation or divulge unsolicited personal information.

'Did you have a good time?'

'I liked the art and architecture,' Ruth said. 'I took hundreds of photos.'

'I bet it was amazing. Are you going anywhere this year?'

'No, I can't leave my dog. He's sick with cancer. He's had treatment, but the vet says I shouldn't put him through any more.'

'Sorry to hear that,' Kerry said.

As always Ruth's face was a mask. 'It's okay. He's very old.'

Ruth replaced the Italian book on top of the box with the others, but continued to stand there, her hands hanging awkwardly at her side.

'Sue seems worried today,' she remarked. 'Is it about Alex?'

'She hasn't heard from him in ages and he's not answering his phone.'

'He never answers his phone.' Ruth paused, and then she said, 'He's lucky.'

Kerry frowned. Alex was lucky? In what way?

Before Ruth could explain a customer called over to them.

'I'll take care of it,' Kerry said, getting to her feet. 'You go and have your break.'

Kerry headed over to the counter. Ruth didn't go downstairs as she'd expected but remained standing there, staring at Kerry. Kerry didn't have time to wonder why. She served the customer, and when she looked back, Ruth had gone.

Over in the furniture section a couple were arguing over an ebony-framed double bed.

'I don't see what's wrong with this one,' the man said. 'It looks all right to me.'

'It's not what I had in mind for the bedroom. It's heavy and old-fashioned. I wanted a light modern feel.' The woman breathed out loudly through her nose. 'I'm sick of rummaging through these places. I don't see why we can't get a new bed.'

'Because it'll cost us hundreds of pounds,' he said. 'I thought we agreed to do this cheaply.'

'When I said that, I didn't envisage us filling our new home with charity shop junk.'

'It's not junk. It's proper wooden furniture.' He examined a scratch on one of the legs. 'It just needs a bit of love and attention and it'll be good as new.'

The woman rolled her eyes.

'All right, all right,' the man said, raising his hands in exasperation. 'If you're not going to be satisfied with a second hand bed, we'll have to get a new one. But don't complain to me when we're overdrawn and we can't afford a holiday.'

'So that'll be my fault too. Just like everything else.'

'Oh give over, will you? You've done nothing but whinge all morning.'

They went downstairs, still bickering.

Kerry stared after them. The tones of their voices were depressingly familiar: the irritability, the lack of respect. Yet this couple were committed to a future together in their new home, in whatever bed they managed to compromise on. Perhaps despite appearances, they still cared for each other. From the outside it was impossible to know.

In the afternoon she was covering the downstairs till when Gladys entered the shop. Kerry hadn't seen her in ages. She seemed frailer than ever as she advanced across the floor, pushing her trolley in front of her. Gladys stopped beside the bric-a-brac shelves to inspect the latest goods, then she approached the counter.

'Hello,' she said, peering up at Kerry. 'I'm ever so sorry; I've forgotten your name.'

'It's Kerry.'

Gladys cupped her hand to her ear. 'Pardon me.'

'Kerry,' she repeated in a louder voice.

'Oh yes, of course. Could I have a look at the angel?'

Kerry looked blankly at her. 'I'm sorry?'

'The little gold angel up on the top shelf,' Gladys said. 'I noticed him a while ago, but I can't see how much he costs.'

'Oh. You mean the cherub.' She'd almost forgotten he was there. 'He's two pound fifty. Would you like to buy him?'

Gladys fumbled in her handbag. For once she'd remembered her purse. 'Yes please. I think I've got enough. But I can't fetch him down myself.'

Kerry approached the shelf and retrieved the cherub. His snub nose and dumpy legs were even uglier than she remembered.

'Isn't he lovely?' Gladys said admiringly. 'Just what I need to brighten up the mantelpiece.'

Perhaps with her poor eyesight Gladys couldn't see the object properly. Or perhaps she simply saw something different from what everyone else had seen.

'I can't read the inscription with these glasses on,' Gladys said. 'Can you tell me what it says?'

'Omnia Vincit Amor. It's Latin,' Kerry said. 'It means love conquers all.'

'That's sweet, isn't it?'

And it was also a pernicious lie, Kerry thought. A foolish romantic notion that loving someone was enough to overcome all the problems that made your relationship untenable.

'Do you realise his left eye is cracked?' Kerry indicated the shattered glass from when she'd dropped him on the floor. Gladys peered more closely.

'That's all right. He still looks perfect to me. And he doesn't need both his eyes. One will do just fine.'

Kerry found a cardboard shoe box, lined it with tissue paper and carefully laid the cherub inside.

'Is Alex here today?' Gladys asked as she counted out her coins.

'I'm afraid he's not been well.'

'Oh dear.' Gladys lowered her voice to a whisper. 'Is it the black dog?'

'Yes, it is,' Kerry said, surprised Gladys knew.

'It's a darned shame, isn't it? Mind you, my husband Bill used to get the black dog too. Ever since he came back from the war. I'm not one to complain, but he could be ever so difficult to live with when he was down.'

'But you stayed with him?'

Behind her enormous pink glasses Gladys's eyes widened. 'Of course I did, dear. I made my vows to love and cherish him in sickness and in health, didn't I?'

She shouldn't have expected anything less, given the stoical generation Gladys belonged to. Kerry taped up the box and helped Gladys tuck it away in her shopping trolley, then escorted her to the door.

'Give my best regards to Alex, won't you?' Gladys said.

'I will,' Kerry promised. Then it hit her that now they didn't work together any more she might never see him again, and she only just managed to hold back her tears until the old lady had set off down the street.


Next Monday morning Kerry had an appointment at the job centre before her shift in the shop. She got ready in plenty of time and decided to walk so she didn't have to face the stress of the bus being late.

She waited in reception, fearful she'd get the grumpy advisor again. But the woman who called her over was young and friendly. Her platinum hair was streaked with pink and purple.

'How's it going?' Her accent sounded Australian.

'I've been doing the best I can,' Kerry began anxiously. 'I sent off some applications last week and I'm still waiting to hear about those.'

'Have you got a CV? Do you mind if I have a look?'

Kerry opened the manila folder that contained her paperwork and handed the document to the advisor, who read it through.

'You've got some great skills and experience here.'

'Thanks. I know I should have found something by now. It's just that… there's so much competition from people younger than me, and….'

'We understand it's tough at the moment.'

Kerry raised an eyebrow. Did they? That hadn't been her experience so far.

'A lot of qualified people of all ages are struggling to find anything suitable,' the advisor continued. 'So don't worry. It isn't just you.'

Kerry started to let go of the tension the job centre always inspired in her. She leaned back in her chair and uncrossed her legs.

'Then it's just a case of carrying on and hoping for the best?'

The advisor was still reading her CV. She looked up suddenly, as if as if something had occurred to her.

'Have you ever considered self-employment?'

Kerry squinted at her in surprise. 'Not really. I'm an office administrator.'

The advisor pointed to the document with her pen. 'But you've done tons of other stuff. Writing, editing, web content management, press, social media.' She regarded Kerry, taking in her nose stud and her favourite old turquoise tunic with the peacock feather design. 'I'm getting the impression you're the creative independent type. The sort of person who does well as a freelancer.'

She had to admit the idea appealed. She could set her own hours, take time off when she needed to and work from home in a calm environment, without colleagues watching her every move.

'I'll give you some leaflets with more information,' the Australian woman said. 'There's government support available for new entrepreneurs. Did you know you can keep your benefits for the first few months while you get started?'

So there wouldn't be any pressure to earn her living from day one. That was better than she'd thought.

But what services exactly would she provide? And how would she find clients when she hated making phone calls? And what about the anxiety of not having a regular monthly pay cheque?

The advisor gave Kerry the pamphlets and she left, feeling it was the first time anyone in authority had taken a genuine interest in her needs.

It was a bright June morning. The scent of roses in bloom drifted from the gardens as she wandered through the streets towards the shop. Her excitement was growing by the minute. Six months ago she'd never have had the nerve to contemplate such a bold move. But recently she'd experienced an increasing desire to move out of her comfort zone.

The advisor was right. Kerry had acquired skills during her working life that hadn't been acknowledged or rewarded by her employers. She knew enough about copywriting, marketing and promotions to offer advice to small businesses or charities that couldn't afford to hire full-time marketing staff. If she could make freelancing work, she'd eventually be able to study part-time for her literature PhD as well. She would pay off her debts and rebuild her life as a successful businesswoman. Someone like Magda, who didn't need anyone else's love to make her complete.

The minute she entered the shop and saw Sue she knew something was horribly wrong. Sue's skin was pallid, her lips were pressed tightly together and her shoulders were rigid.

'Where have you been?' Sue asked.

'The job centre. Sorry, I thought I told you about it yesterday?'

'I need an urgent word with everyone,' Sue said, ignoring Kerry's apology. 'I'm shutting up shop. The others are already in the staffroom.'

Sue bustled off to lock the front door. Kerry went into the staffroom. Gathered round the table were Dan, Pete, Joe, Elspeth and Yasmeen. She took a seat next to Dan, who gave her a grave nod.

Sue returned. She stood at the head of the table and paused, as if unsure how to begin.

'Shall I put the kettle on?' Kerry said, swallowing hard to ease the tightness that was starting to constrict her throat.

'Not now, love.'

Kerry saw the fear in Sue's dilated pupils. Her heart began to thump in her head.

Sue cleared her throat. 'I'm afraid I've got some very sad news about one of our longest-serving volunteers.'

# 30

No one was looking at Sue any more. All eyes were on Kerry as her ribs tightened like a torture rack. She tugged in a series of short shallow breaths, struggling to draw air into her lungs, then she leaned over the table, overcome with dizziness.

'Are you all right? What can we do to help?' Yasmeen's voice sounded somewhere above her head.

'Tell me it's not true.' Kerry pressed her fingers over her eye-sockets until darkness pooled in front of her.

Sue was talking but Kerry paid no attention until her manager came round behind her chair, bent over and spoke loudly in her ear.

'Kerry. Kerry, listen to me. It's not him.'

Slowly the words dawned on her. She opened her eyes. The solid walls of the room re-emerged. Her lungs filled with oxygen again. 'Alex is okay?'

'Yes,' Sue said. 'I spoke to him on the phone last night.'

Sue stood up again.

'It's about Ruth. There's no easy way to say this, but she was found dead in her house over the weekend. It seems she took her own life.'

Kerry's head swam again. *Ruth* was dead? But she'd only seen her on Friday afternoon. It wasn't possible.

There was a silence as everyone took in the news, then Yasmeen spoke in a strangled voice.

'Poor Ruth. Why did she do that?'

Elspeth's mouth hung wide open and her eyes were full of hurt. Dan was solemn but composed, as if he'd already known. Pete appeared to be examining a crack in the ceiling. Joe looked confused, as if he couldn't make head or tail of what he'd heard.

'Are you allowed to tell us what happened?' Dan asked.

'There'll have to be a formal inquest, but the suspicion is she overdosed on sleeping pills,' Sue said. 'They found a bottle of them near her body and there was no sign anyone else had been in the house. The postman looked through her window and saw her on the floor and he called the police. They phoned me yesterday.'

'And it couldn't have been an accident?' Pete asked. 'Sometimes people take too many by mistake, especially if they've had a skinful.'

'Not likely,' Sue said. 'She'd been on those pills for years, and as far as anyone knows, she never touched alcohol.' She paused and rubbed her nose. 'They found her little dog dead in his basket too. We don't know whether that was from natural causes or whether she put him to sleep as well.'

'Her dog was dying of cancer. She told me just the other day,' Kerry said. A lump was rising in her throat. Next to her, Yasmeen sniffed and wiped her eyes on her sleeve. Sue got up and fetched a roll of tissue, which she placed on the table.

'Did she leave a note?' Pete asked.

'No,' Sue said. 'But you wouldn't expect that from Ruth.'

'Was she depressed?' Elspeth asked.

'It's impossible to say,' Sue said. 'She kept herself to herself, as you know. She had limited contact with her brother, but he says she had nothing to do with the rest of the family. Apparently she was adopted.'

'I can't believe she's gone,' Yasmeen said, tearing a strip of tissue from the roll and blowing her nose. 'It doesn't seem real.'

'How long did she volunteer here?' Elspeth asked.

'Well over ten years,' Sue said. 'She was an absolute godsend, working up there on that floor five days a week and not paid a penny. She never even claimed her travel expenses, bless her.'

'When's her funeral?' Dan asked.

'It won't be for a few weeks yet,' Sue said. 'You're all welcome to go. I'll shut up shop that day. To hell with the sales figures. If Pam doesn't like it, she can bugger off.'

Kerry noticed Joe had still said nothing.

Sue scrutinised them all. 'All right, I appreciate this has been a big shock. If anyone wants to take the day off, feel free. But if you want to stay for a brew and a chat, you're very welcome too.' She turned to Kerry. 'Can you put the kettle on now?'

They all stayed for a cup of tea, then Elspeth and Dan volunteered to cover the tills so the shop didn't have to close all day. Yasmeen, who was still tearful, went home. Pete had a house clearance scheduled and he left in the van. Joe disappeared into the yard. Sue and Kerry remained in the staffroom.

'Sorry about earlier,' Sue said once they were alone. 'I should have realised you'd assume it was him.'

'Don't worry about it,' Kerry said. 'I should have realised if it was, you'd have told me privately. It's just that…'

'He's been on your mind. I'll admit he's been on my mind too. So much so that I never saw this coming. Frankly, it's knocked me for six.'

'Does he know?'

'I left him a message last night and told him to call me urgently, and he did. I was in two minds whether to tell him or not. But I reckoned it would be worse if he decided to swan in here without warning and he heard it from someone else.'

'How did he take it?'

'Not well, if I'm honest. I knew it would be a blow. He blames himself, of course. I told him there was nothing he could've done. He was kind to Ruth, like he is to everyone. But he wasn't having it.' Sue looked at Kerry. 'You know he was asking about you? He was worried you'd be upset. I told him I'd take care of you.'

'What about you, Sue?' Kerry said. 'Who takes care of you?'

'I'm all right, love. I'm a tough old bird.' She patted Kerry's wrist. 'Why don't you get off home? You still look a bit peaky. Have a word with Joe on your way out, will you? You're better at this sort of thing than I am.'

Kerry found Joe sitting on the floor of the yard, his arms hugging his bent knees. She dropped her satchel on the ground, crouched down next to him and waited for him to speak.

'I don't get it,' he said at last. 'That she could have felt so hopeless. I mean, what was the problem? She had lots of money, didn't she?'

'Money doesn't always make people happy.'

'I know that. And I get that she was lonely, living out in the sticks on her own. I tried to talk to her a few times. You know me. I'll chat to anyone. But she blanked me, so I gave up. Now I wish I hadn't.'

'It wasn't your fault. You couldn't have done anything to stop it. In the end it was her choice to make.'

He gave an impatient shrug. 'People say that shit. They don't realise it doesn't help the ones left behind.'

She stared at him. 'This has happened to you before, hasn't it?'

Joe fixed his gaze on the concrete and then looked up at her, his brown eyes wide. Sweat had formed in beads on his forehead and along his thin moustache. 'My dad. Blew his brains out with a gun when I was twelve.'

Kerry's hand crept to her mouth. 'Joe, I had no idea.'

'S'all right. Not many people know. We moved to a new neighbourhood after it happened. Me and my sisters just make out like he left us. It's easier than having to explain, innit?'

'Do you know why he did it?'

'He'd been poor and struggling all his life and he owed money he could never pay back. To people who were never going to let him forget it. And he was ashamed of letting us all down, d'you know what I mean?'

'I'm so sorry.' She didn't know what else to say.

Joe shifted his position and let go of his knees as he balled his hands into fists. 'S'all right. I guess it's made me more determined to make something of my life.'


After she left Joe, Kerry headed along the road towards Fallowfield. Her legs moved as if wading through treacle but her mind was working at the speed of light.

Alex had talked to Sue about her. He'd been concerned about how she'd feel. And as shocked as she'd been about Ruth, she'd nearly passed out when she thought that the most precious thing in her life was no longer with her.

Would she ever experience love like that again?

What she was considering was doubtless a bad idea. Sue and Magda and Fran and her parents and anyone with an ounce of common sense would advise her against it. But today she didn't feel inclined to play the obedient girl. She was in control of her life, not them.

She stood at the crossroads, her hair blowing in the breeze. Cars rushed past. The significance of her decision weighed heavily on her. She squared her shoulders and set off in the direction of his house.

# 31

The cherry blossom was long gone and thick green leaves clothed the trees on the estate where Alex lived. The kids kicking a football against the wall gave Kerry curious stares as she passed the row of houses.

Her courage was rapidly wilting. She should at least have texted him first. Alex hated unexpected visitors, whoever they were. He might be asleep or have someone else in the house. But she couldn't turn back now. He might have already looked out of the window and seen her coming

Panic surged in her chest as she approached the door. The living room curtains were drawn. She rang the bell and waited. At last he unlocked the chain and peeked around the door frame.

His eyes widened. He ran a hand through his untidy sandy-grey hair. His face looked sunken and haggard but he'd managed to get dressed in a checked shirt and jeans, though his feet were still bare.

'Kerry.' He sounded hoarse, as if he'd just woken up. 'You're the last person I was expecting. What can I do for you?'

Her tongue grew thick and clumsy in her mouth.

'Sorry to turn up without warning. I was… I was just passing and thought I'd pop in to see how you were.'

She winced inside. What the hell had possessed her to say that? Alex's house wasn't on her way to anywhere else.

'If it's not convenient, I can go away.'

'Yes. I mean, no. It's fine.' He too seemed to be struggling for words. At least he wasn't annoyed with her. 'Please, come in.'

She entered the dimly lit living room. In the corner the television flickered. A collection of coffee mugs had taken up residence on the table. She sat on one of the sofas. He settled on the other and put his feet on the edge of the table.

'I'm so sorry about Ruth,' she began. 'It's so sad. Everyone in the shop is devastated.'

Alex shut his eyes and sighed. 'I should have realised. I should have been there to support her.'

'Nobody had any idea she was so unhappy. She didn't confide in anyone. She never did.'

'Even so, I should have known,' he insisted. 'I worked alongside her every day. I've been suicidal often enough myself to recognise the signs. But I was too absorbed in my own misery. I let her down.'

'Perhaps Ruth didn't want you to see what was wrong with her.'

'Or perhaps she longed for someone to witness her pain, without having to make herself visible?'

Kerry recalled the conversation she'd had with Ruth over the cookery books. Had it been Ruth's final, desperate attempt to connect with another human being? Had Kerry also been too wrapped up in her own problems to see what was in front of her?

She bit the inside of her cheek. 'We'll never know now what went on in her head. We all feel awful that we couldn't help her. But we can't hold ourselves responsible.'

'I suppose you're right.' He rested his head on the back of the sofa and yawned. 'Sorry. I'm feeling pretty wretched. I was in a bad place to start with and the news about Ruth finished me off.'

'I thought it might have. That's why I came. Is there anything I can do to help?'

'Thanks, but I don't think there is. How are you, anyway?'

'Pretty shaken up, as we all are. But otherwise I'm okay.'

'How are you getting on with your job search?'

'I had a good chat with an advisor this morning. I'm considering a complete change of direction.'

She told him her ideas about self-employment, trying to recapture the enthusiasm she'd felt before the subsequent revelation had shattered her mood. Alex listened but she could tell from his glassy eyes that he was struggling to focus.

'I'm sure you'll make a success of it,' he said when she'd finished. 'You've got so much going for you.'

'Thanks. Are you ever going to come back to the shop?'

'At some point. Sue kept ringing me. I felt guilty for not calling her back, but I've not been able to face talking to anyone. You're the first person I've seen since… well, since I last saw you.'

A silence fell. She sought for another topic to divert him from his morose thoughts.

'By the way, we sold the cherub. You were right. Someone did fall in love with him and take him home.'

'Was it Gladys?'

She looked at him in exasperation. 'How do you always know what people are going to do?'

'I don't,' he said with a grimace. 'As recent events have proved.'

Another silence descended as Kerry regretted her tactlessness. She fixed her attention on his rough calloused toes.

'What are you looking at?' he asked.

'Your poor feet. You don't look after them very well.'

He regarded them without interest. 'So what? They've survived long enough, haven't they?'

'That reminds me, I should wish you a belated happy birthday. Sorry I didn't send you a card. I didn't think you'd want me to.'

'I barely remembered it myself.'

'You can't have forgotten your sixtieth birthday.'

'I'd rather not talk about it, if you don't mind.'

Kerry fiddled with her nose ring. How was she going to bring up what she'd come to say? As the silence lengthened Alex yawned and squirmed in his seat, which she knew was his way of hinting it was time for her to let him rest. She decided it was now or never.

'Alex, I've been thinking. This business about Ruth.'

'It's awful. I know.' He yawned again. 'Though at least she can't feel the pain any more. In some ways I envy her that.'

'You know what makes me so sad? That she had no one in her life to care for her. Not a friend or a relative or a partner or anyone. Only her dog, who was old and about to die. It breaks my heart to imagine it.'

He said nothing. Kerry hesitated, then took the plunge. 'Anyway, I was thinking. That when you *have* found love in your life, perhaps it's worth fighting for?'

Alex closed his eyes, lay back and gave a long, exasperated sigh. 'I *told* you I didn't want to have this discussion.'

'I know. And I did my best to respect your wishes. I really did. But I can't let you go so easily. Not when you mean everything in the world to me.'

Her voice was shaking. He glared at her. His tone became irate.

'You told me you came to see how I was. Not to try and talk me into a reconciliation I've made clear isn't going to happen. Do you have any idea how painful this is for me?'

She picked at the cuticle of her thumbnail. Maybe she shouldn't have barged in uninvited and re-opened wounds that had barely begun to heal. But she couldn't have lived with herself if she hadn't given it one last try.

'I understand you're upset about Ruth,' he said, more kindly, 'but I'm afraid her death has no relevance for us. It's not some sort of lesson to make us re-evaluate our situation. It's a tragedy and a senseless waste of life. That's all there is to it.'

'I didn't say it was a *lesson*. I meant…'

'Not all love is beneficial, Kerry. Sometimes it harms more than it helps. I'd rather be alone and miserable for the rest of my life than know I was destroying you too.'

'But you wouldn't be… I mean, we could…'

She closed her mouth. What was the point in arguing? She'd asked and he'd said no. Now she was only compromising her dignity, if anything remained of it after this.

Kerry got to her feet. 'Okay. I accept your answer. I'm sorry if this was upsetting for you.'

Alex didn't reply. He reclined on the sofa, his arms folded, his outstretched legs crossed and his eyes shut, as if he never wanted to see her face again.

'I'll let myself out then,' she said, fearing she might cry. 'Goodbye, Alex.'

She went down the hall. Her hand was on the door handle when she heard his voice.

'Come back here a minute.'

She returned into the room. Alex patted the cushion beside him. She went over and sat at his side.

'Tell me what you were going to say earlier,' he said. 'Just before you got up.'

She wasn't sure now what she'd been about to say. Instead, she opted for the first thing that came into her head.

'You know, I'm not naïve, despite what people think. I know nothing's ever going to be easy for us. At the same time, you've changed my life in ways I never thought possible. So I thought… I thought even though we can't fix each other, maybe we could just be broken together?' She paused to breathe. 'I mean, it's an idea, isn't it?'

He was watching her intently. In the dim light, his eyes weren't amber but a deep, hooded brown.

'I don't know,' he said. 'It's too much of a risk for me to take. It nearly killed me losing you the first time.'

'Then let's not lose each other again, shall we?'

A long pause. Alex took her hand and squeezed her fingers.

'I'll think about it, okay? But please don't rush me into anything.'

'That's all I wanted. For you to consider it.'

He caressed her fingertips. 'Are you sure you still love me?'

'How can you doubt it, after everything I've said?'

'I don't know. Because I'm pathologically insecure,' he said, and laughed.

They sat in front of the television in silence, but it was companionable rather than awkward now. When the news came on Alex reached for the remote control and turned up the volume. A government spokesman was defending cuts to benefits for disabled people. A feature followed on the crisis in funding for mental health services.

As he watched Alex clasped his mottled hands together until the blue veins stood out.

'It sickens me beyond words that anyone can treat vulnerable human beings like this.'

'Maybe you shouldn't watch it,' Kerry said. 'It won't help you feel any better.'

'I need to know what's going on. This is likely to affect me.'

Not knowing how to reassure him, she grasped his hand in hers as they watched the programme. Eventually, sensing he was exhausted, she prepared to depart. It was long past lunchtime and she was feeling light-headed.

'Are you sure I can't make you anything to eat?' she asked him as she retrieved her bag from the floor.

'I'll have a sandwich later. You don't need to worry about me.'

Would she ever stop worrying about him? It seemed as unlikely as the idea that she'd ever stop loving him. She leaned over and kissed him on the cheek.

'When will I see you again?' he asked.

'When you're ready, you know how to reach me.'

She smiled, then forced herself to go into the hall, open the door and leave.

Three interminable days passed without any word from him. Somehow Kerry restrained herself from texting him. It had to be his decision, made without further pressure from her.

In the meantime she worked in the shop, where the mood remained sober. Even Pete had adopted a respectful demeanour in the wake of the tragedy. The volunteers discussed Ruth's demise in hushed voices, covering the same ground over and over again. Why did she do it? What could they have done to prevent it? Questions that seemed destined to remain unanswerable.

Not only was Sue grieving, but also she was struggling more than ever to fill the rota now Ruth was gone and it looked like Alex wasn't coming back any time soon. Then to everyone's surprise, Colin turned up and announced he'd got a job in a warehouse that produced mass mailings. He was thrilled someone had given him a second chance.

'They liked my CV,' he said to Kerry, blinking rapidly. 'The one you helped me write. Said it was very professional, they did.'

That afternoon Kerry helped Sue print out some posters to put up around the local area to recruit new volunteers. She herself took on extra shifts and spent much of her time covering the till on the top floor, though nowadays she found it a disconsolate place.

To distract herself she started researching her business idea. The more she looked into it, the more it became a distinct possibility. She'd need to take some professional courses to boost her credentials but she already had the key skills she needed. Once it got off the ground she'd team up with a graphic designer and eventually offer a full service agency.

Even the prospect of making calls to potential clients wasn't as frightening as she'd imagined. Somehow it felt less daunting when she was promoting something she was invested in. Had it been a blessing in disguise that she'd lost her job and been unable to find another? It had led her to a pivotal moment in her life: the opportunity to free herself from the constraints of office life.

On Thursday her phone beeped with a message.

'Kerry, I've been doing a lot of thinking about what you said and I need to talk to you. Could we meet tonight in the pub? I can be there for 7pm.'

She shut her eyes as disappointment stung her. He was going to refuse her suggestion. Why else would he have chosen somewhere public to meet instead of inviting her to his house? And the message itself was so guarded. As if he was preparing her not to get her hopes up.

What was the point of putting herself through this? She texted him back.

'Alex, you don't have to go to the trouble of meeting me. If the answer's no, just say so. It'll be less painful for us both.'

He replied. 'I'd rather speak to you face to face, if that's okay.'

Of course, he was old-fashioned; he'd never been entirely comfortable communicating by text, and he'd consider it a disrespectful way to turn her down. And perhaps if she were honest, she did want to see him one last time to say goodbye. However soul-crushing it turned out to be.

As evening approached she dressed in jeans and the silky top she'd bought to wear on their first date, simply because she couldn't think what else to put on. It would be over soon, she told herself as she applied her make-up. Then she'd go home and cry herself to sleep, and tomorrow morning she'd get up and get on with the rest of her life.

Kerry arrived at the pub at five to seven. She scanned the room anxiously but there was no sign of him, so she approached the bar and ordered a double gin and tonic. Their usual seat in the corner was occupied and the only empty table was near the television, where men were watching football.

'You all right, sweetheart?' one of them said as she sat down. 'You look worried.'

'I'm fine thanks,' she said, twisting the strap of her handbag.

She waited for fifteen minutes, conscious of the men looking at her, and increasingly infuriated with Alex. If he was going to insist on dragging her here to dump her for the second time, the least he could do was be punctual. She got out her phone for the hundredth time to check for a message.

'Late, isn't he?' one of the men said. 'If you were my girlfriend, I'd never leave you waiting like this.'

Ignoring them, she got up and walked stiffly out of the television area towards a quiet seat beside the window that had just been vacated. Then she saw him.

He was sitting outside on a bench, his shoulders hunched and his elbows resting on the wooden table. Next to him sat a half-empty pint of beer. He must have got there before her and they'd failed to notice each other as she went in.

As she continued to watch him, he put his head in his hands as if in despair. And suddenly it was as if all her bitterness and anger and possessive desire for him flowed away. All that remained was an overwhelming wish for him not to suffer any more.

She got up and hurried outside.

Alex turned to see her. His mouth dropped open.

'I didn't realise you were out here,' she said. 'I've been waiting inside the pub.'

'I thought you weren't coming. I've no idea how I could have missed you.'

'It doesn't matter. We found each other in the end.'

Kerry sat beside him and put her hand on his arm. Her words tumbled out.

'Alex, I know what you're about to tell me, and it's okay. I don't want you to feel guilty or sad any more. If we're not meant to be together, then that's the way it is. I'll never forget you and I'll always be grateful for the time we shared.'

He didn't answer. He seemed perplexed, almost dazed. Was it the alcohol affecting him?

'Are you okay?' she asked.

Still he said nothing. He shook his head, as if to wake himself. At last he looked up at her. 'I can't do it.'

'I guessed as much.' She squeezed his arm. 'Like I said, it's all right.'

'No, I mean I can't do what I came here to do. You guessed right: I was going to tell you our relationship was over. I was too scared of not being good enough for you. When you didn't arrive, I assumed you'd stood me up. While I didn't blame you exactly, I thought it was out of character. And then you walked over here and took me completely by surprise.'

He drew a breath and continued. 'Even though you knew I was going to hurt you, you still were able to show me compassion. And I thought: here's a beautiful, kind, amazing woman who truly, unselfishly loves me for who I am. What kind of ungrateful fucking idiot would I be if I chose to walk away from her now?'

Kerry couldn't speak. Her hand gripped his arm tight.

'Do you know what else I just thought?' he said. 'Remember that thing you said? Even though we can't fix each other, perhaps we could be broken together?'

She nodded. 'I remember.'

'Kerry, you're not broken. And neither am I. We don't need to be fixed. We're fine as we are.' He took her hand in his. 'I'm sorry for everything I've put you through. Can you ever forgive me?'

She put her arms around his neck. 'Oh love. There's nothing to forgive.'

He held her close, and she rested her on his shoulder, and then they got up and slowly wandered home.

# 32

The subsequent days were among the happiest Kerry had known. She'd always been breathless with excitement whenever she was due to meet Alex, but now she had renewed faith in his love. At the weekend they spent the mornings lying in bed and the afternoons sitting in cafes talking. He decided he was well enough to return to the shop.

Then one evening he arrived at her flat trying to pretend nothing was wrong, but his gaze darted around the room and he kept raking his hands through his hair.

'What's on your mind?' Kerry said as she sat down beside him.

'Something I've been dreading for ages,' he said. 'I got a phone call from the Department of Work and Pensions to arrange a work capability assessment.'

It was what they'd both feared would happen. 'When is it?'

'Next week. I've known for a while it was a possibility. They got me to fill in a questionnaire first. I hoped that might be the end of it, but they want to see me.'

She took his hand in hers. 'I'm so sorry you have to go through this.'

'You know I've never avoided working out of laziness. I'm not consistently well enough to hold down a job. The last time I tried it almost killed me. I'm terrified of it happening again. I've heard too many horror stories of people dying from heart attacks or driven to suicide because they were wrongly declared fit for work.'

Kerry squeezed his hand.

'I'm sorry to burden you with this,' he said.

'Don't be.' She kissed him. 'That's what I'm here for.'

'I hate having to prove I'm not a scrounger or a liar.'

'But you've got two well-documented medical conditions. Can't you get a letter from your psychiatrist or your doctor explaining the situation?'

'I'm sure I can, but that won't let me off going for the assessment. They use their own "experts" to decide. I'm scared that once they find out I volunteer, they'll assume I should be able to cope in the workplace.'

'But it's not the same. The demands on volunteers are different. I know how exhausted you are when you've been in the shop, and that's on your good days.'

'I know, and Sue's very careful not to overwork me. I can't expect an employer to show me the same consideration.' He paused. 'Once I'm looking for work like you, I'll have to take whatever I'm offered. And it's not like I'll have much to choose from, considering I'm old and I've got no up-to-date references or training.'

She pressed her palms to her eyes in frustration. 'I wish they could just leave you alone. You've found a routine that suits you and you're contributing to society. It's like they don't care whether they make you ill or not. You'd think they'd at least want to save the state the cost of your healthcare.'

'It's so they can add another number onto the employment statistics,' he said wearily. 'And because half the voters in this country would look at me and see that I can walk and talk, and decide they don't want their taxes paying for me to stay at home.'

For the rest of the evening Kerry tried to focus on other things, but Alex struggled to maintain the conversation. He went home early.

'This is nothing to do with you,' he said, kissing her with tenderness at the door. 'I love you more than ever. But I need to be on my own right now.'


On the day of the assessment she went to his house afterwards, where it was clear he was in a state of extreme agitation. She sat rubbing his shoulders in silence until he was ready to tell her about it.

'That was one of the most humiliating experiences of my life,' he said. 'And, trust me, I've had a few.'

'What happened?'

'Firstly, the assessor was fixated on how I got to the interview. Whether I could travel independently on the bus or if a carer had come with me. Then she asked how I managed alone in the house. Whether I could make a cup of tea by myself and use the cooker safely.'

'But none of that is relevant to you.'

'You should have tried telling *her* that. I explained as clearly as I could that I don't have a physical or learning disability. But some days I'm so low in spirits and energy I can't lift my head from the pillow, however hard I try.'

'What did she say about that?'

'Nothing. She asked if I had any hobbies or pets.' He gave a bitter laugh. 'As if that has anything to do with it. I asked what the point of these questions was, and she said she was trying to find out more about me. But when I started to tell her about myself, she rushed on to her next question so I didn't take up too much of the allocated time.'

'What did she say about your volunteering?'

'She asked how many hours I worked and whether I had problems getting on with the other volunteers. I could tell from her face what she was thinking. That this was going to be an easy one to tick off her list.'

'And that was it? She didn't ask about your depression at all?'

'She asked if I thought I was a risk to other people, and I said no. Then she asked if being in work could put me at risk of harming myself, and I said absolutely, yes it could. So she asked me how many times I'd attempted suicide in the past. But all in the same mechanical voice, as if she was doing a consumer survey in a shopping centre.'

'That's outrageous. You'd think they'd get better training to do that job. Do you think she'll recommend you for work?'

'I'm certain she will. She said employers would make allowances to help me do my job. Which is fine in theory, but in my experience, once you've had more than a week or two off, they start looking for ways to fire you. And I'm not sure I've got the energy left to fight for my rights any more.'

The distress in his face twisted Kerry's heart. She gave him a long hug. 'Whatever happens, I'm going to support you all the way,' she said. 'We can appeal against the decision.'

'Perhaps. Or maybe I've got this all wrong. Maybe I should stop being so fucking weak and get on with it.'

'Alex, do you remember what you said to me when I first told you about my anxiety? You told me never to think of myself as weak. And you were right. You've fought this illness every step of the way. That shows strength most people can't imagine.'

He smiled and squeezed her hand. 'Thank you for reminding me.'

Was it the right time to bring up her idea, she wondered. She glanced at his face. The tightness in his muscles had slackened since he'd related his story and been listened to.

'Alex,' she said tentatively, 'I've got a suggestion to make. It's fine if you say no. I don't want to put more pressure on you. But I'd like you to listen to it first.'

He looked at her, intrigued but alarmed. 'Go on.'

'I was thinking,' she said, 'about what a brilliant photographer you are.'

At once he dropped her hand. 'No, Kerry. We've been through this before. That part of my life is over. I can't go back to it now.'

'Just hear me out, okay?'

His jaw tensed, but he nodded.

'You know I'm planning to set up my freelance marketing consultancy. And eventually I'd like to offer graphic design as well. But quality images are an essential element of promotion. The world is so visual now. And I thought, what if I could offer my clients professional photography too, for a reasonable price? Small organisations struggle to afford it for their brochures and events. It would give you some income and stop you having to do a job you'd hate.'

He was watching her closely, his eyebrows knotted.

'But what about when I'm ill?' he said. 'It always comes back to the same problem. I'd be too afraid of letting you down.'

'I've thought about that too.' She'd stayed awake late into the night running over the details. 'I'd find a network of other freelance photographers who could cover for you. That way you'd never have to face the stress of losing your job when you were sick. I'd handle the whole business side. And I don't think I'd be too awful to work with, would I?'

Alex said nothing, but continued to frown, tapping his fingers on his thigh.

'Is it such a crazy idea?' Kerry said.

'No. I was just thinking how different you seem from when we first met. You've always been strong, I know that, but your courage is shining out now.'

She smiled. 'I feel like I'm just starting to understand what I'm capable of.'

'I'll think about it. I really will,' he said, but she heard the trepidation in his voice.

'What is it you're scared of?' she said. 'Is it about us working together? Or having a paid job after such a long time? Or have you lost confidence in yourself as a professional?'

'All of those things.'

'Well, I have complete faith in you. I've seen your work and it's stunning. As for us working together, it's a risk; I can see that. But it feels right to me. We could try it, and if it doesn't work out we accept it and look into other options. At the very least it would get the DWP off your back for a while.'

His expression grew thoughtful. 'I'd need to get a new camera and lenses. They won't be cheap.'

'We'd be eligible for a loan. I've been doing a lot of research and writing a business plan. Whatever we need, the support and information will be out there somewhere.'

He was catching the fire of her enthusiasm now. She could see it glinting in his eyes and hear it in his sharp intake of breath, and the way he clasped his hands together in his lap.

'I never thought I'd be able to work again doing what I love,' he said. 'But this is giving me hope.'

'We wouldn't be at the mercy of employers' whims any more. Once the money starts coming in, we could make time for being creative too. I could study for my PhD and we could start selling your art photographs. I think it'd be good for us, don't you?'

He seemed lost in thought.

'What do you think? Is it worth a go?'

Alex stared into her eyes, then he cupped her face in his hands and kissed her on both cheeks and on her lips. 'Let's have a look at the business plan tonight, shall we?'


That night as they lay together in her bed, a dream disturbed Kerry's sleep. She was standing on the edge of a pit, looking over its edge into a deep black hole.

'You have to climb down the stairs,' said a voice she didn't recognise. 'It's the only way to get to the bottom.'

What stairs? She leaned over the hole and with her palms felt a series of rough steps, uneven, damp and slippery, hewn into the ice-cold rock.

'But there's nothing to hold onto,' she said.

'No,' the voice said calmly.

She peered into the blackness. There was no way to tell how deep it went.

'And if I slip and fall? How far is it until I hit the ground?'

'Nobody knows. No one's gone this way before.'

Dread prickled along her spine. 'I can't do it. There must be another way.'

'There isn't another way.'

Shaking with fear and cold, she lowered her feet over the side, groping for a foothold. She took a few steps down, still clinging to the edge of the hole. One step further she froze, because now she was holding onto the wall only by her fingertips. She didn't dare down go any further but without any grip she couldn't pull herself back up either.

'Is anyone there?' she called out, hoping the voice would reply, but her words echoed on silent stone.

'Have faith,' she whispered to herself.

Her body trembling, she lowered her foot and took another step, and another. And at last she came to rest on a solid floor, and light flooded the chamber she was standing in, and she saw the pit wasn't so deep after all, and that even if she'd fallen, she'd have had no broken bones. And she was glad then that she'd made the journey, though she awoke in Alex's arms before she learned what she'd been hoping to find.

# 33

When Kerry went into the shop for her shift she found Sue sorting through a heap of clothes, her lips pressed tight. She hadn't seen Sue smile once since Ruth's death. Kerry picked up the pricing gun and began to help.

'There's something I want to ask you,' Sue said. 'I've had some more unexpected news.'

Kerry froze. 'Something bad?'

'Dan's going to be leaving us at the end of the month. He came in yesterday afternoon to hand in his notice.'

'Oh. I see.' Poor Sue was losing her staff in droves. And Kerry hadn't dared tell her yet about her and Alex's plans.

'It's because his little girl's being bullied at school, bless her,' Sue said.

'I remember he told me that a while ago.'

'Dan tried to sort it out with the school, but it's still going on. Now Libby's refusing to attend at all. He and his boyfriend have decided it would be best for Dan to home school her.'

'That makes sense. I can imagine you'll be sorry to lose him.'

'Oh aye. Dan's been a godsend. But he's not the only good person I've got.' Sue peered over her rimless spectacles. 'Kerry love, I'd like to offer you the job.'

'Me?'

'Don't sound so surprised. You've done well here. I thought you were a bit shy when you first started, but you've come on in leaps and bounds. I'd feel very confident leaving the shop in your capable hands.'

'Wow. Thank you. I'm very flattered. How many hours is it?'

'Twenty-one a week. You could either do three full days or spread it out over the week like Dan does. I'll be honest, the money isn't great, but it would give you a regular wage instead of being on benefits.'

Kerry ran quickly through her options. Perhaps it would be sensible to earn some income while she paid off her debts and got her business up and running. And she wouldn't have to say goodbye to the shop, the place that had meant so much to her, just yet.

'I'd love to accept. Thank you.'

Sue's face broke into a smile. 'That's smashing. I'm sorry I can't make it a full-time position.'

'Part-time suits me better. You see, I've got an idea.'

With reluctance, she explained her plans for her new venture. As she'd anticipated, Sue was sceptical.

'I don't mean to be rude, Kerry, but are you sure you've thought this through?'

'I haven't worked out every detail yet. But Alex was positive about it, once he got over his initial doubts.' She looked at Sue. 'Though I can see you're less enthusiastic.'

'I'm not going to bullshit you, love. I think you're asking for trouble setting up in business with anyone as ill as he is. Never mind the fact you're sleeping with him too. Your relationship got off to a rocky start and you've not been back together five minutes yet. The pair of you's got enough on your plates without putting all your hopes into something that might well fail.'

Kerry glanced down as her insides squirmed. Was Sue right? Was she making a huge mistake?

She shook her head. She couldn't allow herself to be crushed by someone else's negativity.

'I want to give it a try, and so does Alex. We both know the risks involved.'

'To be honest, I can see *you* doing it,' Sue said. 'It's him I'm worried about. He's so vulnerable to being burned out.'

'Alex will be forced to get a job anyway.' Kerry told Sue about his assessment. 'Isn't it better he does something he enjoys for someone who cares about him?'

Sue puffed out her cheeks and exhaled. 'Then I suppose there's no point arguing, if you've set your heart on it. You will look after him, won't you?' she said, almost pleadingly.

'Of course I will.'

A silence followed. Sue pulled a face as she held up a quilted satin jacket covered in bright yellow moons and stars. 'D'you reckon anyone would wear this?'

'It's not my taste. But someone else might love it.'

Sue tagged on a price label. 'Right, that's that pile done. Can you get this lot out on the floor, please?'

Kerry hung the clothes on the big rail and wheeled it onto the shop floor. As she was putting them out, the door swung open and Mo shuffled in for her daily visit, wearing her split leather boots and dirty frayed rucksack. Mo approached the rail and muttered as she rifled through the new stock, and for the first time it occurred to Kerry to ask her what she was looking for.

Catherine North lives in Manchester, UK, where the story is set. *The Beauty of Broken Things* is her debut novel.

www.northcatwriter.com

Twitter, Facebook and Instagram: @northcatwriter